BROTHERS

J.Z. NIEVES

Published in the United States by Architect's Archive Press

First Architect's Archive Press Edition, 2025

ISBN: 979-8-9936457-0-4

Publication Date: November 11,2025

Edited by Laura Jane Zimmerman

Cover art by Mushfiq A. K.

DISCLAIMERS

THIS IS A WORK OF FICTION, Y'ALL

Brothers is a work of fiction and it's consumption is for entertainment purposes only. The role played by historical figure, Mary Mallon, in this work is entirely fictional and is in no way intended to be a historical depiction of her actual person, dialogue, events, or situations. Although the locations, North and South Brother are real and a condensed history of the islands was briefly included the situations, characters, and incidents are the product of the author's imagination. Any resemblance to actual persons living or dead, or actual events is purely coincidental.

DO NOT ATTEMPT TO GO TO THE ISLANDS ON YOUR OWN.

For more information on North and South Brother islands visit https://www.nycgovparks.org/park-features/north-brother-island/visit

Content Warning

This book contains scenes of sensitive topics such as suicide(S) and body mutilation(BM) which may be offensive to some readers and inappropriate for children. Trigger warnings(TW) will be under the titles of the chapters that include the sensitive content. Reader discretion is advised

A Note About The Character

Nalini Sharma is a legally deaf character, her dialogue is written as an interpretation of ASL (American Sign Language) unless otherwise specified.

DEDICATION

For my boy, Harrison, and everyone who stuck with me along the way.

Painting By Harrison Serna-Zahn

Dog Harrison and painter Harrison have no relation,
just a nifty synchronicity.

CONTENTS

CHAPTER ONE

THE BROTHERS PROJECT

"Where are my shoes?"

Arel looked up from his feet and waited for his eyes to adjust to the dim light of the moon. He stood on cold laminate flooring and from his feet, he followed the sight of scattered glass and debris to the surrounding windows. Vines had begun making their way through the broken panes and across the walls. Overturned tables and chairs littered his line of sight in every direction. He was positioned exactly in the middle of a room, which judging by the state of its contents hadn't been in use for decades. When shifting his weight he felt small bits of rubble from the fallen ceiling working between his toes.

'*Where am I?*' He thought. Trying to mentally retrace his steps, he leaned forward to inspect the furniture on the floor; a gurney.

"Hospital?" He spun to look behind him to find an open doorway leading out to a wealth of trees. The majority of the light in the room shone through that entryway and its surrounding windows. He could see clear through the trees with the rays of the full moon.

Arel turned his attention to the other side of the room, directly ahead of him was another doorway that opened to what looked like a hallway. On both sides of the door remained large windows still intact despite their decrepit surroundings. He walked toward the entryway but stopped himself a few feet from it, listening to a small voice in his mind telling him not to go any farther. There was nothing to be found in the black and shadow beyond that opening. As he turned away from the door before him his peripheral vision picked up movement in the hallway. He snapped his head back to the doorway, daring whatever it was to move again. Frozen in place with only the sound of blood pumping in his ears, he watched as the shadows shifted in the dark as if there were still people walking the halls. The sight made all the skin on his body explode into goosebumps.

"Good call, Rel," he whispered to himself.

Beginning with a large step backward, he made his way toward the door behind him that led outside not wanting to turn his back on whatever was pacing in the darkness of that hallway. He'd take his chances out in the trees where at least there was light. As he reached the center of the room again, the sound of debris crushed under foot echoed off the walls as he was cast in shadow. Something was behind him.

He turned quickly to see a large figure, so massive, that it blocked all of the moonlight from shining through his only way out. It wasn't a man, it had to be an animal but its shape wasn't like anything he was familiar with. The only defining feature that stood out from its unusual silhouette was its eyes. He could focus on nothing other than the bright flame of its orange eyes that bore into his from across the room. Arel stood frozen as he braced himself for the creature's attack, but then it did something he hadn't expected. The figure spoke, its voice a familiar sound.

"Keep them from the Brothers." The words washed over him like a warm wave, deep and calm.

"Brothers?" he peered up at the eyes that towered over him.

Before he could receive a reply a cold wind swept across the back of Arel's neck. He quickly looked from left to right to see the trees through the broken windows undisturbed by any wind. The air outside was still. The sensation of primal fear rose to cloud his senses and his body made the involuntary motion of turning to face the advancing threat from behind him.

The pacing shadows had begun flooding into the room from the hallway. Out of the black mass protruded a barrage of disembodied arms, viciously clawing at the floor to reach him. Arel stood paralyzed, the ember of courage left in his chest fought to ignite his frozen legs, but the creature that blocked the exit extinguished his fire. He watched in terror as the gruesome horde etched closer. His only chance was to make a break for one of the windows.

As he lifted his foot to run, he felt something wrap around his torso. He didn't have a chance to look down to see what it was before he was pulled back with such severity that all the air in his lungs was thrust from his chest.

★★★★

Arel's eyes flew open and for a few seconds his eyelids were the only part of his anatomy he allowed himself to move as he focused on calming his breathing. He felt surrounded as if the creatures had somehow followed him out of his dream, waiting to strike the moment he shifted his weight.

'*This is ridiculous,*' he thought.

He closed his eyes tight then opened them as he took one last deep breath before urging the rest of his muscles to move. He pushed himself up against the headboard and rubbed his eyes. As he brought his hand down from his face, he clocked a shadow in the vague shape of a man. He felt his whole body tense.

"C'mon man, it's your imagi-" he stopped speaking as the shadow began to move toward him from the chair in the corner of the room.

"SHIT!" In one swift move, he launched himself from the bed while simultaneously grabbing the one thing on his nightstand and holding it out in defense. In his panic, his fingers fumbled to find the lamp switch, distracted by the familiar sound of his blood pumping in his ears and the adrenaline flooding his system. Finally successful in turning on the light, his eyes dashed wildly to each corner of the room. Nothing. Everything was exactly as he'd remembered before falling asleep. Harrison, his black labpit mix, popped his head up from the foot of his bed. He studied Arel with worried eyes, his ears at attention putting the ear that remained torn in two places on full display. An injury inflicted before he found him.

"It's ok, bud. I'm alright," Arel said, debating on whether or not he was reassuring himself or Harrison.

"It's nothing," he said through a heavy breath.

He looked down to see what he grabbed in his frenzy, a book. As he looked over the cover, he snorted a humorless laugh.

"Yeah, *The Romance of Mathematics* was really gonna help me with a hallucination." He turned the book over to view the photo on the back cover. A black and white photo of an older man with a large smile stared back at him.

"Sorry, Dad."

He tossed the book back onto the nightstand but debated reading a few pages to stop himself from thinking about the dream. Being only a few chapters in, there was added pressure to finish it soon before his father called for the verdict on his 'love letter' to the universal language. He let himself fall back onto his bed and allowed whatever adrenalin left in his system drain from his muscles.

"Not tonight," he exhaled, raking his fingers through his black curls and viciously scratching the entirety of his scalp. Harrison got up from his dog bed and Arel listened as he shook himself off, comforted by the unmistakable sound of flapping ears. He looked up in time to watch Harrison launch himself onto the bed, curl up along his legs, and rest his head across his shin. Harrison was never one to sleep on the bed but Arel was thankful for the extra security. A sense of calm came over him and it wasn't long before they both faded out of consciousness once again.

Arel was lulled awake by the music playing from his phone, followed by Harrison's whine of annoyance. He wasted no time opening the blinds of his windows, still unnerved by the idea of shadows, even in daylight.

He took a few deep mindful breaths to ground himself as he took in the view of the east river and the islands that lie therein. It was calming, but today his sight was drawn to the islands and lingered there until he heard Harrison grumble.

"Oh yeah, sorry buddy." Remembering Harrison's need to do his morning business. Arel quickly threw on a hoodie over his pajama bottoms, put Harrison's collar on him, and they made their way to the elevator. Anxious to get outside to breathe in the fresh air, he found himself pressing the down button every few seconds. As he waited, a strange sensation came over him, something was standing to the right of him just over his shoulder. He strained his eyes to look out of the corner, not wanting to make any obvious movements. To his utter alarm a figure loomed in his peripheral vision, its form almost undetectable, apparent only in the disturbance of air. The ripples of heatwaves manifested from unseen fire. He began to feel a warmth build and snapped his head to the right to find the space beside him empty. Adrenalin hit him again and energy rushed through his limbs urging his body to turn this way and that to find the source of the heat but there was nothing and no one else in the hallway besides him and his furry companion.

"It's in your head, Rel," he mumbled.

Out of habit, he looked down as he reached out to pat Harrison's head to find his dark brown eyes already staring up at him with a furrowed brow. When Arel looked up he let out a yelp, spooked by his blurry reflection in the elevator door. Followed by an involuntary jump as the doors opened accompanied by the cheerful sound of a 'Ding.'

"Come on," he whispered furiously. Frustrated by his jumpiness, he let out an exasperated breath and they stepped into the elevator.

As they walked out to the courtyard, Arel breathed in like he was coming up for air. The sun was just rising over the building, he positioned himself in its rays and let the warmth fall over his body. Most dreams he could shake off as soon as he woke up, but he hadn't had a dream like this since he was in college. He still felt like he was surrounded by that gruesome hoard but did his best not to let his mind focus on the disturbing aspects of his dream. He slid off his color-worn flats and stood barefoot in the grass. The cold ground sent a calming wave through his body, relaxing his tense muscles. The combination of the warm rays from the sun with the cool dew-covered grass under his feet helped him empty his mind and bring his thoughts back into his body. He wasn't sure how long he stood with his eyes shut, counting his breath. When he finally opened his eyes Harrison was sitting in front of him, waiting patiently.

Arel knelt and smiled at Harrison. "It's a good thing I have you, buddy," he said as he scratched Harrison around the ears. He then looked around to see what he'd have to pick up.

"I can't say the same about that," Arel sighed. Harrison wagged his tail.

★★★★

The rest of the morning went by in a blur, moving absentmindedly through his routines. As he reached for the door to head out to the office, he stopped and wondered how he got there. Not even remembering picking out his clothes for the day

"Autopilot," he sighed. "Get it together, Rel," he mumbled as he stepped out and locked the door behind him.

The walk to the office was a short one. He was glad to be able to travel to work without a heavy jacket and breathe in more of the morning air. He needed it to get his head right before his first appointment. It was a full schedule today, and his patients deserved a clear-minded and fully present psychiatrist.

The walk-in was a bit off for a Thursday morning, not the usual traffic. Harrison kept in perfect stride with him and stayed close which was a bit out of character, but he assumed it was because of the night they had. Harrison has always been attentive and Arel noticed early on the calming effect Harrison had on others, so he wasted no time getting him registered as a therapy dog. His patients loved Harrison and he had been a major factor in the success of his practice; they were a team. At least, that's how Arel saw it.

Arel thought it strange not seeing anyone else in the lobby or waiting for the elevator, but shrugged it off when the the doors opened. They stepped off the elevator to the floor of his office suite and Arel felt an unsettling feeling for the second time this morning. He walked up to the dark office suite and unlocked the door to the small waiting room. Arel hesitated at the threshold but when Harrison pushed past him to examine the empty room, he followed suit.

"Dylan's never late," he muttered as he walked behind the desk to check the time. The clock read 7:30 AM, he was half an hour early. Not once, from the moment he opened his eyes did he look at a clock or his phone.

"That makes sense," he thought aloud recalling his relatively quiet walk into work. Thankful for a bit more time he'd have to get himself together. He started the day by putting on a pot of coffee and drawing back all the window shades in the office flooding the space with light. He stopped to observe the street below coming to life with his usual morning traffic.

"It's going to be a beautiful day," he affirmed to himself. The office building was a little closer to the boardwalk, so he had a clear line of sight to the water and he was looking forward to enjoying his coffee while taking in the view. Since Dylan wasn't expected for a bit longer, he put on his headphones, turned up the music, and fixed his eyes on the islands that were settled in the middle of the East River.

✷✷✷✷

Dylan walked up to the office and saw the lights already on. He paused and experienced a moment of panic before frantically pulling out his phone to check the time, he was early. Breathing a sigh of relief, he walked into the waiting room and observed shades drawn back and the smell of freshly brewed coffee wafting from Arel's office.

'*Okay?*' he thought, walking farther into the waiting room to the desk. Harrison strolled out to greet him. Dylan knelt to give him a good rub around the ears. Giving Harrison a last pat on the head, Dylan noticed Arel quietly singing. He lightened his steps, gently dropping his bag against the desk as he approached the office and leaned against the door frame. Half a minute went by waiting for Arel to notice he was no longer alone before coming to the conclusion that he wasn't going to snap out of it on his own. Dylan began to wave his arms and walk toward Arel's desk.

Arel jumped and sat up. "Jeez!"

Dylan stifled a laugh and Arel removed the headphones from his ears, releasing the music into the room.

He let out a sigh of relief, "Hey, sorry Dylan," flashing an embarrassed smile.

Dylan noticed along with Arel's jumpy demeanor that he had dark bags under his eyes. "You alright, Rel?"

"Yeah." Arel squeezed the bridge of his nose and blinked in rapid succession to bring the moisture back to his eyes and let out an exasperated laugh. "Just a long night. I made a full pot of coffee," he said, eagerly trying to change the subject.

Getting the feeling Arel didn't want to elaborate Dylan nodded, agreeing to shift the conversation quickly. "Yeah, coffee, that's initially why I came in here." He walked over to the kitchenette. "You should come in early more often," he joked, pouring an excessive amount of sugar into his coffee.

Arel smirked at his jest. He appreciated Dylan's ability to keep the office energy light. No one walked into his office without so much as a grin since his father recommended Dylan for the job.

"Alright well, let me know if you need anything. The first appointment is in fifteen," Dylan said quickly, before taking his first sip and strolling to the door.

Before exiting, Dylan turned back and began waving his finger, "By the way..." Dylan paused to take another sip of his coffee. In his anticipation, Arel raised his eyebrows, the universal expression for 'What?'

"You have a lovely singing voice," Dylan teased, walking backward out of the office while simultaneously giving a thumbs up.

Arel laughed, something he was in desperate need of at the moment. When his father told him about one of his students who was looking for a job and that he thought would be a great fit, Arel was a bit apprehensive. That changed as soon as Dylan came in for the interview. It was as if he'd known Dylan for years, he felt like a little brother but quickly learned Dylan was better than any brother. He would drop the whole "walk in on you singing terribly" thing and never bring it up again. Maybe it was out of fear of being fired but Arel hoped it was out of respect. Either way, he was happy to have Dylan on the team.

By the time his first patient arrived, Arel had pushed his troubling dream to the back of his mind. The day was business as usual. All of his patients for the day had been with him from the start of his Port Morris practice. It was optimistic but he viewed a lot of their appointments as progress reports at this point, it was almost effortless. He loved witnessing their improvements and it was the boost he felt he needed today. Harrison spent most of the day in the office even when Dylan attempted to lure him out with treats, which Arel found strange but didn't dwell on it. Harrison finally left his side for his afternoon walk with Dylan, always before the last appointment of the day.

Arel heard the door open and got up to greet his last patient.

"Olivia, Hi!" he hollered as he walked out to greet her in the waiting room.

✸✸✸✸

Harrison's pace was quicker than usual, once around the block took half the time. He dragged Dylan the whole way back to the building. Dylan struggled to hold Harrison as he impatiently muscled his way into the building before Dylan completely opened the door. Finally through, Harrison ran for the elevator so fast the leash ripped from Dylan's grip.

Standing facing the elevator doors was a tall man in a tailored blue suit. He turned around as he heard the echo of paws on the marble floor and revealed a large smile. Harrison launched himself and the man braced for impact, allowing his messenger bag to fall to the floor. He caught the 70-pound labpit at full speed with ease and laughed as Harrison licked his face. Dylan picked up the pace to meet the pair at the elevator.

"Hey Caro, sorry about that," he said, trying to take hold of Harrison's leash.

"Hey Dylan," chuckled the now disheveled man as he put Harrison back down on all fours.

"The only person to call me by my last name was my high school coach." The tone of his voice was light as he brushed himself off and adjusted his glasses.

"Yeah, that was weird, sorry. Eugene? Gene?" As he threw out each name he lifted and lowered each hand like the plates of a scale, gauging Eugene's comfort level.

"Gene is fine," he answered, picking his bag off the floor. The elevator doors finally opened and they stepped inside.

"So what did you play?"

"In high school?" Eugene set his bag down on the floor again to wipe off Harrison's remaining hair and straighten his dress shirt and tie. "Lacrosse, we both played. Rel and me." As he spoke, his foot nudged the bag and its contents slipped out onto the elevator floor. Dylan knelt to scoop everything back into the bag.

"That's cool, I played in high school too." Dylan instantly felt more relaxed when he noticed the name of the book among the folders and papers.

"How are you liking Dr. Sharma's book?" Dylan asked, locking the bag's flap into place.

"I liked it, the way he ended it was interesting. Oh, sorry, did you finish it?" Eugene asked, raking the mahogany waves of hair out of his eyes. He moved to pick up the strap to his bag only to see Dylan holding it out for him to take.

"Thanks," Eugene said, slinging the bag back over his shoulder.

"No, I haven't yet. I'm a bit behind with work and classes," Dylan said, unconsciously rubbing the back of his neck to ease the tension in his shoulders.

"I won't spoil it then, but it has an interesting conclusion," Eugene said with a half smile. "Did he make you read it for class?"

"No, he only mentioned it a few times while in class. You know Dr. S, he won't push it."

"Yeah, and how many of your classmates got the book when it came out?"

"Everyone. He's gone out of his way for all of us at one point or another, we wanted to support him."

Eugene nodded and they stood in silence for a moment.

"What was-" Dylan was cut off by the ring of the elevator doors opening.

As soon as the door opened, Harrison took off toward the office. Neither Eugene nor Dylan ran after him. There were three other offices on this floor and everyone in them loved Harrison. As expected, he stood in front of the office suite door impatiently drumming his front paws on the floor and giving them a look that screamed, "You're not moving fast enough!"

Eugene opened the door and Harrison flew past him and disappeared into Arel's office. Realizing the session was still going on, Dylan ran to quietly close the door behind Harrison.

Olivia greeted Harrison and reached out to pet him, but he blew right by her and circled Arel's desk as if he were hunting for something. Once satisfied that there was no immediate threat, he settled himself at Arel's side. Arel apologized to Olivia for Harrison's abrupt entrance but she just smiled and waved her hand to say 'It's fine.' Their session was nearly over and she was in high spirits.

She was a pretty woman with chestnut brown hair and green eyes.

"I'm happy to see you doing so well on the lower dosage, Olivia. Continue to take steps to empower yourself and create healthy boundaries. You're still doing something for yourself every day?" Arel asked, moving his hands from Harrison's head back to his notepad.

"Yes, I take walks every day along the shore of the river, it's so nice now that it's been cleaned up."

Olivia's eyes shined with enthusiasm.

"I do my breathing exercises there and pick rocks the water washes up. I think of them as gifts." She looked down as she spoke, for a moment unsure if her statement made her sound silly. Relief came over her when she lifted her head again, glad to see he was smiling back at her.

Olivia had always been worried about sharing her thoughts so openly. She was slowly learning not to be afraid when she spoke in her sessions with Arel.

"A-and, like we talked about, I think of something to be grateful for. It really has made a difference. It's like I'm seeing things through a new lens." She moved her hands as she spoke, then turned her attention to the window, looking as if someone had just called her name.

Glancing at the time, Arel spoke to bring her back.

"That's great, Olivia, you should be very proud of the progress you've made. Keep celebrating your victories, big and small," he said with a reassuring smile.

Olivia smiled and nodded and did her best to hold back tears. "Thank you," she said, as she wiped away the single tear that escaped her eye. Harrison walked over and put his head on her lap.

"You take the steps, you are the one improving your life with every choice you make. You," he finished with a proud smile.

Olivia took Harrison's face in her hands. "You're right," she declared and kissed Harrison's head before giving his face one last pet. She took a deep breath and then stood up straight. Looking as if she never shed a tear.

"Alright! That's what I like to hear." He spoke as he walked around the desk to see her out.

"You'll have to bring me one of those rocks next week," Arel joked.

"Sure thing," Olivia laughed.

Arel opened the door to find Dylan and Eugene talking to each other from across the room. Dylan was packing his things to head out for the day.

"Hey, Olivia," Dylan said at the tail end of a laugh, placing a book in his bag. Olivia's gaze was locked on Eugene but quickly glanced toward Dylan to acknowledge his greeting.

"Hi Dylan, how are you today?" she said absentmindedly. Her full attention was on Eugene, her expression in awe. Eugene often had this type of effect on people. He looked like an ethnically ambiguous GQ version of Clark Kent.

"I'm doing good," Dylan said, glancing from Olivia to Eugene, analyzing her fixation.

Eugene noticed the way Dylan's eyes were darting between him and Olivia. He turned his attention to her and flashed a welcoming smile. He got up from his seat, walked over, and extended his hand as he greeted her.

Arel quickly offered an introduction. "I'm sorry Olivia, this is my good friend, Eugene Caro," he said, unphased by his patient's behavior toward his best friend. This was all too normal when Eugene was around.

"It's nice to meet you, Eugene." Olivia sang the words as a smile lit up her face.

"Likewise, Olivia." When Eugene spoke there was no denying the genuine intent of his words.

Olivia giggled, beaming as she made her way toward the door, ignoring Dylan as she walked by. All three men stood and watched as she continued to the door in her trance.

Dylan, amused by this effect Eugene seemed to have on Olivia, broke the silence. "Have a great night, Olivia," he said, pulling her out of her daze.

She turned, quickly realizing she hadn't acknowledged anyone but Eugene.

"Oh! Good night, all," she giggled nervously and waved.

"See you next week!" Arel called after her. He and Dylan waved in unison until she was out of sight.

"Wow," Dylan exclaimed. Arel couldn't quite tell if Dylan was feigning surprise or if he was truly taken aback by her swooning over Eugene. Dylan looked out the door then back at them both.

"I've never seen that in real life," he said flatly, flinging his backpack over his shoulder. Eugene flattened his mouth into a sheepish sort of smile as Arel laughed.

"I'll see you guys," Dylan said, as he made his way toward the door.

"Hey, you should meet us for drinks later," Eugene said stopping Dylan before he passed the threshold.

Dylan turned with excitement but shot Arel a hesitant look.

"Yeah, we're gonna be at Slate around eight." Arel felt a twinge of guilt never having offered.

"Alright, yeah, see you later," Dylan said enthusiastically, knocking on the door frame twice before disappearing down the hall.

"Gotta grab my stuff," Arel said, walking back into his office.

Eugene followed making a beeline for the window and stared thoughtfully at the scene below.

Arel felt heaviness rolling off his usually riant friend now that they were alone. Eugene did his best to keep his troubles to himself, but Arel knew him too well.

"Help me finish that pot of coffee before we head out," Arel said, walking to the kitchenette and grabbing two mugs.

"Sure, I'm not in a rush," Eugene responded without looking away from the window.

Arel placed the mugs on the coffee table and Eugene sat across from him. "How are you holding up at work?" Arel asked, looking over his coffee mug.

Eugene, with a mouth full of coffee, responded by hand signing the letters 'O''K' He took his time before continuing his thought.

"It's not as awkward as I thought it would be, honestly." Eugene looked down at his coffee, his mouth curved into a tired smile.

"I haven't seen Lin yet. I wanted to give her space. The last thing she needs is her brother digging into your breakup."

"She probably wouldn't tell you anything. You know her, ever the one to suffer in silence," Eugene said, shaking his head slightly and playfully rolling his eyes.

Arel, with a mouth full of coffee, narrowed his eyes and pursed his lips, annoyed by his sister's bullheaded tendency to go at everything alone.

"Well, it still sucks, for both of you. I'm sorry, Gene." Arel spoke looking down at his lukewarm coffee.

Eugene tilted his head upward and smiled half-heartedly. "I'm not, man," he said with a sigh.

Arel went rigid, frozen by the sudden wave of anger on his sister's behalf, but he waited for Eugene to finish his thought before reacting defensively.

Eugene continued, "I'm glad that it happened now," he said slowly. "I'd never want to get to a point where we'd resent each other. There are things I want and things that she wants that just don't line up for a future together," he paused for a moment, "I'll always love your sister, but we've just come to the end of our road."

They sat in silence as they both let his words reverberate through the room and settle into reality. Eugene broke the silence to praise Arel's sister's strength and determination to continue their working relationship through their current situation. Arel's mind couldn't help but drift. His sister had always been a rock in terms of her emotions. He couldn't help but worry about her internalizing any negative thoughts or feelings. Eugene's voice had begun to drift into the background of his mind and was close to completely disappearing into the crowd of his thoughts until two words rang clear through the noise.

"Sorry, what did you just say?" Arel sat up and leaned forward, his heart beating faster.

"The Brothers Project, Nalini finalized it with the city yesterday."

CHAPTER TWO

ORANGE-EYES

"Wait, what's the Brother's Project? What is that?" Arel spoke so quickly it sounded as if it were all one word.

Eugene's brow furrowed with confusion. "It's the development of the North and South Brother islands." Eugene got up, walked over to the window, and pointed to the two islands settled in the middle of the East River.

The islands Arel had been fixated on from the moment he looked out the window that morning. Eugene watched Arel's eyes dash from left to right, but at nothing in particular, as if he were working out an invisible math problem in front of him. As he was running through the events of his dream, Eugene walked back over, sat down, and waited patiently. Arel finally brought his attention back to look at Eugene.

"So...?" Eugene didn't have to finish his thought, his expression spoke for him. *'You wanna tell what this is about?'*

"Yeah, so-"

Arel proceeded to tell him about the dream he had the night before, describing every detail and what happened after he woke up. Eugene sat expressionless taking in all the information being thrown at him.

He knew Arel's history with dreams, how strange they could be. There had been many times in the past he would dream of things that turned out to be true. Dreaming of people he'd never met only to meet those same people at a later date or getting messages from people who have passed away.

Eugene thought he couldn't be phased by anything anymore. Arel finished the rundown of his dream and waited for Eugene's verdict.

Eugene rubbed his chin in thought. "Yeah, that's, uh, that's a new one. I'm kind of creeped out, actually." He wasn't looking at Arel as he spoke, his eyes were on the islands. A chill moved through Eugene's limbs, his body shook it out.

"Right?" Arel agreed, relieved his friend shared his sentiment. "I've had this weird feeling all day, like, a part of the dream woke up with me."

Eugene leaned forward and rested his elbows on his knees as he thought. "Like that time you dreamed of your roommate's deceased grandmother and she hung around till you gave him her message?"

Arel snapped his fingers and pointed at him. "Exactly! Wait, I don't remember telling you that one." Arel's voice rose slightly, surprised.

"Dude, you didn't have to. Everyone was talking about how they didn't want to be your roommate after that." Eugene didn't intend his statement to be funny, but it broke the seriousness of the moment, and they shared a short laugh.

"I didn't want a roommate after that! She didn't have to show up like that. She WAS NOT a pleasant woman. I still can't stand to hear the song 'Big Yellow Taxi.'"

The vision of the old woman flashed in his mind. The blood pooled to the side of her face in large blotches at her jaw and then dissipated into freckle-like formations up the left side of her cheek. An indication of how she fell when she collapsed and died. The sight of her barred teeth, to show him her rotting green gums, and then the taunting way she sang that song.

'*Don't it always seem to go, that you don't know what you've got till it's gone*'

It gave him the heebie-jeebies all over again. He shook his head to clear the thought, stood up, and walked over to the window. The sun shone directly toward the building, casting everything the light touched in gold. He crossed his arms as he pondered solutions. He can figure out what this is all about, nothing like this ever stuck around for too long. '*Maybe I can wait it out?*" he thought, but then another idea crossed his mind.

"I have to talk to my sister-"

"You should talk to Lin-"

They threw out their conclusions at the same time as if they were having the same mental conversation.

"Yeah, I'll send her a text first thing in the morning and see if she has time to talk, I don't have any appointments until noon." They looked at each other and nodded. With his sister being the head of The Brothers development project, he could at least learn more about it and why he got the warning. Maybe that would appease whatever was hanging around, like his college roommate situation. It was a plan, for now. Arel stood a little taller, a bit of weight had fallen off his shoulders.

Eugene looked at his watch. "We should get going if we're gonna hit Slate. You still up for it?" he asked, grabbing his bag.

"Yeah, I have to drop Harrison back at home," Arel said, walking back to gather his things. "Go, I'll catch you later."

Eugene bent over to pet Harrison goodbye. "Yeah, I've got to get out of this suit. It still has your hair all over it," he said holding Harrison's face in his hands.

Harrison gave Eugene a sullen look as he kissed him on the head and walked through the door, giving the door frame two knocks before disappearing.

Harrison was now laser-focused on every move Arel made.

"You ready, buddy?"

He looked up to find Harrison staring at him from across the desk, with a look on his face that Arel understood to be betrayal. Arel ignored his attitude, they went through this every time he was left home alone.

✶✶✶✶

Harrison took his sweet time walking home. Arel tried everything he could to convince his four-legged companion to move faster, even bribing him with a hot dog, it didn't work. Harrison refused to walk and eat, forcing Arel to sit on a bench and feed him the hot dog piece by piece, he even chewed unusually slowly. They got back to the apartment way later than Arel planned. Now running short on time, he scarfed down the other hot dog he didn't get to eat on their walk as he looked through his closet. Harrison watched miserably as Arel ran back and forth from his bedroom to the bathroom and back again. Arel did his best to tame his wild black curls as he dressed the rest of his body, convinced it would save him time. He gave himself a once-over in the full-length mirror secured to his door before leaving his bedroom. Can't go wrong with a black tee, black jeans, and sneakers to match his maroon bomber jacket, he was feeling confident in his choice of attire. Finally ready to leave, he was halted by yet another obstacle in his way, a grumpy Harrison sitting in front of the door blocking his exit.

"I'll be back in a few hours buddy, you'll be fine," Arel said reassuringly.

Harrison didn't budge. Arel let out an audible sigh as he walked into the kitchen and grabbed a treat. An attempt to bribe him once again, and this time it worked. Harrison begrudgingly stepped to the side of the door to receive his treat and allowed Arel to walk out the door and close it behind him. A wave of relief and excitement came over him as he locked the door, ready to be rid of the weirdness of the day. He got the notification that his Chariot driver was around the corner as he entered the elevator and just like that, the events of the day and night before quickly found their way to the back of his mind.

✱✱✱✱

The car pulled up to the bar and Arel thanked his Chariot driver, not sure if she could hear him over the music. She flashed him a smile and he took it as confirmation.

He walked up to the Slate entrance and focused on the bar's slogan printed on the tinted glass doors. **'Every Night is a Clean Slate,'** In big white letters.

"Right," he sighed under his breath as he opened the door. He walked through the crowded bar scanning the faces. He knew Eugene would most likely be near the bar toward the back, open to the patio. He finally spotted him playing pool with Dylan and as if on cue, Eugene looked up and nodded in his direction.

"I thought something might have gotten to you," he said when Arel was in earshot, only half joking. He took a swig of his drink cautiously eyeing Arel over his glass. Dylan chuckled as he lined up his shot, clearly unaware of his meaning.

"Not yet," Arel threw out casually. "I'm gonna grab a drink, you guys good? Want anything?" Both Eugene and Dylan surveyed their drinks, both having a good deal remaining.

"I'm good," they declared in unison.

He found a spot at the bar and waited for the barkeep to finish several shots for a group to the right of him. Pouring the last shot, they looked up and nodded at Arel, a nonverbal acknowledgment that they'd be with him shortly.

Arel unconsciously shifted his body to the left, his eyes mindlessly drawn to the corner of the bar. He locked eyes with a woman who had already been looking in his direction. Her eyes were narrow like she was trying to figure him out from across the room, he knew that look, she was trying to get a read on him. Arel felt a smile form across his face, an action he was in control of ninety percent of the time. She smiled back, using the beer bottle in her hand, she gestured to the spot at the bar next to him asking if she could join him. He glanced back at his friends who were now in the company of two women. He wasn't being missed. He nodded and invitingly gestured to the empty space next to him. He quickly ordered a gin and tonic and unconsciously glanced toward the corner where she'd been standing although she had already begun making her way around the bar to meet him.

There was now a tall man with an athletic build standing where she stood, staring right at him. Strangely, Arel could focus on nothing other than his eyes, realizing they weren't just light brown, but orange. The longer he looked the brighter they became and time stood still.

'*No fucking way.*'

Arel felt his body tense, he closed his eyes and when he opened them again the man was gone and the woman was now standing beside him at the bar. He felt the tension in his muscles subside, immediately at ease now that she was next to him. In the spot where she stood across the bar, he wasn't able to make out all of her features. Now standing before him, he observed the hair that was obscured by shadow was now illuminated into black locs with highlights of auburn red. The top half of her hair was secured at the back of her head as the rest cascaded over her shoulders, displaying gold beads placed in a different location on each loc. They shone like stars against her midnight hair.

Her beauty was hypnotizing, her strikingly dark eyes, her soft full lips, and the lights shining over her added an amber glow to her warm mocha skin, like the rays of a setting sun. She reminded him of a character out of a fairytale in her olive maxi dress. There was something unreal about her and she felt so familiar, but he couldn't put his finger on it.

"I know you," she said, narrowing her eyes and taking a sip of her beer.

Arel's eyes widened, both surprised and delighted by her forward declaration. "I was just trying to figure out why you look so familiar," he stammered, trying to control his smile.

"Evaine," she said, putting her hand out.

"Arel." He glanced down to take her hand, then quickly back up to meet her gaze. He continued shaking her hand and smiling as if the longer they stared into each other's eyes, one of them would remember something. Beginning to realize how strange this moment was, they both laughed and broke their handshake.

"So, what do you do? Maybe I've seen you around?" She held her beer close to her lips as she spoke and took a swig after asking her question.

"Psychiatrist, I have a practice off of Black Water Street." He watched as she tilted her head and glanced up to the left, trying to recall something.

"Nah, that's not it," she said after a second or two.

Arel laughed, he couldn't help but be taken in by the delivery of her words. The way she spoke had a lightness to it, which seemed in contrast to the velvety tone of her voice. Somehow, she made the dissonance work in perfect harmony, it was captivating.

"Ok. What do you do, maybe we've bumped into each other that way?" he asked with genuine interest.

"I work in parks and recreation, and I would have remembered if you came in and applied for a permit." Evaine squinted as she said the word 'you' and finished her statement with a playful smile.

'*Parks and rec, makes sense,*' Arel thought. She had strong grounded energy, like the rejuvenating sensation of standing amongst a wealth of trees.

"University maybe? Where did you study?" Arel asked quickly. He was suddenly hyperaware of his every movement. So many thoughts were running through his mind. He shifted his weight from left to right and relaxed his shoulders.

"State University-ESF, Syracuse," she stated, matter-of-fact. She set her bottle down and turned to lean on the bar.

"I spent some time around Syracuse, maybe that's it," he suggested cheerfully.

There was a pause as she thought it over.

"But you're not from the northeast," he added with a playfully accusatory tone. As if exposing a not-so-veiled secret.

Evaine laughed, "Sharp observation," she mumbled. Nodding her head, she looked down at the bottle in her hand, impressed.

When she looked back up to Arel's face her eyes had shifted from playful to studious. She was trying to figure him out again.

"What gave me away?" she asked, smiling. She turned the rest of her body to face him leaning her left arm on the bar, making herself comfortable for his explanation.

"You have a warmth not innate in us northerners," he smiled, keeping his eyes locked on hers as he took a sip of his gin and tonic. He watched her smile widen as she brushed her hair off her shoulder.

"You're not so cold."

"My parents are Canadian," he replied quickly, his delivery dry.

Evaine let out a loud uncontrolled laugh and quickly covered her mouth to muffle the sound, he couldn't help but join her.

Her laugh danced in his ears and somehow reminded him that he hadn't been there alone. He took a glance over to the pool tables to see if Eugene and Dylan were still talking to the two women who approached them earlier. A new group had taken over the table where they were playing and he began to scan the rest of the room. He hadn't noticed how dense the crowd had become. He finally spotted Eugene in conversation, the doors blocking whoever he was speaking to. Dylan probably, just out of sight.

In shifting his attention back to Evaine his eyes locked with a pair that was staring directly into his, the orange eyes from before. Hypnotizing, it was all he could see, just those eyes. Like in a dream, the room began to darken, illuminating them further. He felt a strange sensation come over him and he was no longer aware of his limbs as if being pulled away from his physical body. The trance was broken by pressure on his chest pulling him back to his bones. He didn't realize that the sound of the blood pumping in his ears had drowned out all sounds around him, even Evaine as she tried to get his attention.

"Hey, ya'right?" Evaine looked around her to see whatever it was that was causing Arel's face to contort into a fearful mask. Nothing. There was no gruesome brawl or even a salacious scene. Nothing that would cause someone to fall completely out of reality. She waved her hands in front of his face to no avail. She said his name one more time and placed her hand on his chest, over his heart. Evaine watched as life came back into his vacant eyes, then peered down at hers. Arel looked down at Evaine's hand resting just over his heart and placed his hand over hers. Without thinking he interlaced her fingers with his. Like muscle memory. An action that would have seemed too intimate for two people who had met only minutes before. With anyone else, it would have been a bold move. At least that's how he felt, being particular about his own personal space. He looked from their interlocked hands to her face and for a moment he forgot what had happened and where he was. He was safe at least for a moment, with her.

Time had seemed to stop but his calm lasted only an instant. Arel was snapped back to reality when he was hit with an urgency that appeared to come from heat rising from his stomach. Whatever that orange-eyed thing was, it was still there and it wasn't in his head.

"What was that?" Evaine asked, her voice laden with concern.

"I'm so sorry, I have to go," Arel apologized, pulling their hands from his chest but continuing to hold hers. Evaine's expression slid from concern to confusion. Arel looked down at their still interlocked hands and gave her hand a little squeeze before releasing it and allowing it to drop back to her side.

"I'll call you," he said quickly before disappearing into the crowd.

"Oh, okay!" she yelled over that crowd as he disappeared, only to realize once he was out of sight they never had the chance to exchange numbers. She stood on her tiptoes to try and see how far he had gone, but she couldn't find him among the packed bodies. Her gut told her he wasn't blowing her off and she took comfort in it and somehow knew she'd see him again. Evaine downed what was left of her beer and unintentionally slammed the bottle back on the counter, turning the heads of a few people in her general vicinity, including one of the bartenders. Not being one to squander the attention of a bartender, she asked for another.

★★★★

Arel frantically texted Eugene explaining his sudden departure. He was going to see him in the morning anyway. His mind raced as he sat in the back of his rideshare waiting for Eugene's reply.

'*What is this?*' he asked himself, thinking back to his past experiences with anything that could be classified as 'supernatural.'

Nothing he'd ever encountered has ever been this aggressive. On high alert, he kept looking up at the rearview mirror half expecting to see the driver glaring back at him with orange eyes. He took in three deep breaths, slowly counting down from three after each exhale, willing his muscles to relax. It worked, when he reached number one he had managed to get his leg to stop bouncing. He closed his eyes and continued to repeat the process until the driver reached the front of his apartment building. His nerves were back to normal as he walked up the incline to the glass doors. He even debated if he should just go back to the bar, convincing himself it was just an anxiety-induced hallucination brought on by exhaustion. After coming to that conclusion, he felt it was best just to head up to the apartment and get a good night's sleep before meeting up with his sister in the morning.

The fluorescent lights in the lobby bothered his eyes more than usual. He kept his eyes closed and pinched the bridge of his nose as he waited for the elevator to reach the lobby floor, continuing his deep breathing.

By the time the elevator doors opened on his floor, he had calmed himself to the point that he was ready to drop as soon as he walked into his apartment. Arel stopped just outside the elevator doors before continuing down the hall.

"What is it with hallways? How can they be well-lit and have a creepy dark tinge at the same time?" he mumbled as he reached into his pocket to get his keys. Before inserting the key in the lock he remembered Harrison needed to go out before he could get to sleep. He let his head fall back and released a defeated sigh, before turning the key and pushing his apartment door open in one swift motion.

As the door swung open, it took him a second to realize Harrison wasn't there to greet him.

His apartment was pitch black, not even a light from any of the appliances. He hesitated in the doorway before stepping inside.

"Harrison?" he called softly. *'Maybe he's asleep,'* he thought reassuringly to himself.

That didn't explain why the entire apartment was pitch black.

"I don't need this right now," he whispered into the dark, taking another cautious step. He pushed the door all the way against the wall to allow as much light from the hallway into his apartment as possible.

"Harrison!" A mixture of fear and anger painted the tone of his voice. Silence. He didn't hear the jingle of his collar like usual or the sound of his ears flapping when he got up to shake himself off. Arel's breath began to quicken and his stomach started to cramp with emotional panic. He started to run toward his bedroom no longer fearing what could be waiting for him in the dark. He stopped dead a few steps from his bedroom door when he heard the soft squeak of the front door and then its subsequent close. He didn't dare turn around, fear temporarily paralyzing his legs. He began to run through his choices at the moment. Option one, make a break for his bedroom, barricade the door, and call for help. Possibly getting the responding officer hurt or killed. Or option two, turn around and face whatever was blocking his way out.

"The latter," he exhaled.

He knew he was near a light switch and slid his trembling hand up the wall to find it. Slowly he willed his legs to move. They were heavy and he felt the uncomfortable tingle of sleeping limbs. He could hear it now, breathing as he prepared to turn and face the thing that had followed him out of his dream. He counted down from three and made an about-face.

Arel kept his head down, terrified of the orange eyes that were waiting once he looked up. He started to feel his stomach contract, its contents rising to burn his esophagus. He struggled against his tightening chest to take a breath and now his emotions betrayed him as he fought the urge to cry. His body did not know how to react to the fear in this situation. Whatever stood in front of him was unlike anything he had ever encountered. The fear he was experiencing wasn't formed by circumstance or ingrained by evolution. Arel knew this was something that existed beyond the realm of men. He could feel its expanse as it began to engulf his senses and suddenly he was overcome with the suffocating notion of being completely alone. That single notion pulled all the warmth from his body. He fought to take hold of his thoughts as he felt himself shutting down. He couldn't think of anything, not a memory, or smell that sparked a feeling of warmth.

Warmth.

His mind took hold of the word and focused until his mind created a visual.

Light.

He saw an ember in his mind and focused on its growth. He focused on it moving down his arms into his fingers, slowly bringing enough life back to move them.

He remembered where he was and lifted his eyes from the floor, not sure how long he had been in that position. There they were, the same orange eyes he saw at the bar, they were brighter now that they met his gaze in the dark. They made his mind swim. There was always a definitive line between realms, there were rules, boundaries, and choices.

Boundaries, his mind hung on that word. The light that had brought life back to his idle body had turned into an angry fire. No longer afraid, he flipped the light switch on.

The light from the switch only illuminated the room between them creating a comfortable barrier. The hallway to the front door was still cast in shadow. He let his eyes adjust, the orange eyes were nowhere to be found. The light that extended into the hallway now exposed a shadow that was making its way across the floor to him.

Chapter Three

THE BEGINNING

"Harrison?" Arel called out hesitantly. He held his breath as Harrison walked into the light and sat just outside the shadow of the hallway.

"Christ!" he exclaimed, letting the top half of himself fall over to lean on his knees. "Woo, you scared the shit out of my buddy," he said with a sigh of relief. Harrison stayed in place, studying Arel as he paced the room to work off the adrenalin before collapsing on the couch in a huff.

"Deep breaths, Rel."

The words came out of thin air and sent Arel flying off the couch searching furiously for its source. At lightning speed he ran through the apartment and turned on all the lights, only to be left wanting for answers. He walked slowly back to the living room, one phrase repeating again and again, *'It's just a trick, it's just a trick of the mind.'*

"Sit down," the voice said calmly. This time Arel looked right at the source. He looked down at the black labpit and watched as his eyes flashed fire orange.

Arel screamed and grabbed the candle pillar off his coffee table and held it up over his head ready to throw.

"WHAT DID YOU DO TO MY DOG? WHERE'S HARRISON?" His words came out in a shrill jumble.

"It's me, Rel, I'm Harrison. I need you to calm down. The neighbors are going to call the police if they hear anything else." Harrison's face remained expressionless matching the clinical voice Arel heard in his mind.

"Wh-what?" Arel's voice shook, feeling the scratchy pain of his screams. He lowered himself slowly to the couch again taking slow deep breaths to bring down his heart rate, all the while staring into Harrison's now orange eyes.

"I have to be dreaming," he assured himself, at the same time, the events of the evening rewound through his mind. Not a moment of consciousness was lost.

'*What's happening?*' he thought, holding the candle he had in hand up to his nose and breathing in the comforting scent of coffee, bourbon, and books. The smell was soothing but he still felt an overwhelming lightheadedness.

"Listen, I'll tell you everything you want to know, but right now the neighbors are on their way over here and I need you not to freak out." The voice spoke as if instructing a child.

"Not to frea-" Arel's voice cut out mid-word as he watched Harrison turn from his small dog form into a seamless replication of himself. He felt his head swim and struggled to keep conscious as he watched himself walk toward the front door and convince the neighbors that everything was fine. The last thing he heard was the sound of his doppelganger laughing with his neighbors as the world faded to black.

✸✸✸✸

Arel awakened to the dark, once again not knowing where he was. He commanded himself to blink, to which his body did not obey.

'*Don't panic, don't panic,*' he repeated to himself. '*Am I in a coma? Stop, Arel. You're fine.*' It proved difficult to keep himself from breaking down. The doom chatter from his monkey mind was throwing out all the worst scenarios to be considered in his present condition.

'*Focus.*' he thought. A focal point, something he could use as a tether to ground himself to his body. He began to concentrate on the rise and fall of his chest, breathing steady and deep. That worked in calming him down so he tried again to open his eyes but nothing happened. All he could do in this state was observe so he shifted his attention to what he could feel and brought his awareness to his arms. They were heavy as they rested on his legs, and it hit him, he was sitting up. The realization gave him a rush of excitement but there was something off. This body felt alien, it was lighter and he felt the slight weight of something resting on his right shoulder. He could feel the comfortable heat of the sun on his head and back, the wind blowing loose hair across his face. '*Oh, ok. I'm definitely dreaming,*' he comforted himself. '*This isn't my body, okay, but even in a dream I should be able to control the body.*'

Without his instruction, the eyes fluttered open as a voice broke the tranquil sound of the tree leaves dancing in the warm wind. The eyes adjusted quickly to the light of the sun. *Her* eyes. He was finally able to catch a glimpse of the body he was visiting. It was like watching a scene through a pair of binoculars. She focused her sight on a boy walking toward her. This boy was of graduate age with a shaved head wearing, what Arel related to, Buddhist robes. He was moving fast in large strides and exaggerated movements. Arel knew this walk, this is how his sister came at him when they were young. As the boy drew closer the more familiar he became. He was speaking a language Arel didn't understand but, like a radio in a moving car, the words became clearer with every step closer.

"You think you can take my place?" the boy hissed the words like a viper. He was looking for a fight. Arel could feel it coming and worried for the woman whose body he was currently inhabiting. She sat up tall and calm with her heartbeat steady, her muscles relaxed. Arel was impressed by how well she kept herself under control. There were no fluctuations in facial expressions, her face was like a stone as she allowed him to finish his attempt at a verbal lashing. Arel could feel her pity for him, she understood that to this boy she was a threat. A threat to the love, he believed, he would receive through his accomplishments had she not been there to outshine him. He had been blinded by the need for external validation from his peers and instructors. Another trait he'd observed in his big sister. Just as the thought crossed his mind, the boy's exterior faded like a mirage to reveal the younger version of the sister he grew up with. Then a thought dropped into his mind. This boy was his sister from another time, another life. And the reason he couldn't control this woman's body was because he was reliving this moment through the eyes of his past life self. A strange conclusion to come to, but it was a truth he felt at his core.

"I can't take your place or hold you back from what is already yours, only you can do that." She spoke without fluctuating her tone of voice or facial expression as she stood to face him.

'*Oh Shit,*' Arel thought, he watched the boy's expression slide from self-righteous anger to embarrassment. The boy knew she was right and it enraged him, he refused to take accountability for his own feelings of inadequacy. He couldn't stand the way she stood before him, the audacity of her strength. He took it as a challenge.

Arel and this woman could feel the energy build around the boy, she was standing before a storm about to break.

She looked past the boy to a man leaning against a tree, watching them and eating an apple. He nodded to her as he took a bite. Arel was struck with surprise, he'd seen this man before. The man with the orange eyes. He looked exactly like he did at the bar, the same tall athletic build, only now he could see more of his face. He had a downturned nose with a narrow base, a square jaw, and shoulder-length hair. He stood in stark contrast to the surrounding monks.

This man didn't look the least bit worried for her and took another bite of his apple. The woman's attention was brought back to the boy as he moved to strike her face. Arel watched as if it were in slow motion. She gracefully swept his hand away from her face and rolled his arm to lock at his back. He was caught off guard by her speed and when she pushed him away, he tumbled to his knees.

She walked over and held out her hand to help him up. The boy squinted up at her, his expression quickly twisted into anger and embarrassment again. He slapped her hand away and rushed at her, determined to land a blow. Arel watched as she flowed with every strike, it felt as if she were dancing around him, but it didn't take long before he felt her patience beginning to fade. She began to move with more force and stopped flowing in defense, she wanted to hurt him. They were now close to a tree and he made the mistake of throwing a punch to her face that she deflected. As his fist flew past her head, she barely thought as she gripped the side of his face and with a savage cry, drove it with all her might into the side of the tree. The boy's head made a low crunch sound as it made contact with the trunk.

The fight was over, she had finished it. A wave of satisfaction fell over her as he lay still in the grass. The pride of victory was short-lived as she noticed blood flowing from his ears. Onlookers rushed past her to pick up the boy's lifeless body. Arel felt her heartbeat quicken and the sickening pain of regret build in her stomach. She turned to look at the man with orange eyes. He was now standing up straight, his hands behind his back, and in his eyes a compassionate sadness. Arel read his look as clearly as if words had been written on his face. In those eyes was sadness, not only for the boy but for her having to carry the burden of knowing the pain she inflicted due to her lack of self-control.

The Orange-Eyed man never opened his mouth but spoke all the same.

'Time to go, Kirana.'

✸✸✸✸

Arel opened his eyes to the sound of a glass placed on the coffee table in front of him, next to the now-lit candle. His eyes focused in time to see the man with the orange eyes sit down across from him. His body shot up faster than it was meant to and he had to wait for the dizziness to subside.

He stared at the Orange-Eyed man across from him and picked up the full glass of water, gulping it down as if he'd been deprived of it. He stood and began pacing the room, eyes remaining on the Orange-Eyed man calmly drinking his tea.

"There's no need to jump to the worst-case scenario, this is most likely a hypnopompic hallucination brought on by sleep distur-bance."

"You're not hallucinating, Arel," Orange-Eyes said calmly.

"Says the man with glowing orange eyes sitting across from me drinking, what is that? Tea!" Arel snapped.

"Ok, Doc, a hypnopompic hallucination can explain what's happening right now, but how can you explain the bar?" Orange-Eyes countered, before taking another sip.

"A far more serious diagnosis," Arel muttered, more to himself than the perceived mental manifestation sitting in his armchair.

"Ok, where is Harrison right now? If I am indeed a hallucination then he would be here, right?" Orange-Eyes asked, his tone losing its airy calm.

Arel fell back into panic and he frantically ran into his bedroom and then back out into the living room. Confused and afraid, doing his best to rationalize what was happening. He quickly thought back to the moment he arrived back at his apartment. The door was locked. Harrison couldn't have run away and the only other person to have a key was his sister, only for emergencies. Arel pulled his phone out to see if there was a message from her about needing to get into his apartment, but there was nothing. Arel wrote that off as a possibility. He looked back to the man studying him from across the room. "Did you do something to my dog?" he uttered, sitting himself down at the far end of the couch.

"I'd have to be real to do that. So for me to do anything, it would be *you* who did something by your own logic. Very '*Secret Window*' of you," Orange-Eyes mused.

"Nope, this isn't possible," Arel said to himself, dragging his hand down his face.

"Contrary to popular belief, impossible isn't really a thing. Most things that seem improbable are just out of human understanding or technology. You'll get there at some point, hopefully, if you don't kill each other first," Orange-Eyes said before taking another sip of his tea.

"Cut the shit! Tell me what the fuck is going on! First, you scare the shit out of me in that dream with that cryptic fucking message!

You follow me to the bar and WHAT WAS THAT PITCH BLACK, CLOAK AND DAGGER BULLSHIT JUST NOW?" Arel caught himself and stopped speaking. He didn't realize he'd stood up and was leaning across the table that separated him from this thing that had been torturing him. He looked down at his clenched fists, released them, and let the shaking abate.

"Who are you? What are you?" Arel asked, defeated, allowing himself to fall back onto the couch.

"Humankind call us, dragon," Orange-Eyes said matter-of-factly as he traced his fingers along the top of his mug.

Arel lifted his head from his hands. "Get fucked," he mumbled, letting his head roll back and hit the wall behind him with a soft thud.

"Will you let me finish?" Orange-Eyes asked.

"Do I have a choice?" Arel snapped back.

"You always have a choice. You can let me help you or you can deal with what's coming on your own," he sat back and settled into the chair unbothered, "So are you ready to listen?"

Arel reluctantly nodded, not knowing what to believe.

"You asked who I am and the short answer is we're family," Orange-Eyes started and waited a moment for an outburst or a smart-ass remark but Arel just stared at him and waited for him to continue.

"I lived among the stars, observing the cosmos until I saw an explosion of light come from the earth. That light was you. I was drawn to Earth when you touched down on this planet for the first time. Unfortunately, when you were born the light you radiated also attracted other entities to you. Your birth family was lost and you were orphaned that same night. I raised you and you became part of my journey as much as I am a part of yours," Orange-Eyes paused and his expression went blank as if he was processing information, "What you just saw while you were sleeping was a glimpse of that first life and I've been with you in every life after."

"So the dream I just had about that woman kicking that kid's ass, that was me? I was that woman?"

"Yeah, no one incarnates as the same gender or within the same culture every time, it would be like living in different shades of the same color. A soul can't grow that way," Orange-Eyes said quickly.

"No, that's not what I meant, I get that, I'm just doing my best to ground this whole situation," Arel said, staring into his empty glass.

"So, how are you able to look human?" he asked skeptically.

"I'm a multidimensional being, I can take any form or no form at all. We're not bound by the physical limitations of this reality," Orange-Eyes answered without skipping a beat.

"Ok, so what about how dragons appear in stories and art?"

"The forms depicted in art and literature are how our true form manifests in this dense 3D reality. Obviously, we all look different." Orange-Eyes set his tea down on the coffee table.

Arel nodded and narrowed his eyes, thinking over everything he'd heard so far. He wasn't expecting the answers this Orange-Eyed man was giving, nor did he remember hearing anything like this in the past. This whole situation was complicated and elaborate and if he had been ill or delusional, someone would have mentioned a change in his behavior. At the very least, Dylan would have noticed something at work. His reluctance to believe was beginning to wane as he continued to listen to Orange-Eyes' story.

"So what do dragons do then? Are you all like guardian angels? Does everyone have one?"

Orange-Eyes couldn't tell if he was being sarcastic but he decided to go with it, "Ok, let me start from the beginning," Orange-eyes started

"How far back is 'the beginning?'"

"The first colonies were called Edens, where the first of your kind were created."

"Oh, we're going *all the way back*. Okay," Arel interrupted.

"It's kind of important to where we are now, so yeah. Anyway, humans were made of the earth, and counterparts were tasked with populating the planet. Humans were not like how they are today, they held considerable power. They lived long lives to the point where no one is sure if the originals that survived ever knew death at all."

"Survived?"

"I'll get to it. These human beings knew no pain, no hunger, or sickness, and were able to manipulate matter with thought. Many of my kind lived among you as teachers and guardians. It was a beautiful time of peace, growth, and knowledge. Now, you're thinking 'what happened,' right? Adam, Adam happened."

"Adam? Like Adam and Eve?" Arel asked, skeptically.

"Adam had a wife before Eve known infamously as Lilith, amongst other names. She was his original counterpart. Adam felt his physical strength entitled him dominance over his partner and demanded her submission. To which Lilith rightfully responded 'Fuck you. I'm out,' leaving Adam to the embarrassment of a failed partnership in Eden, as all others lived in harmony with their partners. A few neighbors offered to go find Lilith and try to convince her to return but after finding her and hearing her side of the story, they decided to honor her decision and wished her well on her journey. After she refused to return, Adam prayed to the Creator for another partner, one that would be subservient to him. But as he did not honor the partner he was blessed with, his request was denied. Now here's where shit goes downhill.

"Adam says, 'Fine I'll make my own partner of my flesh, and she will obey me,' so Eve was created by Adam. This enraged all who lived in Eden as he defiled the natural order for the sole purpose of dominance and control. Adam and Eve were expelled from Eden and were stripped of all the power they were graced with, as he could no longer be trusted. And so, the world fell out of balance after the first murder was committed by his son, Cain. Adam, overcome by his rage and grief over the death of Abel, laid blame on his expulsion from Eden and his first wife, Lilith. The death of Abel was the beginning of Adam's mission to eradicate Edens from the face of the earth in retribution. His rage was primarily taken out on the feminine counterparts with the help of some who joined him. Few Edens survived his sieges with the help of my kind and others. The fall of the Edens snowballed into all-out wars between brothers, all for the sake of possession and dominance. Adam's rage and greed created a ripple effect that resulted in the drive to possess what was valued."

"Fuck, they didn't cover that in the 'World Religion' course," Arel interjected.

"Powers that be would never admit the truth, they'd lose control. Anyway, this is what began the suppression of the feminine or yin. If masculine, or yang, is the drive then yin is the direction. Without direction, there is chaos. Power became the driving force with no other aim than to gain more power, plummeting this world into a series of vicious cycles. Dragons are keepers of the knowledge of the cosmos, so people began hunting us to harvest our meat, hide, and bones. All in the belief it would give them access to the power and knowledge we hold. Few were lost, but we agreed to step back from humanity. Some of us returned to the stars, others took to the comfort of the oceans and mountains. Few took on human forms to try to fight this imbalance head-on. In falling out of balance, humans have forgotten how to connect with the divine, they forgot all they were and would not hear us." Orange-Eyes then released a deep breath, shut his eyes tight, and opened them again. He'd spoken while staring at the unlit candle and hadn't blinked. He looked at Arel to find him staring back at him, eyes wide in awe, his mouth had retracted into a small thin line.

Arel broke the silence. "Well, shit. That's quite the story," he said as he stood up to bring feeling back to his legs. He started pacing back and forth again.

"So what happened to Lilith? Did he find her or did she really go on to become a baby-eating demon that gave men wet dreams," Arel joked, in an attempt to loosen the tension.

"Vicious rumors Adam spread to anyone that would listen," Orange-Eyes shrugged, "A scribe caught wind and took off with it."

"So what's the deal with the apple? How did that become a thing?" Arel asked, stopping his pacing to look at the Orange-Eyed man.

"You really think that asshole was going to take responsibility for being expelled from Eden? He spewed so many different stories blaming Eve, but that was just the one that stuck. Poor Eve, he abused the shit out of her," Orange-eyes said, shaking his head.

"I'm still having trouble wrapping my head around all of this, let alone the idea of bible characters actually being responsible for the fall of humanity," Arel sighed and there was a long pause before he spoke again. "Can we go back? Why is this happening to me right now?"

"Oh, yeah. I kind of went off track, my fault. Go ahead."

"You said 'my light' brought you here, What does that make me? Am I a dragon?" Arel asked, partly joking.

"No dragons don't incarnate as humans," Orange-Eyes replied emphatically, "Certain celestial entities, like some would call Angels or Devas do, it's usually in short terms though." He threw out that last bit as if it were an everyday fact he left out.

Arel stopped again, turning to face Orange-Eyes again, his eyes wide in disbelief, he opened his mouth to ask but was cut off.

"No, you're not an angel." Stifling a laugh as he watched Arel's face drop.

"So what's the deal then? How exactly do I fit into this?" he demanded growing slightly annoyed.

"We call souls like you 'Beacons.' People like you are often drawn to healing professions. Your soul gives off a healing light that reaches across realms, in this 3D world, it manifests as a type of magnetism. It's why you're so successful in your practice, your light draws in the broken and lost. In turn, your light draws out their own, helping them heal their blockages and traumas, and ultimately balancing their internal masculine and feminine. On the flip side of that, as a light in the dark, you attract the greedy and selfish, who want to use your light to their advantage." Orange-Eye's voice finished with a sympathetic tone.

"That would explain 75 percent of relationships growing up," Arel mumbled, mindlessly biting his thumbnail. He thought about the revolving door of friends and lovers that came to him broken and then dropped him cold when they no longer needed him. The worst was when they'd come back and try to manipulate their way back into his life, a painful lesson learned. He retraced more of his memories for anything else that he overlooked in his adolescence that possibly fit this new insight.

"My dreams," Arel spoke the words as if they were the answer. Forgetting for a moment he was engaging with his delusion. Orange-Eyes nodded his head.

Arel's mind was automatically brought to a particular dream he had when he was fifteen years old. It was a dream he never understood and one he had never forgotten. He recalled walking through a door only to find himself in the pitch-black living room of his childhood home. After a moment, realizing the only reason he could tell he was in the living room was because the light was emanating from him and extending two feet in every direction. He remembered the fear as pleading arms reached out of the dark to grasp his hands and shoulders and the feeling of being surrounded. For a moment he was back there in the fear, sadness, and desperation for hope.

Arel looked back to Orange-Eyes, and he finally grasped what that dream was. He felt the heaviness of guilt rise to his chest as he put his head in his hands.

"They were real?" His question was a whisper, Orange-Eyes nodded wearily.

"A family died in a fire not far from you, you were the first light they saw when they left their bodies," Orange-Eyes explained, choosing his words carefully, "There was nothing you could do."

"They reached for me and I slapped them away," Arel protested.

"You can't punish yourself for what you didn't understand in the past. There are times we have to let others find their own way and grow their own light, you did nothing wrong," Orange-Eyes assured him.

Arel remained quiet, going back and forth on whether or not he was just making this all up. He sat staring at the flame of the candle, moving deeper and deeper into his memory, his dreams, and night-mares. There were so many dreams that ended up shaping his waking life, were they dreams at all?

'*What else have I missed*?' Arel wondered.

Orange-Eyes began to explain as if he asked his question aloud. "Dreams serve many functions, some were messages from me and sometimes they were memories of your previous lives. Other times, they were used as a platform to communicate with your higher self or with other souls. When you sleep your mind reaches higher frequen-cies, other planes of existence, you have access to more information but it has also made you vulnerable to other entities using those same frequencies." Orange-Eyes' words took a bleaker tone, unsure.

"Is that what happened last night?" Arel asked, looking up at Orange-Eyes now completely unphased by his ability to read his mind.

"Last night was different from any interactions you've had in this lifetime. I didn't put you there, you did," Orange-Eyes said with a grimace. His eyes darted back and forth trying to work it out in his mind.

"Astral projection? I put myself there?" Arel's voice rose to an unusually high octave, Orange-Eyes winced.

"Your sister, it's her direct involvement in the project. Because you are energetically tied to her, you can access whatever she comes into contact with, whether you consciously feel it or not. Like a ripple effect. Once the ripple reached you, you took yourself to the source of that...disturbance."

"Are you telling me I felt a disturbance in the force?" Arel asked flatly.

"If that's how you want to relate it. You going there, even energetically, put you out in the open, you've been seen. Now they'll be coming for you and anyone connected to you. If I hadn't pulled you out when I did, they would have snuffed you out then." In the progression of his message, Orange Eyes' tone began to harden in concern. He watched as Arel's eyes filled with an urgent panic.

"Who are 'they?'" Arel spat, impatient.

"When I followed you to bring you back to your body, I, nor anyone else on our frequency was aware of the state of the islands were in. They've attracted low vibrational entities from across realms."

"What do you mean? How can vacant islands attract anything?" Arel felt like he was talking in circles.

"The Islands have known nothing but sickness and pain since their inhabitance in the late 1800s. People with incurable diseases were taken there to die. The North Brother Island became home to people till their deaths, one of those people you know by the moniker of Typhoid Mary. Over one thousand souls perished near their shores when a steamboat caught fire. The ones who survived the fire drowned before reaching land. The islands then went on to house the wounded men brought back from a frivolous war and finally, the islands became home to the tortured souls of addicts."

"Okay?" Arel interrupted.

"My point," Orange Eyes began through gritted teeth, "Is that events like these leave marks of their own. They build on one another creating a wound on the land and its surrounding waters. And like any wound left to fester, bacteria set in. There are entities that feed off the imbalance of human souls and revel in their destruction and pain that began so long ago. They can not only inhabit people but places themselves. Like a moth to a flame, dark non-human spirits began to flock to the Brothers' shores in the promise of torturing and feeding off of the lost souls that reside there."

"How though? How could this have gone under the radar with that much happening to human souls? You mentioned angels, right? Why didn't they do anything?" Arel spoke fast as he asked his questions, annoyance coloring his tone.

"Neither I nor any ethereal being can interfere with human affairs, only upon request, and even then there are limitations due to the confines of this reality. This is *your* realm; humans are beings of free will, remember? There are factors that cannot be disregarded. There is karma through choice, a cause and effect that causes a chain of events. No matter how painful it is for us to witness, we cannot break that chain." Orange-Eyes no longer sounded like the man Arel had been conversing with, his voice had dropped deep into his chest. The sound didn't match its vessel and Arel was hit with the striking realization that he was not sitting across from a flesh and blood human being. Orange-Eyes' presence had expanded beyond his form and Arel, struck by its magnitude, felt himself begin to shrink.

Orange-Eyes saw fear return to Arel's eyes and brought himself back to center. They sat in silence and let the charged energy in the room settle back to normal. Arel sat on the far end of the couch again, as far away as he could sit from the thing across from him.

"It's at times like these that living in the light has its disadvantages, things in the dark move under the radar. Places aren't like human beings." Orange-Eyes spoke as if he were thinking out loud, staring at the candle flame and running his fingers over his mouth as if he were trying to wipe away the words.

"What do you mean?" Arel felt himself drawn forward again.

"Light and dark cannot occupy the same physical space, like liquids with different densities, oil and water for example. The only place this is possible is within the human soul."

"Are you talking about the concept of Duality?" Arel interrupted.

Orange Eyes brought his long thin finger to the tip of his nose and tapped it twice. "That's what makes human beings different from any other being in the universe. Made of both light and dark, with the freedom to choose and move from one to the other, that is your design." Orange-Eyes then took another sip of his tea.

"So if I hadn't projected myself to North Brother you would have never known what's there, not until the project broke ground. What would have happened if I never went?" Urgency and fear shook Arel's voice.

"Dark entities are like parasites, they will latch onto one person, take what they want, and jump to the next. But unlike parasites they not only affect their host but also the people around them by insti-gating further imbalance, lowering their vibration, in turn, inviting more low vibrational entities. They will move like a virus, sadistically infecting every person they come into contact with inciting murder, suicide, and madness." Orange-Eyes had the tone of someone who had seen this play out, or after millennia of watching humans rage war after war, it wasn't a stretch as to what would happen.

"Ok. Hypothetically, because I'm still on the fence, how are we- I to deal with this?" Arel asked aggressively rubbing his eyes. Frustrated with himself for abandoning his logic.

"To start, you have to be mentally unshakeable and completely balanced. They feed on fear, guilt, and pride. If they pick up on any trace of low vibrational energy, they'll go deep, lifetimes deep. So we'll have to go deep. It's gonna take some digging."

Arel's mind reeled, it can take years to uncover patterns, situations, or triggers that create certain emotional responses. Now lifetimes as well? He knew they didn't have that kind of time.

Listening to Arel's inner dialog, Orange-Eyes interjected to ease his spiral into panic. "You have help, you set energies in motion when you set out on this path. You'll be experiencing more visions of the past that will help you address any past traumas, you've already begun attracting more of your soul family, and you have me," Orange-Eyes said, doing his best to console him.

"Right, okay. You know what? I think I'm just gonna go to sleep now. Hopefully, tomorrow I'll wake up and this will all have been a dream," Arel said, his voice tired and defeated. He rose slowly from the couch and began to make his way to his bedroom.

"Tomorrow we go see your sister first thing in the morning," Orange-Eyes called after him.

Arel nodded thoughtfully, an uneasy sting hit his abdomen. It wasn't only for whatever this is.

"Come on, Harri-" Arel cut himself off as he remembered this four-legged companion was no longer there. "Nope, You know what? This is insane, I'm gonna wake up and Harrison will be in his dog bed."

"Arel, this is real. I understand this is a difficult transition to get used to," Orange-Eyes acknowledged apologetically.

Arel breathed in deep through his nose and let out an audible breath tears welling in his eyes.

"I will not call you Harrison, not when you're like this," Arel declared in defeat, gesturing to Orange-Eyes' present form.

"I mean, you cou-"

"No."

"A long time ago I was called, Lóng Rú or just, Rú."

Arel turned around without another word, walked sullenly to his bedroom, and shut his door.

CHAPTER FOUR

KARMA

Olivia focused on the sound of her shoes hitting the planks of the boardwalk, slow steps to keep pace with her breathing. It was a warm morning and the cool wind off the river seemed to whistle a low melody over the rhythm of her feet. Coffee in hand, she was coming up to her favorite spot to stop and pick up rocks. As she walked closer to the stairs' upper landing, the melody on the wind built into a symphony that overpowered all her senses, drawing her mindlessly to the staircase. Hypnotized by the song on the wind, it carried her down the steps to the rocky bank below. The current was stronger this morning and the water higher than usual, not that Olivia took notice. In front of her stood a man knee-deep in rushing water masterfully playing the captivating melody on his violin, his fingers moving delicately along the strings of its neck. To anyone not privy to his song, a bare-chested man in designer trousers standing knee-high in the East River playing a violin would have been, at the very least, strange. To Olivia, this was an enchanting dream with the most beautiful man she had ever seen.

"Eugene, you play the violin."

Her dazed words were heavy on her tongue. He didn't look up as she took careless steps into the water slipping and stumbling to reach him. She watched as a smile began to form over his stoic face and widen the closer she got. Standing before him now she reached out to touch his glistening skin, the sun seemed to fight through the clouds to shine off of his mahogany locks. She saw him as unmoving as if his feet were rooted in the ground under the water but he was moving, floating deeper into rushing water. She moved with him clutching her purse to her chest, oblivious to the rising water, bewitched by his beauty and song. He ran his bow over the strings for the last time and let the notes hang in the air. Olivia felt a wave of elation as she watched him open his eyes revealing striking hazel irises. As the last note of his song faded, the warm greens and ambers in his eyes grew dark and descended to the deepest black. The spell had lifted, the beauty and comfort of his song had drawn her helplessly into the clutches of unimaginable fear. She watched in silent terror as his Adonis-like figure contorted into feeble decaying limbs, with flaps of grey and green skin hanging off of rotting muscle. Her throat clenched as she attempted to scream, choking on the thick stench wafting from his flesh and gaping maw. It smiled revealing blackened teeth and oozing green gums as it reached out to encircle its once idyllic arms around her petrified frame. Once the creature had her by its iron grip she did her best to fight and kick to keep from sinking beneath the rushing water. Olivia kept her eyes to the surface silently praying to see rays from the sun as the creature dragged her down into darker waters. The moment she let go of her prayer she watched rays of light break through the surface of the water only to be blocked by the sight of floating bodies.

★★★★

Arel was startled awake at the sound of crashing pans from the kitchen, hit suddenly with the memories from last night. He moved slowly getting out of bed, feeling the painful pull of his tense muscles from laying in the same position all night. For a split second, he expected to be pummeled by a 70-pound Harrison, only to be reminded of last night's events to their fullest extent. He stood slowly and made his way out to the source of the commotion, every step heavier than the last.

"Sorry, I dropped the pan." Rú was standing at the stove, spatula in hand. Arel hesitated before sitting at the breakfast bar separating him from the stove, his rational mind still fighting the reality he was facing. He didn't respond to Rú, only sat down and let his head fall into his hands. The pressure on his eyes created patterns against his black eyelids. The moving shapes lulled him back into relaxation. Falling deeper into ebony clouds, he began to hear voices in the distance but couldn't make out what they were saying. He didn't fight to make out their words, it was soothing him deeper into a sleep state. He opened his eyes to a new scene, he was standing across from a visibly distraught man and a half-packed bag. Arel looked down at the bag and caught a glimpse of himself in a small mirror. Kirana. This is the first time he'd seen himself as another person, it was familiar and surprisingly comforting. One side of her head was shaved up to her temple and narrowed to a point at the back of her neck, the rest of her hair was swept back in a braid that fell over her shoulder. Her dark brown eyes fell under a furrowed brow, in the dim-lit room, they looked completely black. Her full lips were pressed into a thin line hiding a clenched jaw. She was drawn from her reflection at the approach of another figure and looked up to meet orange eyes.

Arel was pulled out of his vision when he felt the thud of a mug placed before him. It had only been a few minutes since he sat down at the breakfast bar.

"Sorry to interrupt," Rú said as he pulled his arm back to plate Arel's scrambled eggs.

He flung his head up from his hands, one eye still closed, and examined the cup of coffee in front of him before taking a sip. Smooth and rich, with the perfect amount of cream so as not to overpower the flavor.

"How is this so good, are you moonlighting as a barista too?" Arel jabbed.

"You just make shit coffee, how do you do that?" Rú snarked.

Arel wasn't prepared for that response and choked back a laugh.

"Finish that and hurry up getting your things together, we're meeting your sister at 7:30," Rú said as he put the pan in the sink to wash.

"We?" Arel asked through a full mouth.

"Yes, you and 'Harrison', we have to keep up appearances." Rú had thrown air quotes around his former name.

"Right," Arel agreed unenthusiastically and took another bite of his eggs.

✴✴✴✴

Nalini was in her office by 7:00 AM every morning. She kept a strict schedule down to the minute. Wake up at 4:30 AM, laps in the pool, have breakfast, then get ready for work. She has always prided herself on the decisiveness and execution of whatever task was put in front of her. Headhunted out of MIT, she rose quickly through the ranks of Xelas Corp. But it was her work on the Port Morris initiative that landed her as the head of the North East office. A position that would give her access to the most exclusive projects in New York City and its heads of government. It was she who planned and implemented the changes to Port Morris that transformed it into the social and economic hub it is today, which the city was currently profiting off of. She could have any project she wanted and she had plans for the North and South Brother Islands.

She was looking forward to seeing her brother, but not sure if it was because it had been a while since they'd seen each other or because she just missed Harrison. She appreciated her brother keeping his distance after her break-up with Eugene, but couldn't help but wonder if that was part of the reason he wanted to see her this morning. The last thing she wanted was her psych brother overanalyzing her choices. That thought stuck with her and she imagined him walking in looking down his nose at her decision to walk away from his best friend. She created different ways this conversation would go in her mind, and each one made her more defensive and angry. By the time she got the text that he was in the lobby and on his way up, she had already psyched herself up for a fight. In preparation, she slid off her speech bracelets, in case someone else came in early to the office, she didn't want anyone to hear their conversation. Assuming, of course, the conversation went in any of the directions her mind took her in.

Arel and the transformed Rú made their way to Nalini's office at the end of the hall. Rú stopped ten feet back, picking up on the mood seeping from her office.

'Tread lightly, Rel, she seems to have let herself spiral into a confrontational mindset,' Rú spoke directly to Arel's mind.

He closed his eyes and took a deep breath before continuing to step on the mat in front of the door. He saw the sensor light on her desk flash twice and waited for the green light to flash next to the doorknob before walking in. He opened the door to let Rú in first, he knew it would soften her up, she loved seeing 'Harrison.' Although he missed Harrison the way he had known him, Arel was beginning to appreciate the ease of two-way communication. Rú seamlessly slid back into his Harrison facade, running over to jump on Nalini and letting her rub his ears and kiss his face. The smile she had on her face was wide and genuine as her attention was on Harrison but her smile was quick to fall from her eyes as she looked up to acknowledge her brother. Meeting her gaze he was once again taken back to the boy from his past life, the flash of defiance and a need to defend himself. The sting of a heavy heart struck his chest, he wasn't sure if the pain was his or hers but without another thought, he crossed the room and pulled her into a hug. He felt her muscles tense and then relax as she lifted her arms to hug him back. She loosened her hold to let him go, but he held on to her squeezing her shoulders tighter. He felt her heaviness lift as she laughed and tapped his back twice to release her. Pulling back and letting her go, Arel looked down to see Nalini's speech bracelets lying over a small stack of papers. A rush of excitement hit him and he stepped back so she could see his face and hands.

"What's that?" he signed quickly, his eyes wide and mouth open. He reminded her of a child who had just discovered a hidden present.

Nalini laughed and walked behind her desk to put on her bracelets and began signing. The bracelets sprang to life as she started to move her hands.

"Pretty cool, right?" The bracelets sang the words as she continued with a smile that lit up her entire face. "Gene didn't tell you?"

"No, he probably wanted it to come from you. Mom told me a little about it but I didn't think they would be finished this fast," Arel spoke as he signed, not realizing he was practically shouting in excitement.

"They surprised me with them when they promoted me to head of the North East Office. Xelas is now in the business of transformative technology as well as development. They will be on the market by next year along with caption contacts and glasses," she signed.

Arel was very impressed by the bracelets' accuracy and how they kept up with her speed. He stood eyes open wide with his hands in prayer position against his lips, the warmth of pride swelling in his chest.

"All because of you." He felt himself getting emotional. He had watched her fight the rest of the world her whole life up until now. To see her standing completely in her power in a company that fully supported her filled him with hope.

"We're also working on navigating glasses that use AI in real-time for those in any stage of blindness. Xelas, we see an opportunity, we take it." Nalini's bracelets seemed to speak with a tone that expressed the same pride displayed on her face. A trick of the mind, he thought.

Just like that, Arel was reminded of why he had wanted to meet with her in the first place. The buzz of excitement quickly left him. He tried to keep it light.

"Yeah, Eugene told me about the Brothers Project." He moved his hands slower, unconsciously matching the rhythm of his speech.

Nalini walked around her desk and sat down like a queen on her throne, he followed suit and sat in the chair across from her.

"It's going to be a lot of work, but it's going to be worth it," she signed, her mouth sliding into a confident smile.

"Lin, do you know the history of the island?" Arel was cautious with his movements as well as his words.

"It's why I chose it, to give it a new life." There was a passion in her eyes as she emphasized the words 'new life' with her hands. She had a mission, she was going to make her mark. Arel struggled to find the words to bridge this conversation, he shifted uncomfortably in his chair.

"*A noble intention-*" Rú chirped, settling in to lie down next to Arel.

"*Not helpful,*" Arel thought.

"Hasn't the city tried to go in and revitalize it before? There hasn't been anyone that has succeeded. It's dangerous, I mean there's a reason they left it abandoned." Arel tried to keep the delivery of his facial expressions as neutral as he could. The brightness in her face dimmed and she slid the bracelets off of her wrists.

"What is this about, Rel? Why are you here?" Her eyes were like daggers. He knew this look, she was shutting him out. Looking at her was like looking at the boy from his vision. In her eyes was the same sentiment, that he was trying to take this from her.

'You're losing her, Rel,' Rú warned.

Arel quickly ran through his options of how to breach this and just decided on the truth. "*Fuck it,*" He thought.

"Lin, there are things on those islands, parasites that will infect anyone who steps foot onto them. People will die!" he finally exclaimed.

'*Now she thinks you're just jealous and crazy, congratulations,*' Rú thought.

'*Well, can't you change? Help me out!*' Arel thought back frustrated.

Nalini, unaware of the silent exchange, understood enough to make up her mind as to why her brother had decided to visit her, and she wouldn't tolerate it anymore.

"I have a meeting, you and Harrison need to leave." Her movements were sharp and dismissive. She stood and walked to open the door. As she moved to walk past him, he pleadingly grabbed her wrist. She looked down at him with a look filled with anger and betrayal, it broke his heart. He let her go and by the time he stood and turned to leave she was waiting with the door open. She refused to make any eye contact with him and only moved to pet Harrison as he walked out the door. Arel turned only to have the office door closed in his face.

Seething and frustrated, Arel stormed toward the elevators with Rú trailing his heels. Rú could feel the explosion coming. Arel pressed the elevator button, relieved to see the doors open immediately. He looked around hoping there weren't any cameras but found himself out of luck when he spotted one in the right-hand corner of the elevator doors. He cursed himself.

'Re-' Rú was cut off before he could finish his name.

"NOPE!" Arel barked, keeping his head down away from the camera. "We're not having this conversation here," he hissed. He kicked himself as soon as he said the last bit of the sentence aloud. He hoped these cameras didn't have two-way speakers and hoped there was no one on the other side of the monitor.

Rú knew everything Arel was going to say but he was going to let him say it anyway. They waited in silence for the elevator to reach the lobby floor then made a beeline to the front doors. Arel accepted they weren't going to be able to talk properly until they reached his office, and was determined to calm himself down. Walking outside into the morning air, Arel threw his head back and took a deep breath releasing the tension from his shoulders. It was going to be a long trip back to the office.

By the time Arel and Rú got back to his office, Arel's anger had lessened to annoyance, with a touch of hopelessness. He had about an hour before his first patient, and Dylan wouldn't be in till noon. It was safe for them to talk.

"That was a fucking waste of time," Arel blurted out, tossing his bag on one of the chairs facing his desk. He walked straight for the coffee maker.

"Stop." The word wasn't in his mind. Arel turned around to see Rú in human form, slightly thrown by how he was dressed, like he walked off a Tom Ford runway.

"No one needs to be drinking your shitty coffee right now," Rú criticized, walking over and grabbing the coffee pot out of Arel's hands.

"You're gonna roast me about coffee, right now? WERE YOU NOT LISTENING BACK THERE?" Arel stopped talking when he saw the smirk on Rú's face. "WHAT'S FUNNY?" he roared, flinging his arms out from his sides.

"'Roast you about coffee." Rú had a hard time saying it without chuckling.

"Are you fucking serious? Coffee jokes?" Any visual expression of anger dropped from Arel's face, his inquiry was less of a question and more of a dare.

"First, that coffee joke was a self-burn. Second, Lin was never the solution to fix the problem and, at most, would have only delayed the inevitable. She has her own motivations and with the history between you two, I figured it was a long shot." Rú's voice was almost completely monotone. Before Arel could verbalize the question, Rú tapped his ear twice to answer it.

"Wait, the fight? The boy lost his hearing, you mean that echoed into this life? That's why she's completely deaf only on her left, that's the side of his head that hit the tree." Arel felt like he received a punch to the gut. He walked quickly over to his chair and let himself fall into it. Everything was coming into focus, the competition, how she always kept him at arm's length, and why he'd always felt the need to make amends.

"That fight created a connection between the both of you, it introduced lessons that were supposed to elevate you both differently. All actions have consequences and yours have followed you both into this lifetime to be resolved. You lost control and you've had to continue to live with the damage you inflicted. For Nalini, her actions stunted her self-worth progression and she has failed to recognize that it was her own feelings of inadequacy that led her to start that fight. You're both here to end it, to forgive each other and yourselves," Rú explained as he carried over two full mugs, leaving a trail of steam as he walked over and set them on the desk. He sat and held the burning mug with both hands.

"We didn't go there to stop the project, you took me there to confront my karma," Arel surmised, reaching for the freshly brewed coffee. Rú nodded and took a long swig of the scolding coffee. When he breathed out a cloud of smoke flowed from his mouth as if he'd just taken a drag from a cigarette. He noticed Arel's eyes widen through the rising cloud.

"Warming up, a dragon thing," Rú said, answering the confusion on Arel's face. Arel shook his head and continued his train of thought.

"That's why you didn't transform in her office," Arel concluded, finally taking a sip of his coffee. Rú was right, it was way better than if he made it. The warmth moved through him soothing any tension remaining in his chest and shoulders.

"That would have been using my will to manipulate her decision," Ru elaborated, knowing that's where his statement was taking him.

"Ok so, what was supposed to be accomplished there? I mean, nothing happened." Arel turned to look out his window and glared at the small islands in the distance.

"How did you feel, seeing your sister after you had your vision," Rú asked, he sounded like Arel in one of his patient sessions.

Arel rolled his eyes slightly but then caught himself. "I felt guilty. At first, all I saw was him, the boy from my vision, and then I blinked and saw her. It was like I was seeing her and the boy all at the same time. I could see and feel everything, his anger, her strength, his pride, her determination. I could feel the need she had to defend herself and the need for acceptance, even after everything she's accomplished. It's strange, after observing everything, I was, am, in awe of her. I understand now that her experience in that life and this one has built this fire in her that has spread and become a light to so many, including me. Even with our remaining karma, I was proud of her. I AM so proud of her and all that she is today, even if she kind of hates me right now." As he was speaking, he was coming to grips with what he hadn't realized in the moment. In her office, he had been so focused on the mission in his mind, that he wasn't conscious of the healing taking place.

"And if she doesn't move past it from her point of view, and can't forgive you?" Rú asked.

"Well, I can't force resolutions, so all I can do is be understanding of her feelings and be there. Getting angry or impatient because of where she is on her journey is counterproductive. It'll keep us running around in circles." Arel was definitive in his answer and it made him breathe easier.

"Good, then it's something that can no longer be used against you. As I said, dark entities use any guilt or sadness to break down your will, anything to make you doubt yourself. Doubt is a door to fear." Rú's words hung in the air as they finished their coffee in silence.

Arel looked at the clock and shot up from his desk chair, running to unlock the waiting room entrance.

"My first patient is supposed to be here in five minutes." He shouted over his shoulder and he disappeared from the room. After swinging open the office suite doors and not finding his first patient of the day waiting he let out a sigh of relief.

"Hey I'm gonna need Har-" Arel stopped talking when he saw a black labpit in place of the 'Human' Rú.

"Cool, thanks," he called from just outside his office. He hadn't noticed the man walk up behind him.

"Hey, Dr. S, who are you talking to?" The man inquired peeking around Arel, only to see what he knew as Harrison looking back at him.

Arel paused for a moment and tried to think of an excuse but couldn't think of anything.

"Uh, Harrison. How are you doing today, Jason?" he deflected quickly, moving aside to let his patient pass him before following him into the office and closing the door.

Opening his office door to walk Jason out of their session, Arel was surprised to find Dylan sitting at the reception desk. Dylan exchanged pleasantries with Jason as he was leaving and once out of sight, he turned to Arel, only to be met with a look of confusion. "What are you doing here this early, I thought you had a presentation?"

"Canceled. How you feelin'? You never came back from the bar, Gene said you got sick." Dylan's tone was light but hinted at suspicion, he had seen him talking to a pretty woman at the bar. He leaned back in his chair and crossed his arms.

"Yeah, I was just hit with a panic attack and had to get out of there," he answered. "I'm good though, thanks, I just needed some sleep." Arel saw the concern leave Dylan's face and he relaxed again. There was no reason to assume he knew the truth of what actually happened but Arel was still on edge.

"That sucks, man, did you at least get the number of the woman you were talking to?" Dylan asked hopefully, he perked himself up in his chair.

"Ye-" Arel began, then stopped abruptly after a quick mental rewind through his encounter with Evaine. He never got her number.

His shoulders slumped forward and he let his head fall back, contorting his face into a wince.

"Shhhhhit, I never asked for her number," he whispered, loud enough for Dylan to hear but not enough that someone just walking in would hear. "I'm an idiot," he groaned, raking his hands down his face.

"I got you, dude. What's her name?" Dylan chirped, turning to face the computer, fingers at the ready hovering over the keyboard.

"I don't condone cyber stalking and I never got her last name," Arel admitted, silently cursing himself, just as his next appointment walked into the waiting room. "We're going to have to talk about this later," he whispered, stepping aside to allow his 11 o'clock to pass him.

"Oh um, Olivia called, said she needed to see you today," Dylan quickly called before Arel closed the door.

"I had a cancellation for 4 PM, I can see her then," Arel answered.

Dylan gave him a thumbs up in confirmation and picked up the phone to call Olivia back.

CHAPTER FIVE

OLIVIA?

The day seemed to fly by and for a while, it felt like business as usual. Arel got a text from Eugene during lunch to give him an update on Nalini and the progression of the project and that he'd head over to his practice around 5 PM. Arel figured his meeting with Olivia wouldn't take long, she'd been on the up and up.

Rú played his part, going in and out of the office, spending time with Dylan, and letting the patients pet him and rub around his ears. From Arel's point of view, his being able to go from one reality to the other so seamlessly was wild, but then remembered Rú is a dragon. The realization that he lives in a world where dragons actually exist gave him a headache and he tried not to think about it too much. To his core, between his past supernatural experiences and now Rú, he didn't think anything could surprise him at this point.

3:50 PM, he had a few minutes before Olivia was to arrive, and then back to the world of weird. Now that he was no longer completely blind to what hides in plain sight, he was starting to prefer the weird. It may have been terrifying but at least it wasn't a lie.

Rú wasn't keen on leaving with Dylan to go on their late afternoon walk but they were keeping up with appearances. Their walks were usually about 20 minutes or so, they'd be back before his meeting would be over and Arel hadn't had a moment to himself within the last 24 hours. He wanted at least a few minutes alone with his thoughts. After watching the pair leave, Arel went to his kitchenette to drink what was left of the coffee Rú had made. Just in case, he brewed a fresh pot on the off chance Olivia was interested in a cup. He had just sat down with his coffee when he heard the suite door open.

"Hey Olivia," he hollered, getting up to greet her. He made it halfway to the door when the dread hit his stomach and it was when he reached the door frame that a full wave of fear came over him. He saw the woman standing in the middle of his waiting room. She looked like Olivia but this was not the same woman he had been treating for the past year. Her face had a translucent hue and it seemed to hang like a mask, hiding the root of whatever seemed to distort her features. She was smiling, an expression that did not meet her eyes, they bore into his with sinister intensity. The hem of her jeans was wet and ripped. Her frame had an unsteady appearance as she stood, waving back and forth. As she took steps toward him he noticed the gate of her walk was off. Her legs dragged with every step as if she were fighting sleeping limbs, twitching and jerking with every move.

"Hello, Dr. Sharma. Thank you for seeing me today." Her words sang unnaturally as she spoke and landed heavily on Arel, he felt ill and she was too close for comfort. He worked to compose himself.

"We're alone, how about we sit out here," he said, trying to keep his voice normal. Everything in him told him not to turn his back to her and there was no way he was going to venture into a smaller room with whatever this *thing* was. '*Rú will be back any minute,*' he thought to himself.

"I'd feel more comfortable in your office," Olivia chimed, the softness of her voice chilled him. It was like watching the human equivalent of a ventriloquist dummy. Arel fought to keep the fear from affecting his breathing and increasing nausea. Relief hit him as he saw the door open, but disappeared when he saw it was Eugene. Arel quickly threw up his hand, a signal from him not to come any closer.

Eugene froze in place heeding his silent warning and turned his attention to the woman between them. She turned her upper body fast without moving her hips, resulting in a loud crack that made both men jump.

"Oops," she cackled, proceeding to adjust her bottom half to match the top of her. Both men watched in silent horror as she forced her hips to turn, creating a cascade of snaps and cracks. Between the two of them, Eugene was holding his composure better than Arel. His face was serious, if you didn't know him you wouldn't know he was terrified.

"I know you," she crooned, moving to take a step in Eugene's direction. "You're the one she saw." Her head began to sink between her shoulders like a lion crouching to pounce, a sick gurgle emanating from her throat.

"Who Olivia? Who is she?" Arel yelled out, hoping to take her attention away from Eugene and draw out more information. Her head wobbled as she turned to face him.

She lifted her finger and pointed to her face, confirming his fears that the thing standing in front of him now wasn't Olivia. She watched his face drop in realization and his eyes grow wide with fear. Her smile spread wider across the grotesque mask of Olivia's face, releasing blood-laced drool that had been pooling in her drooping cheeks.

Eugene hoped to go unnoticed as he tried to move behind the reception desk. He needed the security of something physically separating her from him. It was like she had eyes in the back of her head, as soon as he extended his foot behind the desk her head snapped back to face him. Eugene jumped, flattening himself against the wall behind him.

"It was your face that drew her to me," her voice rang out with excitement, wrapping her arms around herself and swaying back and forth. She closed her eyes and released a satisfied sigh. Eugene's repose gave way to a combination of horror and confusion.

The look on Eugene's face was enough to clear the fear from Arel's mind.

"HEY!" Arel roared, stopping her advance on Eugene. She turned her attention back to where it started. She stood still for a moment staring into Arel's unwavering eyes, waiting for his newfound strength to fail. He felt a fire ignite in his chest and took a step toward her.

The thing masquerading as Olivia took this as a challenge and lunged toward him releasing a blood-curdling scream, cut short by the soft pop of punctured flesh. Rú stood behind her, his claws protruding through the front of her throat, then pulled back his hand from her neck and let the body drop to the floor. Arel looked from the body on the floor to Rú to his half-transformed arm. His hand was covered in rough rounded scales and at his fingertips ended in long coarse claws now covered in a brownish/green sludge.

The silence was broken this time by a scream coming from the door of the office suite. Dylan stood in the entryway holding a dogless leash still attached to the collar, now lying on the floor. He continued to scream looking from Rú to the body on the floor and then to Rú's transformed arm. The situation proved to be too much as he quickly dropped to the floor unconscious.

Arel quickly looked to the corner of the room to find Eugene petrified against the wall, his glasses hanging dangerously low on his nose.

"Gene, you're ok. He's not going to hurt you," Arel assured him, walking around reception to push the chair over to the corner so Eugene could sit down. Eugene kept his eyes on Rú as he walked over to scoop up the out-cold Dylan and place him on the waiting room couch. Rú then walked back to the door to see if there was anyone in the hall. It was close to 5 PM and the floor cleared out pretty quickly on a Friday. The halls were clear, so he proceeded to close and lock the door, they got lucky.

"Wha- I, Ha -Harrison?" Eugene finally stammered, fixing his glasses before slowly lowering himself into the chair Arel had brought to him.

"Hey Gene," Rú said, disinterested in Eugene's current shock as he walked over to inspect the now oozing body on the floor.

"Rel, what the fuck is happening? I just watched Harrison turn into a dude with claws!" Eugene rambled, his cool demeanor flying out the window. He leaned over, put his head between his knees, and tried to inhale deep long breaths. "I'm gonna be sick, he just killed her! It! WHERE'S THE TRASH BIN?" he demanded hysterically, shooting up from his chair and running into Arel's office to throw up in the kitchenette sink.

Arel stood at a loss of what to tackle first. Since one of his friends was currently throwing up his lunch and the other was out cold on the couch, it was safe to focus on the oozing body masquerading as one of his patients. Rú was leaning too close to the body for Arel's comfort, he stayed back a couple of feet crossing his arms, subconsciously creating a barrier between him and the oozing carcass.

"It's dead, right?" Arel gulped, holding his hand over his mouth and nose. The thick green fluid pooled on the floor was emitting a rancid odor akin to rotting fish.

"It's gone," Rú assured him, picking up its head to get a closer look and inspect the eyes and mouth. He took care to set the head down gently before moving on to inspect its arms and hands. Rú's brows drew together and his eyes darted up and down the body.

"What was it?" Arel asked, registering the recognition on Rú's face.

"It's a type of water spirit, a shapeshifter…" His voice trailed off and his face fell somber.

"What?" Arel demanded, now worried by the sudden change in his demeanor.

"Olivia…" Rú started but was interrupted by Arel's attention shift to the couch behind him. Dylan sat alert, eyes wide with what Arel assumed was shock from what he had just witnessed. Dylan then looked down at his shaking hands. He had come too soon after passing out but decided to stay quiet. He wanted to get the full story of what was happening in case they decided to lie to him when he woke up but he couldn't stay quiet at the sound of Olivia's name.

"I know what happened to Olivia," Dylan spoke low and was careful to enunciate his words through his breaking voice. "They found her body on the banks a little after 10 AM this morning, drowned," he sniffled, wiping away a tear that had spilled over his lashes.

"It, uh, was on the news at the falafel stand while I was out with Harrison." Dylan's unsure eyes fell on Rú at the mention of Harrison and Rú nodded in confirmation of his unasked question. Dylan's gaze fell back to Arel.

"That's when we booked it back here, to tell you she wasn't coming." His emotional tone dropped to a monotone as his eyes fell back to the corpse on the floor.

Arel stood frozen, he had hoped it had just taken her form, that it had just been a perverse trick. He was brought back to the present when Eugene walked into the room having heard everything Dylan had said.

"I'm sorry, Rel," Eugene uttered from his office doorway. He was at a loss for words, what would be comforting after such a grotesque scene? Eugene looked to Rú for any direction only to be met with an apologetic stare.

"This thing killed her to get to me?" Arel asked finally, his voice surprisingly stern.

"Yes," Rú answered quickly

"This is not your fault, Rel," Eugene said, side-eyeing Rú for his bluntness.

"Yeah," Arel agreed thoughtfully, he stared down at the corpse that seemed to be breaking down unusually fast. "She was a pawn to them, a move on the board." His voice was gruff, his sadness hardened to anger. As he walked closer, the body was drying out and parts of it were beginning to solidify.

He looked at its face and, for a second, he only saw Olivia. His resolve fell back into sadness and tears began flooding his eyes. He watched as its skin rapidly dried, stretch into a thin paper layer, and finally crumble into dust. He looked down at the layer of dust that sat on top of the ooze that remained on the floor. The only thing left of the true Olivia was her purse, now lying off to the side of the mess.

"What just happened?" Arel asked, looking up at Rú.

"Water spirits don't do well out of water for long, it was already beginning to break down when it got here. With the spirit gone from the physical form, the air broke it down at a more rapid pace."

"If it's a spirit how can it have a physical form at all?" The question had come from Dylan still sitting on the couch behind Arel and Rú, he was joined by Eugene silently nodding next to him.

"Some spirits are strong enough to possess a magic that can make inanimate matter and even other animals into forms they can inhabit for a time. It's not common, as it takes a tremendous amount of energy," Rú explained as he walked around the mess on the floor of the waiting room. He walked into Arel's office and walked back out with paper towels and a bucket filled with bottles of cleaning solution. Arel bent down to pick up Olivia's purse, causing a small rock to roll out as he lifted it from the floor. He froze and tears began to flood his vision.

"That explains the dock smell," Dylan noted his nose wrinkled in disgust, oblivious to Arel's realization.

"Shut up," Eugene snapped at Dylan. "Rel, what is it?" he asked, urgency coloring his voice.

Arel stood up slowly, dropping the bag as he stared at the small reddish rock in the palm of his hand, unable to form words through the sudden onslaught of grief.

"Olivia liked to stop and pick up rocks when she went on her walks," Rú answered as he set the bucket down and walked over to Arel. "In their last appointment she told him she would bring him one," he said as he helped Arel over to the couch and sat him down next to Eugene.

"I'm so sorry, Rel. I di-" Dylan stopped his sentiment. As he choked back his own sobs, Dylan moved to Arel's other side and wrapped him in a hug. It was a few seconds before Arel returned the embrace, squeezing tight the rock in his hand allowing himself the physical release of his pain. Eugene placed a hand on Arel's shoulder, a comforting gesture that encouraged him to relax his grip around the rock's smoothed surface. Dylan held onto Arel a little longer before releasing him at the same time Eugene recoiled his hand. The three of them sat in silence as Rú worked to clean the mess that was Olivia's imposter,

Arel kept his gaze on the rock in his hand. The guilt he felt for Olivia's Death began to build a painful weight in his chest, he couldn't help it from creeping into his mind.

"Don't do that," Rú said aloud, wiping the last of the ooze off the floor. "This is not your fault. Don't make that guilt yours"

Eugene and Dylan looked from Rú to Arel with confusion, Arel ignored their inquiring looks.

"And how am I expected to do that?" Arel asked slowly through gritted teeth, working to compose his anger.

"By putting the blame where it belongs. Mourn her, remember her, honor her by fighting for what was taken from her, but do not do her the disrespect of making her death about you." Rú's words were firm but compassionate. He stood and made his way over to the couch to address him directly. "You know the damage guilt can do, it offers no justice and no resolve," he finished his statement as he knelt and placed a hand over Arel's closed fist.

Arel looked up from his hands to meet Rú's blazing eyes, they were warm and had a depth in them no human eyes could convey. They held the weight of immeasurable knowledge, truths witnessed and solidified by time.

Without another word, Rú stood back up and returned to the bit of mess still waiting to be cleaned on the floor. Leaving Arel to sort out his thoughts and to get his mind right. Dylan and Eugene were silent as they watched Rú put all the soiled paper towels into a lavender-scented trash bag. Arel noticed Dylan and Eugene watching Rú with mixed expressions of confusion and curiosity. He could tell their minds were teeming with questions that neither of them was willing to come out and ask. He took a deep breath and thought about how he was going to approach this explanation. There was probably a right way to address the dragon in the room but at the moment his mind was still on overload and this will be a lot better when everyone is on the same page.

Arel raked his hands through his hair and interlocked his fingers at the back of his neck, he drew in a deep breath and exhaled loudly, letting his arms fall to his sides.

'*Here it goes,*' he thought. "Guys I should formally introduce you to Rú, you've known him as Harrison." He sounded almost apologetic, like admitting to a lie. He knew there was no reason for feeling like that, it just came out that way.

"Yeah, we both saw him change into THAT." Dylan retorted, gesturing to Rú. "I don't wanna speak for Gene, but how and why is Harrison now an impeccably dressed man with retractable claws? And what the hell is going on, Rel?" Dylan's tone escalated from sarcasm to genuine hysterics.

Eugene sat silently and nodded in agreement with Dylan. Although Eugene had known about Arel's history of paranormal experiences he had never experienced any. There was a security in being on the outside that allowed room for question or a choice to believe it or not. That choice was no longer on the table. He was running over every dream and experience Arel had ever shared with him. He wondered if he had encountered all that Arel had growing up, would he have turned out as well adjusted as Arel was today?

"Does this all have to do with that dream about the Brothers project?" Eugene's voice was tense and the words just came flooding out of his mouth.

"What's the Brothers project?" Dylan asked, curiously looking from Eugene to Arel.

"Yes," Rú answered Eugene, ignoring Dylan's question entirely.

"Guys, what's the Brothers Project?" Dylan repeated impatiently, his voice edgy.

Arel was coming back to equilibrium and jumped into an explanation without the least bit of apprehension. "It's the new development project by Xelas Corp," Arel answered as he rose to his feet, needing to stretch his tense muscles. "They're gonna do a complete overhaul of the North and South Brother Islands. My sister's spearheading it." Arel began to pace back and forth as he laid out the mundane aspects of this situation.

Dylan leaned forward and rested his elbows on his knees, his arms still crossed over his chest. "Mhmm and what about a dream?" Dylan added, extending his index finger to point at Eugene next to him. An acknowledgment of the slighted detail in Eugene's original question. A detail that seemed to offer more prevalent information.

"Yeah, okay." Arel clapped his hands together and held them to his lips, thinking of how to sum up his dream in the best way. "Long story short I had a dream the night before yesterday that put me on one of the islands. I got a glimpse of what was on the island and it got a glimpse of me. Rú showed up and pulled me out."

"So you're the orange-eyed monster that told him to stop the Brothers project?" Eugene directed his question to Rú.

"Dragon," Rú quickly corrected. Both Dylan and Eugene did a double take.

Neither Dylan nor Eugene responded right away. Dylan's mouth fell open in confusion and his eyes slid from wide with wonder into a suspicious squint, unsure of the information just dropped on him. Eugene leaned forward resting his elbows on his knees slowly interlacing his fingers in front of his mouth and closed his eyes. Exhausted by the cascade of events that happened within the last hour alone. Dylan was the first to break the silence in the room.

"Dragon," Dylan repeated in a small voice. "Okay, sure. I shouldn't be too surprised after that," Dylan said, pointing to the trash bag. He leaned back to rest his head on the wall behind the couch but shot back up to attention with a revived vigor. "But how can you look human, though?" he shouted with genuine curiosity.

"He's a multidimensional being, he can take any form. He's not bound by the physical limitations of our reality," Arel threw out the explanation before Rú had a chance to open his mouth, it was almost verbatim to Rú's explanation the night before. Arel realized he had cut Rú off from his own explanation and looked over to clock his reaction. Unphased, Rú just nodded in agreement.

"Wait, does this mean that zombies and vampires are real?" Dylan asked fully animated.

"This is what you want to address right now?" Eugene interjected, returning his attention to the conversation, annoyed by the direction Dylan was headed.

"Listen, you and I have just received information that has changed the very fabric of reality and witnessed the most terrible ordeal I could imagine. I want to be prepared for any possibility, let me have this." By the time Dylan finished his rant, the look in his eyes was that of a crazed man in the search for truth at any cost.

Eugene conceded and waved his hand as a gesture to proceed. "Fine," he mumbled. In unison, they all turned their attention to Rú for answers.

He rolled his eyes but obliged with a sigh, "Zombies exist, yes, it's very sad. Do they eat people? No. Do blood-sucking vampires exist? Yes, but they're less 'Twilight 'and more 'Descent.'" It took a second for that imagery to settle in their minds but clicked all at once as they all made the same repulsed face.

"Great," Dylan uttered, his tone slightly veiled with a tinge of disappointment.

"They live deep underground mostly," Rú continued.

"Okay," Dylan said, a plea for him to stop expanding on it. He rubbed his forehead, figuratively trying to rub the imagery from his mind.

"Yeah, I never understood the desire to romanticize a parasite," Rú concluded with a shrug.

"Okay, are we finished? Is everyone good on questions?" Arel's queries were less questions and more declarations that they were moving on. Dylan shrugged and nodded in agreement.

"Good," Arel said, glad to get them back to the situation at hand. "Eugene, you said you had some info about what was going on with the project."

"Um, Right…" Eugene mumbled, adjusting his glasses and trying hard to put his thoughts in order to remember the details of the project's next steps. The middle of the day had seemed like light years away from the present moment, his world had turned completely upside down.

As he began to recall the events before coming to the office he remembered the assignment he was no longer keen on completing. His eyes widened with fear as he began to speak.

"Lin put me in charge of getting the permits and visiting the properties. I'd have to go to the islands in person to oversee the assessments." Eugene let his head fall into his hands and anxiously raked his fingers through his mahogany waves, digging his nails soothingly into his scalp.

"It's fine. You're not alone, and honestly, I wouldn't let you go alone anyway." Arel was surprised by how calm he felt as he assured Eugene. He felt a rush of familiarity, almost like deja vu without the vision, they've done something like this before. He never wanted Eugene or Dylan to be involved in this situation but, it would seem, the universe had other plans.

"I'm going to call my patients and cancel all appointments for the next few days. In light of Olivia's death, it's best this gets resolved before anyone else is hurt." Arel's tone faltered over Olivia's name.

"Dylan, can you help me out with that?" he asked somberly.

"Of course, man. I'll pull up everyone's info and start making calls." Dylan was off the couch and halfway to the reception desk before he finished his sentence.

Arel reached out to stop Dylan as he passed him. "Thank you."

Dylan nodded and forced his mouth into a half smile. "We all loved Olivia," he declared, looking from Arel to Rú before moving behind the desk to turn the computer back on.

Arel turned his attention back to Eugene, his olive complexion looking abnormally green. He could tell Eugene was having trouble wrapping his head around everything. Eugene had always been the one to problem solve and find solutions to any situation that had come up in life. He loved structure and rules, he thrived in the lines. Arel knew it was going to take time and patience to learn to see the world in this new way. For Arel, he'd always had one eye open to this world whether he was aware or not it was easier for him to accept. For Eugene, it was like being tossed out into open water without a life jacket.

Rú felt the tension that was coming from words unspoken.

"I'm gonna go lay some barriers around the building," Rú announced, as he swiftly headed for the suite door. Dylan and Eugene needed the space to talk to Arel without him in the room. "Be back in a bit," he said before disappearing behind the door.

Arel walked over and sat on the couch next to Eugene and waited for him to be comfortable enough to speak.

"How are you doing this, Rel?" Eugene asked, sounding slightly defeated.

"Dude, I freaked out when I saw Harrison turn into Rú. The neighbors almost called the cops because of all the screaming," Arel recalled. Eugene laughed quietly and Arel found himself joining in. "Yeah, it's funny now."

"Almost called the cops?"

"Well, the neighbors came over to check on me, I was hysterical so Rú morphed into me and dealt with them at the door. I, uh, fainted when I saw him turn into me," he confessed with an embarrassed laugh.

"Christ, this is insane." Eugene's demeanor lightened and he spoke with a bit of a chuckle. He sat back and closed his eyes.

"There's no protocol for this, no right way to react, but we can deal with this. I never wanted you or anyone else to be in this with me. I hoped I could do this on my own but, honestly, I don't think I'd be able to. What does that make me?" Arel admitted, his question was more rhetorical and didn't expect Eugene to answer him.

"Human," Eugene sighed. "It makes you human, Rel. No one wants to go through anything alone and no one should have to. And it's probably for the best, if I didn't find out now I would have been headed to those islands blind. The office originally set up meetings to pick up the permits today and walk the grounds for tomorrow, Saturday, but I pushed the pickup till tomorrow and came here instead. I guess some shit happens for a reason. I'm glad I know, as fucked as this is, it's better than being in the dark." Eugene seemed to have calmed himself down by his own reasoning, his voice was steady now.

"I don't think shit happens for a reason. I think you listened to your instincts and that led you here, now. You listening to your gut kept you out of danger, kind of, it put you on a trajectory where you're more informed, as terrifying as that information is. In this case, you made that shit happen." Arel finished his statement looking confused by the delivery of his thoughts. "I hope that makes sense to you cause it made sense in my head."

Eugene smiled. "Yeah, I got you, but I don't know how I'm gonna sleep again though," he concluded as he leaned forward and let his head fall into his hands, pushing his palms into his eyes.

"You can crash at my place for a while," Arel offered. Eugene lifted his head and looked at him like he had just said the most ridiculous thing at that moment.

"No shit, there's no way I'm going back to my dark empty apartment when you have a fucking dragon living in yours," Eugene said, half joking.

"Me too," Dylan chimed in from behind the desk, all they could see were his eyes and the top of the phone on his ear as he dialed the next patient.

"Fine, I've got one blow-up mattress and Dylan can take the couch." Arel agreed.

"Why do I have to take the couch?" Dylan griped, covering the speaker with his hand.

"Rock, Paper, Scissors for it then," Arel said sharply. The day had been a roller coaster and his energy was dropping, he was hoping nothing else came up tonight, for all their sakes.

Rú walked through the door with two duffle bags and a half-eaten falafel. "We all good?" he asked, taking another bite. Dylan and Eugene eyed the bags clutched in his right hand with curious expressions.

"Yeah, we're gonna swing by their places and pick up some thi-"

"No need," Rú interrupted him, tossing the bags at their feet.

"How did yo-, you know what, never mind." Eugene was too drained to deal with any more outlandish explanations and decided to let it go.

Arel was still curious, "How did you know? You weren't here when we talked about it." Before he got a chance to finish his thought Rú cut in.

"Calculated guess, you guys forget that I know you." He lifted his right hand to gesture toward Dylan. "There was no way Dylan was staying at his place alone, he keeps his eyes closed during horror movies. It's gonna be a while for him, you might want to look into a two-bedroom." He was only half joking about the two bedroom but Dylan looked over at Arel with wide pleading eyes.

"No," Arel dismissed.

"And Eugene would think his way into a paranoid mess, putting a giant energetic target on his back. It wouldn't matter how many barriers I set up around his building. Plus, his apartment had bugs." Rú finished his explanation by taking the last bite of his falafel and tossing the wrapper into the bin across the room.

"My apartment doesn't have bugs," Eugene said defensively, crouching down to check the contents of his duffle bag.

" Not regular bugs, spirit bugs," Rú said, picking a piece of lettuce stuck between his teeth. "You ever notice little black spider-like things that scurry in and out of your peripheral vision? Those are spirit bugs, they're energetic ticks that latch onto your chakras, throwing you out of alignment and creating physical pain and mental imbalance in prolonged cases."

"That explains a lot, actually," Eugene whispered to himself, adjusting his shoulders.

Rú nodded, "So, I'll ask again, are we good? I want to see if I can gain more information on whatever else has traveled to the islands and check in on your parents and Lin," he said impatiently.

"Wait, I thought nothing could get off the island without being attached to a person or something," Arel said nervously, standing quickly to make his way into his office to grab his things.

"It's a precaution, after Olivia I just want to be sure," Rú reassured him calmly and Arel nodded silently.

"I ordered a Chariot, it's downstairs," Rú said, holding up a phone with a notification that read, '*Your Chariot Awaits.*'

"When did you get a phone?" Arel asked.

"I didn't, it's yours. I took it before I left," Rú answered with a smile.

The car ride back to the apartment was a quiet one, no one trusted themselves to say anything in the presence of the Chariot driver, and the silence carried until they reached Arel's apartment. Rú waited until they were settled before leaving. They planned to be at the parks and rec offices when they opened at 9 AM to postpone any visitations to the island. Arel was so preoccupied with their present mission he hadn't thought of the possible reunion between him and the beautiful Evaine from the bar. It was an inevitable reunion but Rú wasn't going to ruin Arel's pleasant surprise by tipping him off. Things always come back around and it's the perceived happy accidents that help us shine a bit brighter, stronger, and a little more hopeful.

CHAPTER SIX

RÚ'S ROUNDS

Rú's first stop was Nalini's apartment in Manhattan, he debated for a second whether he should don the mask of Harrison but it'd take forever to get there on foot. It had been a while since he spread his wings. It's New York, no one looks up anymore. It was minimal exposure, even if someone happened to look up they'd most likely write it off as a trick of the light or their mind would try to fit the sight of him into boxes of acceptable explanations. People always think themselves out of the truth to fit a narrative they are comfortable with. He had convinced himself.

Rú reached the roof of the building and let the thought of his human skin fall away from his mind. It faded away to reveal metallic black scales that softly reflected the light of the moon. A camouflage that worked well in the night sky. He stretched his wings, their span reaching to both ends of the building's ledge. He had forgotten why he hadn't taken his 3D form in so long until he began to feel the floor underneath him buckle a bit.

'*Mmhm, that's why,*' he thought.

One thrust of his wings would create a force that would leave the apartment beneath him raining pieces of ceiling. This body was too heavy, he'd have to travel in essence. Not as leisurely, he won't be able to enjoy the wind flowing over his face and wings, but it was faster. He reluctantly let this form fall away and decided to forgo any form at all. He wasn't fond of lacking the ability to feel physical sensations but for the sake of time, it was necessary. He thought of Nalini's building and in a blink of an eye, he was outside her apartment.

Other than the people coming and going from their apartments and the residential spirits that still reside there, all was quiet. The barriers he'd set a few days prior were still holding, a little depleted, the dense energies people carry had worn them down when they came and went but the upside was that they took a bit of that energetic defense with them. A protection they didn't ask for but received all the same, like enjoying the safety of a mobile sanctuary.

He didn't have to spend long building the barriers up to full strength and decided to check on Nalini. She was in her workout room going a few rounds with the punching bag. Her thoughts were teetering from Eugene to her brother, creating scenarios that put them against her and made her 'the bad guy.' Projecting her fears built into stronger punches. She was building up an anger high, effective in sending the bag flying farther with each punch and in depleting her internal strength. With each punch, she fooled herself into believing that it was the anger that gave her strength not realizing it was only a channel for her true strength. Rú could see anger's insatiable nature taking its hold and couldn't leave her to dive deeper into it. He wouldn't be able to change her thoughts or stop their progress, but he could give her a message.

Through the chaos of her busy mind, a single phrase broke through the barrage of thoughts. '*You are enough.*' The thought stopped her in her tracks, she relaxed her stance and stopped the bag from swinging.

It worked better than he thought, she was no longer fixated on her anger but was ruminating on the phrase that was now taking up space in her mind. Asking herself why it was something that stopped her momentum. She repeated the thought that dropped into her mind over and over as she walked back and forth feeling her heartbeat slow down. Her thoughts descended from her mind back into her body, she felt the knots and tension in her muscles as she swung her arms and shook out her legs. Now coming down from her high, she decided the rest of her evening was better spent in a relaxing bath. Rú watched as she released the remaining anger, like water evaporating after a storm, as she settled on which book she was going to read.

Satisfied by Nalini's change in mental direction, Rú took his leave to her parents' house.

He closed his eyes and opened them to see he was now standing in front of a stoop leading up to the brownstone on a quaint street in Brooklyn. He looked up and down the street noticing the lights on each end of the block were out. The lights that remained surrounded the brownstone in front of him. He was standing within a barrier not made by him. An old energy. Curious, he closed his eyes and when he opened them again he was standing in front of a wide mahogany staircase and was met by a being in human form patiently sitting halfway down the steps, a smile stretched across their beaming face.

"It's been a minute, Sunny," Rú said, shifting himself into the astral form of his human body.

"That's a clever use of units to gauge a relative concept in a boundless universe," The Being chuckled as they stood and took the remaining steps by two.

"Well, I guess it has felt like a minute for you," Rú said with a smirk. "What are you doing here?"

"I like to check in," The Being said, now standing in front of him with a smile even wider than before. Their shining smile was in stark contrast to the navy hue of their skin.

"So you're aware of what's happening with Arel?" Rú asked, looking past the being, to see Arel's father walk across the hall.

The Being's smile fell into a thin line. "I know. I've noticed the parasites circling the house," they said, turning away from Rú and walking down the hall to the dining room where Arel's parents were enjoying a late dinner.

"I didn't think their reach extended this far inland," Rú said, now standing next to them.

"They're motivated," The Being responded with a humorless smile. The look on their face was one of a parent in confrontation with a child desperately trying to push their buttons.

"What are you doing here, Sunny?" Rú asked again.

"I was invited here, Bahuvida is working on another book," The Being answered, shifting their tone to one of pride. They looked back at Arel's father and smiled. "He asked for help getting his ideas in order and for light to be shed on things he may be missing. And Ayra is working on a new program for her class," they nodded toward Arel's mother covering her mouth as she laughed.

Rú looked at The Being for a moment taking in their unbothered demeanor as they watched the laughing couple, happily oblivious to the darkness on the fringes of their block.

"Will you help us?" Rú asked tentatively.

"I have been helping. If you're asking me to interfere, then no, I will not," The Being said plainly. Rú went quiet, conflicted by the concern he felt and the reason behind The Being's stance.

"You're too close to the situation, you do them no service by taking on their doubt. Do you doubt Arel's will? Who he is?" The Being already knew the answer, but they wanted Rú to remember its truth.

"I have no doubt," Rú said confidently.

"Good, neither do I. So, I will not do him the disservice of underestimating his strength in the face of fear and neither should you," The Being paused to look at Rú directly. "They all need to learn they are capable of facing anything in this world," The Being finished. Gesturing to their surroundings as the radiant smile returned to their face. "And you don't have to worry about them," they said with a nod toward the giggling couple.

"I felt the barrier you set on top of mine," Rú said, in acknowledgment of their handy work keeping the shadows at bay. The Being laughed, "That wasn't me," they said pointing an index finger toward the couple again.

"The darkness of fear dare not tread where the strength of love dwells, it will be its undoing," The Being said.

Rú smiled and felt his worries fall away from him, The Being was right, he was too close to the situation, ignoring the higher perspective. This was not an insurmountable threat but a stepping stone, a challenge he knew Arel was more than capable of conquering.

"Thank you, Sunny," Rú said thoughtfully, before disappearing.

The Being smiled and bowed their head without a word.

Rú made it back to the apartment building a little before dawn. The guys should still be asleep and there was no point sitting around a dark apartment waiting for them to wake up. He decided to spend the remainder of that time on the roof to watch the sunrise.

✮✮✮✮

Eugene sat awake staring at the ceiling fan, he slept as much as his body would allow. He was surprised by the absence of nightmares he expected to have but thankful for the peace all the same. He looked over to the couch to see Dylan still knocked out, mouth wide open. Eugene stifled a laugh, shaking his head slightly. A weightlessness rose to his chest that sent electricity through his limbs, urging him to move. He looked at his phone, it was almost 7 AM, and thought it was probably best to get going before they were all fighting for the shower. Getting up from an air mattress without making any noise can be almost impossible, but he quickly succeeded in standing without waking up Dylan. As Eugene was cleaning his glasses lenses he heard Dylan begin to mumble from the couch and turned to find him still sleeping. He hadn't noticed Dylan talking in his sleep during the night, it would have woken him up as he was a light sleeper. He didn't give it another thought as he put on his glasses and began to go through the meticulously folded items in his duffle bag. Eugene pulled out his black cashmere crewneck sweater that he usually paired with jeans but was surprised to see that Rú hadn't packed any. Instead, he pulled out his charcoal plaid trousers which he thought were a bit dressy but with the way Rú chose to dress himself it made sense that he wouldn't just throw in a pair of jeans in the bag. With all his items and essentials in hand, he stepped lightly through the living room to the bathroom next to Arel's room.

Just as he was about to enter the short hallway Dylan's mumbling grew louder and stopped Eugene in his tracks. Dylan wasn't speaking English and his voice shook in distress as he clutched the blankets over his chest. Dylan's voice was growing louder and Eugene worried he'd wake up Arel. Eugene rushed to wake him up from his nightmare and reached out to shake him awake but Dylan's eyes flew open right before Eugene's hand could meet his shoulder. Eugene jumped back, almost tripping over the air mattress. Dylan was looking up at the ceiling in a dead stare quiet now.

"Dylan?" Eugene whispered, assuming he'd woken up from whatever dream he'd been having. Dylan didn't answer him and continued staring straight up, it was starting to freak him out now. He took another step back and when he did Dylan's head snapped in his direction, his eyes empty and his face void of any emotion. He began to speak again, this time he understood every word.

"You're going to be fine, everything will be fine," Dylan cried out over and over in the unknown language, his voice saturated with anguish, pleading the words to be true. It was unnatural and a grotesque contrast to his lifeless face, it chilled Eugene to the bone. Now thoroughly creeped out, and trying to keep his body as far away as possible, he reached out to jab Dylan hard on the shoulder and chest.

"Dylan, wake up!" Eugene boomed, no longer worried about waking up Arel. Dylan's eyes sprang to life and his expression changed to one of surprise.

"What! What's happening?" he screamed and sat up straight, flinging the blankets off himself in a panic. Eugene stood back in awe, still unnerved by Dylan's sleeping persona.

"What were you just dreaming about?" Eugene asked, keeping his distance.

"I don't remember, you just shocked me out of REM," he said, annoyed. He pressed his palms into his eyes as he let his head fall back down onto his pillow. "Why?" he sighed in an exhausted breath.

"Your eyes were open and you were talking in your sleep. You sounded really upset, b-but your face was... completely blank," Eugene said, still alarmed, his voice high-strung.

"That sounds kinda terrifying," Dylan yawned, closing his eyes again unphased due to his post-sleep fog.

"Can you speak any other languages?" he probed, trying to find a connection rooted in this reality.

"No, why?" Dylan answered lazily, he didn't look at all interested in Eugene's questions.

"You were definitely speaking another language, like Mandarin or something," Eugene said talking more to himself than he was informing Dylan.

"Do you speak Mandarin?" Dylan asked, propping himself up on his elbows, interested now.

"No," Eugene answered flatly.

Eugene turned away from Dylan and took a second, debating finishing his thought out loud for fear of sounding insane. "I understood you, it was the weirdest thing. Like my mind dubbed what you were saying, it's hard to put into words. I just knew."

"Are you sure you weren't the one having a nightmare?" Dylan asked, turning to look at him with wide accusing eyes.

"No! I mean yes! I was awake, headed to the bathroom." Eugene's words slowed to a pensive crawl as he thought about what had happened, it was a lot to wrap his head around this early.

"That's wild," Dylan yawned, eyes closed again.

"What's going on?" Arel asked appearing from the hallway, groggily rubbing his eyes.

"I was speaking Mandarin in my sleep and it freaked Gene out," Dylan explained, with the exuberance of someone relaying the weather.

"His face- his face was dead," Eugene said defensively, waving his hand over his face and doing his best to reenact the look on Dylan's face.

"You speak Mandarin?" Arel asked Dylan, ignoring Eugene.

"No," Dylan replied flatly.

Arel snapped his fingers and began wagging his index, he nodded and took a minute to connect the mental dots. "You're probably remembering a past life," he said, proudly placing his hands on his hips.

"But I don't remember the dream," Dylan said, finally opening his eyes. Now a little disappointed to be left out of his own experience.

"If it was as bad as it looked you might not want to," Eugene chimed in, shaking out the chill he got as the scene replayed in his mind. "I'm gonna go take a hot shower, try to burn the image out of my brain," he said changing the subject, rushing into the bathroom and slamming the door shut.

"Don't take forever!" Arel yelled from the living room. He walked over to the breakfast bar to see Rú in the kitchen filling up the coffee pot.

"Were you here this entire time? You know what? Never mind. How'd it go? Find anything out?" he asked as he walked up to the bar and took a seat. Dylan finished folding up his blankets and joined him at the bar. Rú finished putting on the coffee before answering him.

"I was on the roof, walked in on the tail end of whatever that was. But nothing to report, we're just gonna have to keep an eye out for what might pop up. Your sister is covered and you don't have to worry about your parents, they've got it sorted," he said, grabbing three mugs from the cabinet and placing them on the bar in front of them.

"So there's nothing?" His question was rhetorical, on one hand, disappointed by not having more information on what he might be facing, and on the other hand knowing more might have psyched him out. He was slightly surprised with himself at how at ease he was at present and he wasn't going to pick it apart by overanalyzing.

Rú shook his head in response, pouring coffee in two mugs. "No, there's no big bad demon heading it all up, no dybbuk boxes, or cursed items. That I know of anyway. Sometimes these are things that unfortunately happen over time. Energy builds up, like attracts like, it builds up like a dam and then something comes along that causes that dam to break," Rú explained almost clinically. "But that's why the cosmos has us," he finished with a lighter and more hopeful tone.

Arel nodded, Rú's explanation was a strange comfort, almost like it was a natural phenomenon. Like events that lead up to a landslide or an avalanche. Cause and effect. Feeling a little more confident, he picked up the mug in front of him and breathed in deep its rousing aroma when Rú grabbed the mug from his hand.

"Why." Arel's protest was curt and it was the only word he could muster, more exhausted than annoyed. Right as Rú pointed his finger over Arel's shoulder, he got his answer.

"Shower's free," Eugene said walking up from behind Arel and accepting the coffee Rú had taken out of Arel's hands. "Yes, thank you," Eugene said brightly.

Before Arel could contest, Rú cut him off. "You take longer than Dylan," he said, giving him a dismissive wave and taking a sip of his own coffee.

Arel didn't bother fighting him, instead, he turned and slapped Eugene up the back of his head, sending his nose into the mug and splashing scolding coffee onto the bar.

"Fuck you!" Eugene called over his shoulder, shaking the coffee off his hand. Dylan laughed and took a seat next to Eugene, his eyes never leaving Rú. He was wondering how Rú knew about his timeliness in the morning. Trying to work out if it was some type of dragon mindreading magic.

"It was the time Rel left me with you to go on that weekend getaway with Celia," Rú said, answering the question lingering at the top of Dylan's mind.

"Riiight, right," Dylan nodded and took a sip of his coffee. "Oh, maybe Rú can tell us what my dream was about," he said, nudging Eugene, getting a kick out of watching his expression shift into a grimace.

Rú took a second to tune into the scene Dylan was referring to and thought about the consequences of telling them about the memory that played out in his dream. He decided it wasn't his place, the meaning of this dream is meant to be felt, not explained. The truth is in the feeling, in telling them, their mind would only get in the way of their journey.

"It'll come to you, one way or another. That's an insight you have to find out on your own," Rú finally concluded looking from Dylan then to Eugene.

"Rules?" Dylan asked, disappointment painting his tone.

"I mean, I could tell you but that'll take away from the magic of uncovering your own mysteries. Gaining insight into who you are has multiple layers, the danger in telling you a facet of that information could take you off the path for your highest good and the soul's development." Rú had chosen his words carefully, hoping to offer enough information to satisfy his curiosity without giving too much away.

It didn't work.

"Why?" Dylan asked with the air of a curious toddler. Eugene took another swig of his coffee and propped his fist under his chin, settling in for the exchange. He knew Dylan wasn't gonna let it go easily.

Rú reached across the bar and knocked on Dylan's forehead twice. "That's why. Your mind can shut down information and ideas before the rest of you has a chance to process it if that information goes against any social constructs you were brought up in. The mind isn't the key to understanding your path, it's feeling, it's how the soul speaks. There's some information that is better taken in organically and in its own time as to ease your mind into a new way of under-standing."

Dylan looked straight ahead, processing what he had just been told. His face went back and forth between expressions as he tried to work it all out.

Rú realized what he was trying to do. "It's not gonna happen all at once, Dyl. It'll come when you're in vibrational alignment with the information."

"Vibrational alignment? The fu-"

"Showers free!" Arel yelled from the back. unknowingly cutting off Dylan's profane rebuttal.

"This isn't finished," Dylan said, pointing at Rú before grabbing his duffle and slinging it over his shoulder. Both Rú and Eugene laughed as he walked away.

"Thanks for grabbing my clothes, not the combo I'd choose but..." He shrugged and sipped his coffee instead of finishing his thought.

"You've got some good pieces, I wanted to elevate your look a bit," Ru said, Eugene rolled his eyes.

"How are you holding up?" Rú asked, Taking a gulp of his scalding hot coffee and letting the steam flow from his nostrils. Eugene was taken aback for a second, again forgetting he wasn't sitting in front of a man. Rú saw him go still as his eyes followed the trail of steam. "Happens when I drink hot liquids or hot foods," Rú quickly explained.

Eugene just nodded and continued to answer his question. "I'm doing ok, I guess. I expected nightmares but I didn't have any. Then again, 'please don't have nightmares,' was the mantra in my head as I fell asleep," he confessed with a sheepish laugh.

"That's how they say it goes, isn't it? Ask and you shall receive," Rú said, turning to grab the pot to pour himself another cup of coffee.

"But that's not always the case," Eugene answered with a cutting tone. Rú stopped put the pot back in the coffee maker and turned to look at Eugene. His face was void of any emotion, it was all in his eyes, screaming with accusations and questions.

"Your Dad," Rú said softly. He turned around and leaned over to rest his elbows on the counter across from Eugene, so he could address him face-to-face. "In one of your past lives, your father played the role of your son, in another he fought and died beside you, and in another, he was your little sister. The experiences you have in these lives shape your soul bit by bit, light by fire. Coming back every time a little bit wiser than before, a bit more compassionate, and a little more understanding. Your Dad was the great man you remember and love because of the events and lessons in those lives, good and bad. He finished his journey in this life and lived it well. He left you with a tremendous capacity to love, that is a gift, but you see it as a void to be filled. Who do you think made your mantra a reality?" Rú lifted himself from the bar and turned back to the coffee maker to finally pour himself what was left of the pot. "The ones you love never leave you, Gene." He turned back around to see Eugene resting his forehead on folded hands. He inhaled a deep breath and lifted his head, tracks of tears still on his cheeks.

There were no more words that needed to be said, Eugene just lifted his mug to Rú and downed the rest of his coffee. Rú nodded and lifted his mug in response. It was quiet for a time as they both thought to themselves and Rú put on another pot of coffee.

Eugene was the first to break the silence, "Do I have past lives where I wasn't a good person?"

Rú paused for a moment.

"Here's the thing, human beings are made up of both high and low vibrational energy. When balanced you're in a harmonious state.

The point of coming to live out a life on this planet and experiencing this reality is to learn to come into that harmonious state by choice. Achieving that balance isn't easy. There are the choices you make and the effect they have on the people who surround you. Compromises are made in moments of panic, events that affect you negatively, and then there is the influence of external forces. All these things add up; taint perceptions, condition negative reactions, and create destructive behaviors. However, the universe in its infinite wisdom will always help you learn from misguided choices by sending whatever negativity you put out into the ether right back to you. Sometimes this happens in one lifetime but there are many times lessons aren't learned and it follows them through many lives. That's why it pays to put out positive energy, even in difficult times, it will always come back to you." At that, Rú turned around to check the progress of the brewing coffee before turning his attention back to Eugene.

"So how am I doing with that?" Eugene asked fiddling with his empty mug, nervous to hear his answer.

"You've been around this rock quite a few times and you've done a good job balancing things out. The key is self-awareness and compassion. So, keep it up."

A smile formed over Eugene's face, satisfied with the response but Rú wasn't finished.

"You do, however, have experiences and connections that were cut short in previous lifetimes that have a chance to play out in this one. So, I'm gonna do you a solid and lay out some guidance you can choose to take. Don't let your mind get in the way of what you feel is right for you. Your intuition is right, go with it." Rú peered into Eugene's eyes with specific intensity, hoping his message landed where it needed to.

"Experiences, like what?" Eugene asked, hoping to get a glimpse into his future.

"Nope, That's something you'll get into when you're meant to. Two-faced little monsters, always want to know what happens at the end of the book. A little mystery is good for you!" Rú joked, but part of it didn't land.

"Two-face?" Eugene wasn't sure if he should be insulted or not.

"Yeah," he chuckled, then realized how it sounded. "Oh, no. Not that kind of two-face, not in this instance. The lack of symmetry in human faces, from one side to the other is the physical manifestation of your duality." Rú turned his head from left to right pointing to each side of his face. "Good side, bad side. Two-face."

Eugene sat quietly staring forward with a blank expression, "You're fucking with me."

"Nope."

Eugene leaned back and raked his fingers through his hair and interlocked his finger at the back of his head. "I mean, it kinda makes sense, it's just crazy that something that's a factor of our physical makeup is an effect of the balance in the human soul."

"When worlds collide," Rú said brightly, turning to the finished coffee pot to pour a mug full of coffee before Arel walked into the living room. He sat next to Eugene and picked up the mug set out for him this time.

"So, what are you guys talking about?"

CHAPTER SEVEN

HAPPY ACCIDENTS

On the way to the permit office, they continued the conversation Rú and Eugene started over morning coffee. Extended by Dylan's insistence on being kept in the loop on any new information. They felt comfortable talking as their Chariot driver seemed to have tuned them out as soon as they entered his car and the fact that Rú could tune into whether his attention shifted to them. The mood was light, they made jokes and were in good spirits when the car stopped in front of the office.

Arel was the last out of the car and as soon as his feet hit the ground he was reminded of the woman from the bar. His heart began to beat faster with anticipation, it was like he could feel her even without setting foot in the building.

"You're not wrong, she's working today," Rú said, just out of earshot of Eugene and Dylan, engulfed in their own conversation and a few yards up the walk.

"What? We need to establish some boundaries with this mind reading, man," Arel rambled through breathy words and fidgeting with his navy button-down. He moved to adjust the invisible tie he decided not to put on that morning.

"Your heartbeat picked up, your breathing changed, and as this is her place of work I took an educated guess. Stop fidgeting you look fine, she likes you, calm down," Rú said, pulling Arel's hands away from the top button of his collar that he was repeatedly buttoning and unbuttoning, eyes wide and fixated on the front doors.

"Wait, really? Even though I ran out on her mid-conversation?" he asked, his breathing calmed down and his voice settled into its normal range.

"Yeah, That was my bad, sorry. BUT, she doesn't hold it against you. It did look like you had an emergency." Rú patted Arel's shoulder reassuringly and stepped to the side of the walk to allow Arel to pass by him. "You good?"

Eugene and Dylan had stopped and were waiting just outside the doors for Rú and Arel to finish their conversation.

"What's the holdup?" Eugene called, as Arel and Rú walked up to join them.

"The woman from the bar works here," Rú spilled with a sly smile. It was a smile that said he knew more than what he was letting on.

"Ooohh," Eugene and Dylan said in unison.

"Shut up," Arel said dryly as he walked past them, taking a breath before opening the door. Arel had tuned out the chatter going on behind him as they walked down the hall to the office, absentmindedly rubbing his thumb up and down his palm, the pressure and repetitive action calmed his nerves. Even with Rú's reassurance, he still couldn't shake the pterodactyls flying into the walls of his stomach as he reached for the permit office door.

He held his breath as he walked through the door and was met with the gaze from familiar eyes, but not her eyes.

Behind the desk stood a man who towered over him, the smile on his face met his stormy gray eyes. He looked out of place standing behind the permit counter in leather and furs covering his wide muscular frame with long braided blonde hair. Arel felt all his muscles relax, a strange response, he made mental note of. It was of two minds, knowing full well that what he was seeing wasn't right and at the same time acknowledging the ease of being home in the presence of this behemoth of a man.

The moment the man opened his mouth to speak and sound met air he was gone and Evaine stood in his place. Her locs tied up in a bun, wrapped in a green and gold scarf. The gold in the scarf accentuated the gold beads glinting in her hair. He marveled at the way this woman made a uniform look regal. Rú nudged him forward to knock him out of his daze.

"I knew I'd see ya again," she said smiling confidently, crossing her arms and leaning them on the counter. Arel shook his head and rubbed his eyes, hoping this moment wasn't as awkward as he believed it was as he made his way across the room to her.

"Yeah, I had that feeling too," he said, completely forgetting about the vision of the six-foot-five Viking standing in her place not thirty seconds ago. She let out a laugh, satisfied by his answer.

"I'm sorry I ran out on you, I –" she cut off his apology with a hand wave.

"Don't worry about it, it'll cost you a drink though," she quipped. "But it seemed like it was pretty serious, did everything work out alright?" Her light tone changed to a mixture of concern and curiosity.

Arel was reminded then why he was there. "That's actually why we're here," he said, his light smile sliding into a serious line. Evaine's focus finally shifted from Arel to the three other men who had come into the office behind him. She gave them each a friendly smile, a welcoming gesture that Rú was the last to receive. Her curious eyes lingering on him a moment longer than the others.

"Have we met?" she asked Rú through narrow eyes, he smiled and made the noncommittal gesture of holding out his hand and shaking it to say 'yes and no'. Confused by his nonverbal answer, she looked back at Arel for an explanation but it was Eugene who offered a reason as to why they were there.

"I called yesterday afternoon about the permits for Xelas to begin the inspection of the brothers. Hi, I'm Eugene." He held out his hand and gave her a smile that would have sent any woman into a suggestive fantasy, but the only emotion on her face was concern as she tentatively shook his hand. She glanced back at Arel caution flashing in her eyes before catching herself. It was a shift Arel didn't miss, she knew something.

"Yes, we have everything ready to be signed and can set up transportation for Monday morning." Her tone turned into a polished customer service voice, all the playful lightness gone.

"Evaine, what do you know?" Arel asked, softly leaning forward. She released the tension in her shoulders and let her hands slide off the counter and into her pockets.

"Ever since the Xelas deal, it's like something has changed. The herons don't touch North Brother as it is, but now we haven't seen any around South Brother either. Boat patrolmen have been claiming to see people but won't report the sightings because they don't want to have to set foot on the islands. Personally, I don't think they should be bothered, no need to stir things up." There was a warning in her words.

"Too late," Dylan blurted, standing facing a rack of pamphlets.

"What?" Evaine spat, now alarmed.

"You're gonna have to tell her," Rú said, calmly looking around the room, he stopped when he spotted what he was looking for, "is that recording?" he asked, pointing to the camera in the corner behind her.

"Yes. Tell me what?" she asked impatiently, looking at Arel.

'*She doesn't need to be involved in this,*' he thought to Rú.

'*She was always involved,*' Rú responded quickly. At that, Arel turned to face him, forgetting for a moment they were having this interaction mentally.

"Aight, tell me what?" Evaine asked again, any softness lost to annoyance. Arel scrambled his thoughts dodging his own questions now.

"What time do you get off of work?" he asked quickly, glancing up at the camera. "We'll tell you everything, we just can't tell you here." She seemed satisfied with this response and softened her demeanor again.

"8 to 8 today," she sighed, "Saturdays are usually shorter but the department is understaffed." She was cut off by Dylan now on the other side of the room looking at the community corkboard.

"Government, am I right?" he said, pulling a flyer for underground city tours.

"I'll be out at 8:30, the latest," she finished, her velvet tone had returned and she was only focused on Arel.

"How about I pick you up then and I'll explain everything," he suggested, the words flew out of his mouth a little faster than he wanted them to. As strange as this explanation was going to be he was elated at the idea of seeing her again.

She smiled, "that works for me." She then looked at the rest of the neglected party, cleared her throat, stood up straight, and stepped back into her professional persona. "Is there anything else I can help you with? Any questions about the paperwork?" she asked, sliding the stack of papers across the counter to Eugene.

"No, this is great, thank you," he said, a distracted response as he thumbed through the sheets of paper. "Knowing Lin, she's going to go over every line, this should at least give you till Tuesday," Eugene said, to Arel without looking up.

"Every line? Isn't that a bit much?" Dylan chimed in, finally meeting up with the rest of the group at the counter.

"Attention to detail, it's how she made it to the top," Eugene replied, without turning to address Dylan, instead giving Evaine a thankful smile.

"No one from any of the departments will be making visits to the islands until these forms are returned, correct?" Arel asked Evaine, his tone all business now.

"I can't say for sure, there were a few memos on the possibility of sending a team to walk the island this weekend, in preparation for Xelas crews," she said, addressing them all now.

"Call me if they decide to send a team?" Arel requested, trying not to let the worry of that possibility seep into his tone.

"Yeah, sure thing," she said, a twinge of sarcasm to her words.

"Great, thanks," he said hesitantly, the sarcasm in her response threw him off for a second. He questioned the delivery of his request to call him and worried that she somehow misread his tone to be too demanding or bossy. "I'll see you later," he said, turning away from her, not wanting her to see the mounting insecurity manifesting all over his face.

Evaine waited for him to catch his mistake but decided to speak up as he was halfway to the door and the rest of the group was in the hall.

"Arel, I'm gonna need a number to call you," she said flatly. He spun on his heels to face her and flashed an embarrassed smile, there was no way to play it off differently. He felt instantly lighter and foolish for not realizing that was the reason for her sarcasm. He laughed and unconsciously ran his fingers through his hair as he walked back to the counter where she set out a paper and a pen.

"I can't believe I almost did that twice," he confessed, quickly scribbling his number down.

"Oh, I wasn't going to let you get away without it again," she laughed, stopping herself abruptly. "That sounded less creepy in my mind," she added, rolling her eyes.

Arel looked up at her and smiled, her slip of the tongue had laid to rest all the insecurity he had walking into the office.

"I like hearing what you're thinking," he reassured her.

She nodded in response, "Good." She paused and looked past him to the door, seeing three heads watching through the glass. "I think your friends are getting impatient." He turned quickly just in time to see all three heads drop out of sight.

"Yeah, I'll see you later." Reluctance tainting his voice, knowing it'd be back to the madness of his new reality as soon as he walked out of those doors. He took in a deep breath before turning away from her and she gave him an encouraging smile goodbye.

Walking into the hallway, Arel wasn't surprised to see it empty, and as he made his way out of the building he tried his best to compose the smile on his face. He didn't want to add fuel to the fire of the questions and prodding he'd get about Evaine as soon as he walked outside. He stopped just before walking out the door to massage the muscles in his cheeks to force the cheesy smile from his face. He proceeded to exit when he was confident that his face was back to a neutral expression. As he expected the three were standing just outside the building waiting for him, he braced himself.

"All set?" Rú asked before turning to walk toward the curb. Eugene and Dylan were unusually quiet, Dylan looked as if he wanted to burst but he wasn't about to pop that bubble.

"So what's the plan, Rú-Dude?" Arel asked jokingly, his tone was brighter than he intended and quickly looked over at Eugene and Dylan to see them both with smirks on their faces.

Rú stopped and spun around. "Glad you're in a better mood, but don't call me that again," his voice was flat and final.

"Just rolled off the tongue," Arel teased.

"Don't do it," Rú said, turning away again.

"Oh nope, that one's gonna stick," Eugene joked, crossing his arms over his chest.

"I like Rú-Dude," Dylan chimed in, rubbing his chin.

Eugene nodded in agreement, and Arel pointed to the duo in acknowledgment of their quick responses. Rú could appreciate the light-hearted energy the three were bouncing off each other and let the joke slide.

"Alright," Rú sighed in defeat, like giving in to the demands of toddlers. "Listen, Eugene's gonna go back to Xelas and keep an eye on things there, Dylan's going to go with him and you and I are going to take a trip out of the city."

"A trip where? Shouldn't I be in the city, just in case?" Arel asked, his apprehension had layers and was apparent in his strained voice.

"We'll only be gone a few hours. The guys will be fine at the office and Evaine will be too, I warded the building." Rú stated confidently, sliding his hands into his pockets and bouncing on the balls of his feet.

Arel nodded and forced himself not to overthink it. "Where are we going?"

"Devil's path," Rú's face and tone were lackadaisical as he blurted their destination.

"The Devil's Path? It's gonna take over two hours just to get there and I have to be back before eight!" Arel's tone ascended as he spoke. "We don't have time for an 'into the woods' spirit quest!"

"Relax," Rú held up his hand to stop him. "You won't have to trek up any trails."

Arel didn't say anything, just looked at Rú with an expression that read as a mixture of annoyance and confusion.

"Ok, we should get going right now if we want to make it out in good time," Arel said, walking passed him toward the car now waiting at the curb.

"That's for them," Rú said low, Arel spun back around to face him. "We will be flying."

"What?" Dylan and Arel asked in unison, there was excitement that colored Arel's voice, where Dylan's took a dejected air.

"Wait...wait," Dylan pleaded as Eugene gripped the back of his shirt and pushed him toward the car.

"We'll see you guys later, I'll pick up my SUV so we don't have to keep calling for a car," Eugene called over his shoulder, walking to the waiting Chariot driver. "Have fun on your spirit quest."

Arel all but ignored Eugene's statement and didn't respond, his mind was trying to wrap around the idea of flying on a dragon.

"So how are we doing this?" Arel said, clapping his hands and eagerly rubbing them together.

"I know you're excited right now, but I assure you, that will change," Rú said flatly, focused on finding a spot that was somewhat secluded. Next to the parking lot stood a small cluster of trees big enough for him to take off from. "Follow me."

Arel didn't utter another word and just followed him into the trees. Once settled in the middle of the small grove, he looked around him to see if anyone was around to watch them. He turned back to face Rú expecting to find him in his human form, instead, Arel found himself face-to-face with the creature he'd only seen in movies and read about in books.

Arel jumped back, "JEEZ, that was fast," he said leaning left to right to look at Rú's entire head. The more he looked at Rú in his rightful form the more he saw the comforting face he'd known for so many years. The shape of his snout, the bridge of his head, and even the shape of his eyes now orange instead of brown, it was Harrison. In the place of his ears were horns that twisted out and up, the right one had three distinct notches. He smiled and remembered rubbing that ear in particular when he first picked Harrison up from the rescue. "It's good to see you, buddy," he whispered to himself, reaching out to touch the horn on his nose.

'Come on, we have to get going.' Rú chuckled.

Arel walked to Rú's right and saw a horn on his elbow. He stepped up to it, stretching to reach the base of his wing. The texture of his scales was soft underhand, the metallic short hairs creating a sharp reflective illusion. Rú hoisted his elbow to ease Arel's climb. He settled comfortably between Rú's massive shoulder blades. A trail of horns flowed down his neck from the side of his head descending in size to the base of his neck, giving Arel a comfortable handhold to anchor himself to.

"Ready?"

Arel took a deep breath and thought about what was about to happen, he was about to fly on a dragon, envisioning the closing scene of 'The NeverEnding Story.' "Yeah, I'm ready," he said, tightening his grip. He could somehow feel the smirk form on Rú's dragon face. Rú crouched low and shifted his weight from left to right.

"Don't forget to breathe."

CHAPTER EIGHT

HOME

Dylan stepped out of the car after Eugene and was surprised to see the Xelas offices were located in an older building. Before him stood a quaint four-story historical building with original windows and red brick with a small stoop leading up to double doors. He envisioned a colossal modern tower with the eye of Sauron looming over its peak. Now he was thinking that probably wasn't a fair assumption as he walked up the stoop to the building's original doors. The lobby was the perfect balance of future and past, the only thing in contrast to the original design was the elevator in the back of the building set across from a small reception desk. Eugene greeted the woman behind the desk and made small talk while waiting for the elevator. Dylan occupied himself by looking at the photos that lined the walls of all the projects Xelas had completed across the country. The pictures told the story of the company's founder Waneta Mason and the very first renewal project in Kimilche, Washington in the 1990's. He didn't get too far before Eugene called him to the elevator.

"Pretty cool, huh," Eugene said, a certain level of pride laced his words.

"Huh? Yeah, not exactly what I expected," Dylan said thoughtfully.

"What did you expect, The Umbrella Corp?" Eugene joked with a smirk.

"Kinda," Dylan smirked. "Mount Doom but, yeah, I guess Umbrella Corp would work too."

Eugene laughed, "That was my first guess, I should have gone with that one."

Dylan's eyes grew big. "Maybe you were telepathic in one of your past lives and it's coming back up," he said excitedly.

"God, I hope not."

At that, the elevator doors opened and Eugene could see that Nalini's office door was open. His stomach churned uncomfortably and he looked down at the forms he was about to deliver.

"I'm gonna drop these, wait for me in my office, it's right there," Eugene instructed, pointing to the office in the right corner. He took in a deep breath before stepping through the doorway, placing the paperwork under his arm to free up his hands. Nalini looked up almost instantly and gave him a professional smile, she waved him in and asked him to close the door.

"They could have emailed them." The singing tone of Nalini's bracelets didn't match the look of annoyance on her face.

Eugene played dumb. "That department is a bit behind, and short-staffed," he spoke softly as he signed.

Nalini's expression softened. "Well, maybe that's something we can help them with in the future."

"Are you planning to take over all of New York?" Eugene smiled, only half joking. She could find a way to run this city and probably would at some point.

Nalini smiled and laughed softly, "Have you been talking to my brother?" she signed playfully. The light expression on her face fell as she observed the shift in expression on Eugene's face, he was deciding on whether or not to lie to her. Eugene never could lie to her, not even a white lie like this.

Nalini just breathed in deeply and nodded her head once, she was dismissing him, but he wasn't going to leave it alone.

"He's just worried about you." Eugene's movements were slow and expressions exaggerated, desperate to make her understand. His effort did the opposite, this enraged her. Nalini slipped off the speech bracelets and stood to walk around her desk to meet him.

"Don't you see what he's doing? He's creating a problem to take away from the success of this project. Arel knows what this will do for the city!" Her hands flew furiously, the rage in her eyes was overwhelmingly chilling and its intensity was fortified by her soundless words. If it were anyone else before her they would be cowering in the corner, but Eugene knew her better than anyone. This was about more than her and Arel's sibling rivalry. He walked over to her and stood in front of her and waited for her eyes to meet his.

"There are things you don't know." He never took his eyes off of hers, even when she looked away to watch his hands and lips. She looked up at him in annoyance and stepped back.

"Tell me then," she dared him, before crossing her arms.

Eugene now regretted saying anything at all and cursed himself for not letting it go and walking out when he had the chance.

"You're gonna think I'm crazy," he said out loud as he signed.

"Tell me," she repeated. He started to pace back and forth, trying to find a way to say this without her writing it all off as nuts.

"It's haunted," he decided to just keep it simple. She was still for a moment, he was beginning to feel uneasy as he couldn't read her face.

"That's it? This is New York City, everything is haunted," she dismissed, walking back around to sit at her desk.

He waited for her to sit and look back at him. "This isn't like any other haunting, someone has already died!" Eugene roared as he signed the words, having grown impatient with her unwillingness to truly understand. He was no longer worried about if anyone outside was listening in. He was frustrated with the runaround and the prejudice against her brother, it had no place in this.

Surprised by his outburst, Nalini's face fell into concern, "Who? Did it happen on the island?"

Eugene released a relieved sigh, hopeful he was finally getting through to her, "No, it happened on the boardwalk to one of Arel's patients, Olivia."

Nalini breathed in a deep breath and closed her eyes to center herself before continuing. Her face was calm but the compassion and concern had all but left her face, her eyes were cold.

She chose her words very carefully but her movements forceful. "This is very unfortunate and my heart goes out to Arel and her family but as you said she was a patient of my brother's."

Eugene began to shake his head, knowing exactly the conclusion she had come to but he allowed her to finish.

"If I'm correct, this is the same woman said to have drowned. I do not see the connection between this tragic event and the islands." She finished her statement and let her head fall into her hands exhausted by her restraint. After a minute, her head sprung up as something had come to mind.

"This would explain his weird behavior yesterday." Her face was curious and even forgiving. She could forgive his intrusion on her newest success if it was some kind of mental breakdown brought on by grief. Disregarding the timeline of events entirely as Olivia's body was discovered after their morning meeting.

All of Eugene's patience had gone, now he just wanted to get his point across. "That would have been my assumption too, if she hadn't shown up at his office after they pulled her body from the water," he stressed the word 'after.' "Except it wasn't really her, it was a spirit sent from the islands." Eugene then sat down across from her and waited for her reaction. She stared at him through narrowed her eyes.

"You almost had me, Gene. This is not funny, that poor woman, I have work to get done," she signed, her face exhausted by this interaction.

"We can prove it!" Eugene threw out quickly as a last-ditch effort. "Come to Rel's apartment around 9:30 tonight," he pleaded as he stood not wanting to overstay his welcome. He walked backward toward the door as he waited for her to think it over, stopping just before the threshold.

Nalini looked at him long and hard, weighing the costs of falling for what might just be a time trap set by her jealous brother. But she'd never seen Eugene like this, hellbent, he never took sides between her and her brother and this gave her pause.

"If I agree, will you leave my office?" she signed with a defeated sigh.

"Yes," he agreed, he was in a bit of disbelief but then he'd have to wait and see if she'd show.

She looked away from him and back to her computer. The verdict was tabled for now, she didn't want to waste time worrying about the possibility of monsters. She simply nodded then waved him off, pulling up the website to a local flower shop as Eugene closed the door behind him.

Eugene walked into his office and closed the door behind him, hovering there with his hand still on the doorknob mentally reviewing the conversation with Nalini.

'Yeah, that was the right move,' he thought, debating on whether it was his place or not to bring her in on the situation.

"What was that?" Dylan asked out of the blue, his eyes still glued to the article he was reading on his phone.

"I didn't say anything," Eugene said, looking at him slightly alarmed.

Dylan looked up and shook his head. "Sorry, thought you did, must be hearing things. I guess I'm more stressed out than I thought," he admitted, scratching the back of his head. "I heard you yell though, are you ok?"

Eugene nodded as he made his way around his desk and let his body collapse into his chair. "I convinced Lin to come by Arel's tonight to get the whole story." He looked at Dylan to gauge his reaction.

"Good, from what I heard there's no way Rel could have gotten her on board," Dylan said lightly, returning his attention to his phone.

"Yeah, I don't think she'll be able to write off Rú," Eugene mused, staring at the ceiling and reclining as far back as his office chair would allow.

"Dude, don't remind me, Rel is living out my dream of flying on a dragon 'How To Train Your Dragon' style," Dylan vented, letting his shoulders slump forward.

"Do you think Rú would ever let me go flying?" Dylan asked.

"I think he'd drop you on purpose," Eugene replied immediately.

"You're probably right," Dylan chuckled.

"What were you looking at on your phone?" Eugene asked as he noticed that whatever he was reading had him pretty invested.

"Oh, I was looking at all the photos and stuff downstairs of the Xelos founder Wanetta Mason and was compelled to research," Dylan said, he held up his phone before letting it drop back into his lap.

"Pretty crazy, right?" Eugene said, sitting back up and leaning his elbows on his desk.

"Yeah, her expansion across the US is insane, 5 major block projects in the first year of the company's inception, and how quickly she was able to expand into other states was pretty remarkable," Dylan said as he scrolled back through the article he was reading.

"No, not that, she's kind of a mystery. All that's known about her life before starting the company is that she grew up on a reservation in the northwest of Washington and Mason is not her real surname. There's no record of her before she started the company in 1991," Eugene explained, leaning in as if it were telling a secret.

"Must have been on the second search page," Dylan mumbled, looking back at his phone, scrolling furiously.

"Yeah, there's not gonna be a lot of articles on that but there should be a few about her disappearance," Eugene added lightly looking back at his computer screen.

"Whaaaaaaat," Dylan drew out the word until he scrolled down far enough to find what he was looking for. "Oh yeah, here are a bunch of conspiracy sites that have articles on it." He clicked the first page and skimmed the article before moving to another one. "This IS crazy, how has no one written a book or TV movie about this?" Dylan asked, genuinely baffled.

"Oh, people have tried, she named the current CEO as her executor in her will and he has the full force of Xelas' legal team, they can be pretty scary," Eugene said, his voice distant, distracted by his own internet search. After a minute of silence, Dylan looked up from his phone screen to find Eugene leaning in close to his computer.

"Are you looking her up too?" Dylan asked, getting up to turn the screen so he could see. Eugene slapped Dylan's hand away from the monitor and turned it himself revealing the results of his search of

'New York City monsters' to which most of the sites were of notorious murders and killers in New York.

"Come on, dude," Dylan muttered, response dripping with disapproval.

"I figured while we're here keeping an eye on Lin I could look up what else might possibly be lurking around the city. I know, it's the supernatural equivalent of WebMD-ing your symptoms," Eugene confessed.

"No, your search isn't specific enough," Dylan said, leaning over Eugene's chair, going in on the keyboard, and typing various words pertaining to supernatural entities and occurrences. Eugene felt a heat rise from his core into his chest and his body stiffened as Dylan leaned in close. Out of the corner of his eye, he traced Dylan's jawline and was drawn up to the curves of his mouth when he bit down on his bottom lip. An unconscious act as Dylan furiously typed, laser-focused on his current mission. He smelled warm and sweet, Eugene felt the tension in his muscles begin to melt as the scent swam through his senses. A pleasure short-lived as Dylan dramatically hit the enter button, breaking Eugene out of his daze. The search revealed countless sites dedicated to New York City's frightening underground and its encounters.

Dylan stepped back and proudly pointed at the monitor, "Now there is your supernatural equivalent to WebMD."

At that moment the sensor light on his desk flashed and a knock came at the door. Eugene knew it was Nalini. He minimized the screen and pushed the green button next to the sensor light that gave her the literal green light to enter. Eugene was glad in that moment the office was respectful of personal space, no worry of anyone barging in uninvited, and everyone was on equal standing.

Nalini walked in to see Dylan standing next to Eugene in front of the computer. She wasn't wearing her speech bracelets and held up her finger to indicate she'd be right back. To Eugene's surprise, Dylan sprung into action introducing himself in flawless ASL and shaking her hand.

"I'm with the parks department, we're going over possible problem areas on the islands," Dylan signed smoothly looking over at Eugene for his confirmation only to find him staring at him, mouth slightly agape.

Nalini smiled. "I love that the department is being so proactive, that's wonderful news," she finished and gave Eugene an approving smile.

"I'll leave you to it, nice to meet you," she signed and held out her hand for Dylan to shake again. Before she was completely out the door she turned quickly with her finger in the air, Eugene's heart skipped a beat.

"I want to send flowers to the family of the person we talked about earlier but Arel's not responding to me. Can you call him and get the information from him?" she asked, her face pleasant but composed. Eugene smiled, her compassion and how she was compelled to express it was the one thing he loved most about her.

"Sure," he answered, feeling the gnawing pain grow in his stomach as she thanked him and left the room.

"That was nice," Dylan praised as soon as she shut the door.

"Yeah," Eugene whispered, mentally scrambling to change the subject to get his mind off of Nalini and the pain that came with thinking about their failed relationship. "So what was all that?" he exclaimed, shifting Dylan to his full attention

"I used to do improv," Dylan professed, placing his hands on his hips proudly.

"Not that, the signing," Eugene urged, curious and genuinely impressed.

"Oh, Rel has a few patients whose primary form of communication is ASL and I wanted to talk to them too," Dylan stated lightly, sitting back down across from Eugene.

Eugene leaned back in his chair and nodded. He found himself suddenly overcome with a sensation of warmth, it began to replace the hollow pain of loss he experienced when Nalini left the room. The stark contrast sent his mind reeling, shining a new light on this unfamiliar feeling. The revelation caught him off guard, he had built up walls to filter his thoughts and feelings. Filters that filed all sensory information into preconceived mental boxes that told him how to feel. He knew he liked being around Dylan and now wondered if his mind was trying to put him in a box that didn't fit. He tried to place his newfound feelings, trying to remember a time he had felt this way, even for a second, with Nalini.

It was the feeling of relief, like walking through the door after a long day and being able to breathe in peace. The warmth and comfort of sanctuary. He ruminated on this feeling trying to make sense of its origin and trying to trace it back like a train of thought. He continued to stare into space, falling into the rabbit hole of his mind's chatter that reminded him of his patterns, influences, and adopted behaviors. All the things that could be put on paper that told him who he was, none of it included what he felt to be true. He'd always found himself attracted to other men but he'd been with Nalini since high school, being with anyone else never crossed his mind. The idea of being with someone else stressed him out as it was and he knew there was no reason to be worried about his family and friends and yet discomfort sat heavy in his gut. His thoughts then took him back to this morning's conversation with Rú, the words dropped into his internal deliberation as if by a third party, '*Don't let your mind get in the way of what you FEEL is right for you. Your intuition is right, go with it.*' He thought back further, took a deep breath, and intended to heed the advice. He'd gotten so used to controlling every aspect of his life, fitting things together like puzzle pieces based on what he thought he wanted. Realizing that the pieces he forced together never stayed that way and anything built off of those pieces fell away too. He had been trying to force this feeling into a place where it didn't belong but this time it wasn't his mind taking charge.

"So, what's going on there?" Dylan asked, breaking the silence and pulling Eugene out of his moment of clarity.

"W-what?" Eugene stammered.

"Lin," Dylan clarified, pointing his thumb toward the door. "Saw that look on your face, you guys seeing each other?"

"No," Eugene shut down quickly. He turned to face his monitor giving Dylan the impression there was more to that story.

"No? Why? She's probably the most beautiful woman I've ever seen," he said, pointing his thumb back to the door.

"We broke up," Eugene blurted quickly, hoping to stop the direction of the conversation.

"Oh damn, I'm sorry bud...You guys seem to be handling it well," Dylan added, Sitting back trying to put a figurative space between him and his conversational blunder.

Eugene shrugged, "We've been friends since we were kids," he offered as the reason for the civility between them.

"Still fresh?" Dylan inquired, knowing full well that he was pushing it but he let his curiosity get the best of him.

"You looking to make a move?" Eugene blurted out, instantly regretting allowing the words to come out of his mouth, worried he just planted an idea.

"Oh, nah, not for me," Dylan said, dropping his eyes back to his phone. His apathetic tone of voice threw Eugene. As glad as he was to hear Dylan's answer, he was still curious.

"You just said she was one of the most beautiful women you've ever seen?" What was meant to be a statement came out in the form of a question.

Dylan looked up and tilted his head, his eyes shifting from left to right. He was trying to think of how he wanted to frame his thoughts. "You know how, in just a few minutes, when meeting someone you can tell if you're going to get along?" Eugene nodded in response. "That," Dylan finished, looking back down at his phone.

"That doesn't answer my question," Eugene said, rubbing his eyes wondering where he was going with this.

"Whether or not someone is 'beautiful' is not the best indicator of how well someone is suited for another person, a lot of times it can distract from who they really are and you end up ignoring red flags. People will tell you exactly who they are, you just have to feel it out," he paused a moment. "Nothing against her!" He threw up his arms in defense.

"Alright, how do you know then? How do you know when someone is right for you?" Eugene prodded, throwing up air quotes around the word 'right.'

Dylan looked down at his hands that were restlessly flipping his phone back and forth between the two, thinking again how to put words to feeling. It didn't take him too long to find his answer, he looked up and locked his eyes with Eugene's. "They make you feel at home."

Eugene felt his heartbeat pick up, irrationally worried Dylan would be able to hear it, and did his best to bring it back down to normal.

"So let me play devil's advocate for a minute," Eugene threw out quickly. Playing the opposition would keep his mind off his internal dilemma or bring more insight, it was a win-win.

"Please," Dylan said, welcoming the challenge. He leaned forward ready for the debate.

"One can, and does, experience the feeling of home many times. So how does one really know that said person is 'home?'" Eugene proposed, he leaned back and crossed his arms, waiting for Dylan's reply.

"Good one. Home can be quite a few people throughout a person's life. It fully depends on where you are mentally and emotionally in your life. Say you've met someone today and you feel the comfort and safety of home but over time your life changes. The rooms of that 'home' that worked so well no longer fit who you are or your lifestyle. It was a perfect home for a time and you loved it but you've got all you could from it, so to speak. The problems arise when you think there should be only one home for the rest of your life and try to fit things that don't work with the layout of that 'home.' Things change, people change," Dylan explained, he leaned back in his chair satisfied he answered the way he wanted.

Eugene let Dylan's thoughts float in his mind. The more he spoke the more Eugene felt as if he were settling into himself, uncovering options he'd never thought of. He ultimately agreed with Dylan's sentiments but there was one thing that he hadn't addressed and it was something his romantic heart wanted stipulated.

"So you don't believe there's that one person for everyone," Eugene pressed.

"I think it depends entirely on the person. I believe people come into our lives for a reason and that everyone teaches us something. Sometimes they come and go, and sometimes they stay, it doesn't make them any less 'home,' it was the home you needed at that time," Dylan affirmed confidently. It was a diplomatic answer but lifted a bit of the fog from Eugene's confusion and gave him a bit more clarity.

"Interesting, so let's say you find a home but it's in a neighborhood you're not familiar with?" Eugene continued, wanting to pull another layer off of Dylan.

"Oh ok, we're gonna continue with the 'home' metaphor? Alright, is it a bad neighborhood?" Dylan asked, lifting his left brow in suspicion.

"No it's just, different," Eugene responded thoughtfully, that moment truly understanding the words as he allowed them to come out of his mouth.

"Then it just depends on whether you want to be open to it or not. If you find something that feels right for you, are you going to pass it up just because it's different than what you're used to?"

Eugene nodded. "Been listening in on Rel's sessions?"

Dylan smiled and looked back down at his phone, "No, never."

Eugene's eyes lingered over Dylan, he felt the push and pull of balance of himself and the world around him, welcoming the peace of being truly free.

CHAPTER NINE

SPIRIT QUEST

Rú broke through the clouds and swiftly landed in a small opening a little way off the hiking path, an area not so easily accessed by foot. Arel didn't wait for a leg down and slid off Rú's back landing on all fours. He gripped the ground beneath him to steady his wobbly shoulders, happy to be on the ground again.

"I told you to breathe," Rú said, back in his human form.

"I did breathe," Arel croaked. "The speed. I wasn't ready for the speed. I don't feel well," he said, trying to stand completely straight, sending his stomach into a barrel roll. He leaned over, resting his hands on his knees, and waited for it to settle. As his mind cleared from the haze of nausea, he noticed the uncomfortable cling of his cloud-soaked shirt. He glanced over at Rú, half expecting him to be in the same boat, only to find him sitting waiting on a boulder. He was not only completely dry but fully dressed like he was ready to shoot a men's urban fashion editorial in the woods.

"Dude, how is that appropriate attire for a spirit quest in the woods?" he complained as he peeled the wet fabric off of his skin and laid his shirt over a low-hanging branch to dry.

Rú sighed, "One, this isn't MY spirit quest, what did you expect? Monk robes? And two," he paused and ran his slender fingers through his hair. "I do what I want."

Arel laughed, "fair enough," he clapped and rubbed his hands together in anticipation "ok, how does this go?" he asked as he shook out his shoulders and legs.

"I want you to stand at the center of that sunspot," Rú instructed, pointing to the perfect circle of light a few yards in front of him. "And take off your shoes," he added quickly.

Arel did as he was instructed, kicking off his shoes and standing in the center of the light-filled circle.

"Now clear your mind, and take deep breaths," Rú said, getting up from the boulder and proceeding to walk around Arel just outside the light.

"Ah, grounding, I-"

"Nope, shut up and listen, we don't have a lot of time and I need you to focus," Rú interjected, his tone was steady but Arel could hear the twinge of annoyance.

Arel was used to meditation, often instructing his patients on how to incorporate it into their daily routines. He focused on his breathing and relaxing his muscles, allowing whatever thoughts that came to mind drift away in rhythm with it. Once Arel's heart steadied and he settled into a comfortable rhythm, Rú began his lesson.

"I want you to focus on the sun now, feel the heat, and imagine your skin absorbing the light." The sound of Rú's voice had changed, it seemed to have split into two tones, creating a hypnotic melody as he spoke. "Now imagine the light fusing with the cells in your blood, move with it as it flows through your limbs, and feel the heat as it moves with it."

Arel followed his instruction and could feel the energy and heat as it traveled through his body, it flooded his feet and hands. He felt the heat build, he didn't know how long he'd be able to stand still much longer.

"Now, I want you to move your focus to the grass under your feet. Shift your weight and allow the cool of the earth to rise through your soles, feel the heat meld with the cool energy rising from beneath you. Picture that energy as an electric blue," Rú droned, as he watched the energy around Arel increase.

Arel let the imagery take over his mind, he no longer had to think about it as it was happening in his mind's eye. The coming together of the two energies merging, balancing the coolness of the earth and the heat of the sun, he moved with it as it flowed through his veins.

The forceful energy from the sun was now given direction by the cool energy from the earth, it wanted to move. Arel released any restriction and allowed his body to move where and how it was compelled to. The movements had structure; it was as if his body was living out its own memories without the instruction of his mind.

Arel's eyes remained closed but as he continued to move the vision in his mind began to clear. He felt calm as he allowed his arm to lift and hover over the other in front of him and let his foot step forward. Arel felt his frame lighten as it continued to move. His internal sight cleared releasing the hold he had on himself and he allowed himself to fall completely into his vision.

He was back in Kirana's form in unfamiliar woods, the only light in the dark came from her body. A shadow form was all she could see beyond her light, it was one entity but she felt its reach surround her. It was trying to find a weakness in the barrier of light that protected her, a weakness in her will. In the face of this creature, he was comforted by the calm she held strong too. She dug her feet into the earth and was thinking of the light of the sun, knowing the same light lived in her. Kirana moved her arms in circular blocking motions, allowing her energy to build and expand, drawing the shadow back. She peered into the dark and searched the creature's face only to find eyes darker than the surrounding black. She continued to focus on the two black voids as she advanced one foot in its direction, she felt a pressure come over her. That must have made it angry, he could feel a smirk playing at the corner of Kirana's mouth. The void grew darker then disappeared altogether, the pressure she'd left lifted and the night became still. She had faced off with this shadow creature and sent it running. She felt pride and satisfaction swell within her and she turned around to continue on her way only to be met by orange eyes.

"Ahh!" Arel shrieked, as he was frightened out of his vision and pulled back to the present. He stumbled but was able to find his footing before completely falling over.

"You did the same thing then, there really are some things that don't change," Rú remarked from the boulder.

"What was that? In the dark?" Arel asked enthusiastically, letting his arms shake loose.

"It was a Djinn, some of them can be nasty. To face a Djinn is to face fear itself," Rú stated, crossing his arms

"Like a boggart, from Harry Potter," Arel related lightly.

"Sure, if boggarts took pleasure in torture and ripping you limb from limb," Rú retorted, sarcastically

"Ok fine like Pennywise from 'IT'," Arel amended.

Rú took a minute to run through the synopsis in his mind. "Yeah, that's an apt comparison," he said with a shrug. "Ok, let's talk about what you just experienced, what did Kirana do when confronted by the Djinn?"

Arel closed his eyes and stood up straight, he recapped everything in slow motion allowing himself to feel what she felt in the dark.

"She stood her ground, she literally dug in. It was like she was drawing her defense from the earth," Arel recounted, his face hanging over his body as if he were staring at his feet.

"Very good, why?"

Arel opened his eyes and looked at his feet in the grass. He focused on the pulse in his feet and with every beat he felt a wave of energy rise up from beneath him to meet it.

"Because she knew she wasn't alone, she knew her strength wouldn't fail because she was connected to everything around her and it would not fail her," Arel answered, lifting and dropping his feet and looking at the trees around him. He wondered if he was actually feeling them reach for him or if it was in his mind.

"Yes," Rú said softly, as he continued to walk just outside of the light. "The air in your lungs and blood is purified by trees, the minerals that make up the ground beneath your feet make up your genetic material. The iron in your blood is the very same iron from the hearts of extinguished stars. There is tremendous power in the elements, you witness their devastation every day, and you are made of them all. The power and depth of water, the strength of earth, the expansion of air, and the passion of fire. You are literal beings of heaven and earth, connect to them and the universe will bow before you. You, human beings, have more power than you allow yourselves to perceive."

Rú stopped and stood directly in front of Arel and watched his expressions shift and change as he absorbed his words. Arel began to nod and walk back and forth, making a point to feel the vibration beneath his feet. He stopped pacing and sat at the base of the tree to his right and let the cool bark from the tree calm his muscles. He felt stable at its roots and he surrendered to its imperceptible protection. At that moment Rú's words were reality.

Rú felt the shift in energy that emanated from Arel, it was now in unison with the energy that surrounded him, it created an impenetrable barrier. He could feel the ease flowing from Arel.

Rú smiled. "Very good, now get up," he said, turning away from him and directing him back to the circle of light. Arel begrudgingly lifted himself from the comfort of the tree and stood at the circle's center.

"Ok," he exhaled, ready for the next part of his lesson.

"Now go back into that memory, I want you to focus on the Djinn. How were they acting? How were they trying to break down your defense?" Rú asked, now closer to the tree line.

Back in the memory, Rú's voice felt farther away than before, making Arel feel a bit more vulnerable.

He was no longer seeing through Kirana's eyes and no longer had the comfort of her confidence and experience, it was only him in front of the Djinn. He scrambled to take hold of the security he had in the circle and to remember the strength he had at his disposal was the same as the earth beneath him, he dug his feet in.

"What are they doing?" Rú asked calmly, walking the tree line. It sounded like a whisper in his vision.

"Surrounding me." He moved his head about in every direction. He took a deep breath and fought the fear welling in his chest. "It's not real," he said to himself. As he dug his feet deeper he remembered what Rú had said and began to picture the iron in his blood igniting into its previous form of light, creating a barrier around him. He felt the energy from the earth beneath him and he willed it to merge with the light, urging his limbs to move. He moved his foot forward and allowed his arms to form and flow over one another. His energy began to build and in turn, expanded his barrier, he felt a smirk form across his face as he felt the frustration from the creature in front of him. It tried to increase its pressure on his defense to no avail. The more it tried the deeper Arel dug in. Frustrated, the Djinn stopped its advance and vanished.

Arel opened his eyes to see the sun had moved enough for the circle of light to shift, he was now standing with only one foot in the circle. He looked around to find Rú, he was leaning against the tree whose base he had previously been sitting.

"That was different," he remarked walking over to check to see if his shirt was still damp.

"You needed to fully experience what it was like to face fear and put your knowledge to practice." Rú pushed himself from the tree and made his way to the middle of the opening stopping a few feet from Arel. "What else did you notice?" he asked, crossing his arms.

"I know Kung Fu," Arel said, pushing his arms through the stiff fabric of his sleeves.

"I wouldn't say-"

Arel's eyes grew big and hastily cut off Rú. "I'm the one."

"You're not Keanu Reeves," Rú declared forcefully as he turned away to sit on the boulder.

"What?" Arel said in surprise.

"Do you really think I've never seen a movie? That I stayed home every time you went out?" Rú's tone was emotionless.

"Clearly not," Arel said, gesturing to his present outfit choice. "You have to be the only dragon on the planet with an affinity for high fashion apparel."

"You'd be surprised," Rú said, flicking a bug off his sleeve. "We like nice things."

Arel laughed as he finished fastening the top buttons of his shirt. He pulled his phone out of his pocket to check the time, it was already close to 5 o'clock. He looked up to see Rú gesturing to a smaller boulder next to the one he was sitting on. He trudged over to it and made himself as comfortable as he could.

"Shall we continue?" Rú said, looking into the trees ahead of him.

"We shall," Arel breathed with a snarky undertone.

"What you just witnessed is only one example of what you could be experiencing. So I'm going to ask you again, what was it that kept your defense strong when the Djinn went to surround you? What was it trying to do?" Rú asked, still eyeing the tree line.

Arel paused, going back into his memory, laser-focused. "It was trying to cut me off, it's intention was to make me think I was alone."

"And what was your response to that outside force trying to impose that narrative?" Rú asked. Arel knew what he was doing, it was a tactic he used with patients. Asking them to explain the circumstances or reasoning to understand it at a deeper level, was a way to ground a lesson.

He obliged him, "I thought about being part of the elements. Everything you explained, I believed in it and that I could draw strength from it. The moment I thought of it, I felt like I had an army at my back. I let go of worry."

"Exactly!" Rú exclaimed, launching himself from the boulder. "When you let go of fear it no longer has anything to feed or build upon. When you believe in your own capabilities and connection with the knowledge around you, you are more powerful than anything outside of the boundaries you create. You are always in control of what you allow into your space, energetically speaking," he clarified quickly. "There is always a support system in addition to your own self-belief, whatever that may be; ancestors, angels, universal consciousness, or just the knowledge you are connected to greater forces beneath your feet. It creates a barrier no low vibrational entity can break. The balance of believing you are supported, and focused determination can thwart any threat born of fear. The human will is an incredibly powerful thing and paired with belief, untouchable."

Arel sat quietly, running over scenarios in his head. "So what about that water spirit that took the form of Olivia? That wasn't a purely spiritual encounter, it would have killed us if you hadn't been there," he countered.

"It was actually a pretty good strategy." Rú realized that came out a little more excited than it should have by the look of disgust that flashed over Arel's face. "Of course apart from losing our poor Olivia the way we did," he clarified quickly. "It was counting on surprise and fear to lower your defenses enough to make you vulnerable to attack before it lost form. A lack of fear weakens lower entities in any case. Physically you would have been able to overpower it and now you remember you know how to defend yourself, so..." Rú shugged nonchalantly.

"Ok, so what about if I'm facing off with a person possessed?" Arel challenged.

"Ok let me put your question down, flip it, and reverse it. How would you handle that situation knowing what you know now?" he responded. Rú's face was expressionless and he was pacing with his hands resting against his lips, palms together.

"Did you just work a Missy Elliot lyric into this lesson?" he digressed with a slight chuckle.

"It's stuck in my head, go with it. What would you do?" Rú continued, without losing focus or pace.

Arel got whatever chuckles he had in his system out and brought his thoughts back into the scenario. "I'd focus on the person, try and draw them back out," he surmised, satisfied and convinced that this answer was the only one appropriate.

"And if you can't?" Rú asked, turning to look at him head-on, honestly curious as to what Arel's alternative would be.

Arel didn't think too long on how he'd respond. "Knock 'em out, come back to it later."

"There she is," Rú said, ultimately unsurprised his solution would mirror that of his previous life, he wasn't at all disappointed to see a little more of Kirana shining through.

Rú walked over and gestured for Arel to hand him his phone.

"What happens if it's a poltergeist deal and things go flying," Arel asked lightly, passing Rú his phone.

"You've got fast reflexes, duck and cover," Rú replied without looking up from the phone.

Arel narrowed his eyes at Rú, "Yeah ok, great, thanks."

"Alright, let's get going so we can get back with enough time for you to beautify yourself before picking up Evaine," Rú teased as he handed Arel's phone back to him.

The sunlight had almost disappeared behind the tree line and stratus clouds were moving in for seamless cover, it was going to be an effortless flight back.

Chapter Ten

BLACK-EYED KIDS

Arel enjoyed the flight through the clouds more the second time around, possibly due to the leisurely pace Rú was taking. They were making good time and Arel was feeling at ease with what he'd uncovered about himself and his capabilities, so he granted himself permission to appreciate the present moment of actually flying through clouds. He wasn't going to think about the fact that being up so high it would be impossible to breathe so clearly or why he wasn't freezing. He was riding through clouds on a dragon, the laws of the natural world didn't exist at that moment.

Near the apartment building was a small park with a thin, but dense, line of trees where they could land. It was getting darker and with the clouds floating low it didn't take much reflective energy to remain unseen for Rú to land without alerting possible on-lookers. They hit the ground at 7 o'clock, Arel felt a flutter in the hollow of his stomach as he saw the time. He hadn't allowed himself to think of her while he was away, afraid he'd run away with his imagination instead of focusing on the task at hand.

He looked at Rú as they made the short walk to the building then down at his once again drenched button-down and mentally took stock of everything he had in his closet

"Could you magic me something better to wear?" he asked, holding the door open for Rú to walk in first.

"I could, yes. But no, I'm not going to," Rú breathed, pushing the elevator button and looking straight ahead of him at his blurry reflection. They stood in silence, leaving Arel to stew in thought as to what Rú's reason was. The elevator doors opened and he followed behind Rú in and waited for the doors to close.

"Why?" he asked, no longer able to hold in his curiosity.

"Because you're too much in your head and shouldn't depend on any kind of accouterment for confidence," Rú explained, leaving Arel in the elevator as soon as the doors opened.

"Says the mythical creature in head-to-toe Armani," Arel grumbled as he unlocked his apartment door.

"These?" Rú pointed down to his boots. "Armani could never. And I'm not trying to impress anyone," he said pushing passed Arel to walk through the door first.

Arel was showered and dressed at 8 PM settling on his favorite navy blue crewneck sweater with brown leather patches on the elbows paired with his slate grey slacks and brown boots. As he looked himself over in the mirror a rush of confidence welled in his chest. "Not bad," Arel mumbled to himself, wondering why he asked Rú for his help at all.

8:15 he was checking his phone every five seconds for the arrival text from Eugene and Dylan. At first, his mind went to the worst-case scenario worried that something could have gotten to them, until a small voice in his mind reminded him that they live in New York City and Eugene's building had a valet service that takes forever. The thought calmed him until his mental attention shifted to the idea of Evaine waiting on him. He got up and started to walk circles around his apartment trying to will his palms to stop sweating. He pulled his phone out of his pocket to check the time again, to his relief the screen lit up with a text from Eugene informing him they were downstairs in the SUV waiting.

"Ugh, finally," he exhaled. He looked up to tell Rú they were outside to see him already making his way to the front door. 8:20.

✶✶✶✶

Evaine rushed to shut down the computer and checked the rest of the office, not that anyone had ever tried to stay past closing, but it was protocol. She didn't mind walking through the dark halls at night, it was calming after spending all day under fluorescent lights. Before leaving the building, she stopped in the bathroom to let her hair down, touch up her makeup, and give herself a once-over in the mirror. There wasn't much to be done about her work polo and khakis, but she made it work with her floral bomber. Once she got her hair to lay the way she liked she pulled out her phone to check the time, 8:30 on the dot.

She walked out and scanned the parking lot for any parked cars, even though half the lot was obstructed by a line of trees. The air was still and yet an unnatural chill nipped at her exposed extremities. It gave her pause, before turning to lock the doors she searched to tree line for movement to the right and left of her. After a minute of observation, she was satisfied she wasn't being watched and turned to lock the doors behind her only to notice a slight movement in the trees that blocked half the parking lot. She froze, her eyes drawn to where she saw the motion, just beyond a layer of leaves were two orbs blacker than shadow. She stared unwaveringly into the dark, willing them to move, "Come on," she challenged out loud, but only loud enough for someone close to her to hear. The orbs remained perfectly still, she allowed the tension in her muscles to relax a bit, annoyed she allowed herself to be spooked by shadows. She took a breath to clear the fear from her mind and finally turned around to lock the door. As she turned the key the world went quiet, no rush of cars or chirp of crickets. The air shifted and her ears popped as if she'd just been locked into a pressurized room. She stood motionless with the key still in the lock trying her best to remain calm as a puff of cold air hit her back.

"My ride isn't coming for me, can you let me in to use a phone?" said a small voice from behind her, the two tones of the voice sent an alarming bolt of energy up her spine. First a painful cold then an unbearable heat that worked its way through her limbs like lightning.

"Had to wait till my back was turned," Evaine said calmly, the cloud of fear cleared, replaced by rising anger. She turned to face the small voice and to her surprise, she had to look down farther than she thought. The boy before her appeared to be between the ages of seven and nine wearing a sweatshirt with a deep hood hiding the upper portion of his face. When he looked up at her to meet her gaze, the exterior light from the building illuminated the boy's face. Evaine stepped forward noting his round baby-doll cheeks and small mouth but froze when she saw the boy's solid black eyes, cold and hollow orbs relentlessly searching for any sign of fear on her face.

"Let me in, I need to use the phone." The intensity of the boy's voice grew with each word, the pitch falling into a hypnotizing tone that shocked the senses into the illusion of sinking. The sound cracked her defense sending a chill to her bones and leaving her skin crawling. The boy was aware of it all, her increasing fear rolling off of her in waves. The boy's mouth twisted into a perverse smile, a sight made more unsettling by his lifeless eyes.

He stepped forward only to stop short as if he hit an invisible wall, his smile dropped and his face went blank.

Evaine released the breath she didn't realize she was holding. "No way," she breathed. She pulled a small burlap bag from her purse and held it in her hand for a moment looking from the bag to the boy. She lunged forward, faking a charge and the boy flinched.

"No shit," she laughed out of relief. "Thank you, Mae," she said and kissed the bag in her hand, elated that she had a friend back home who cared enough to make her a protection bag before she left for New York. "Woo, I owe you," she whispered as she tucked the burlap bag back in her purse, clutching it tight to her side. A wave of curiosity came over her and felt emboldened to bend over to look at this black-eyed child. She cocked her head to the side to get a better look at him, the longer she stared the more she realized how unnatural it looked and not quite human. She had the overwhelming feeling that she was facing off with something much bigger than what appeared to look like a life-size porcelain doll. Looking into the abyss of its black orbs she could still feel the isolation, out of her element, like facing off with a great white in a glass cage with no floor.

Then boy's body violently jerked forward sending her flying backward causing her to lose her footing. She threw her arms up to shield her face and shut her eyes, bracing herself for assault on the ground.

"Evaine!"

She opened her eyes to see Arel running toward her and an imposing black mass following behind. Before she could call out to warn him of what was coming up behind him, the mass shrunk into a man-size shadow just as it reached the extent of the dim street light revealing one of the men who was with Arel earlier. She shook her head, trying to convince herself the large mass was a trick of the mind after dealing with that black-eyed child thing.

"Are you alright? Are you hurt?" Arel asked hurrying to lift her to her feet. He cupped her face in his hands, gently turning it left to right checking for any cuts from her fall. She grasped his hands in hers, removed them from her face, and held them against his chest.

"I'm fine," she declared. "But I wish you had come a bit earlier." she gave him a tired smile and released his hands to wipe the dirt off her pants. Evaine watched as the man behind him walked farther into the light. Rú kept his distance but offered her a friendly smile before turning to look around. She found his calm demeanor strange, he had to have seen what just happened and her curiosity of Rú stopped there. Her eyes dashed left and right then behind Arel and Rú.

"Where is it?" she asked frantically moving herself in front of Arel and pushing him behind her at the same time, pulling the burlap bag from her purse again to protect them both. "It could come back."

"It's not coming back," Rú assured her, taking a step forward he could feel the energy from the bag in her hand. "Good thinking," he said pointing to it. "How did you know you'd need it?"

"I, uh, I didn't. A friend back home made it for me, she made me promise I'd always keep it on me. Why, what's it to you?" Evaine, staring daggers at him through narrowed eyes. Rú smiled and put his hands up in surrender, "It's not me you need to worry about, Evaine."

Arel stepped out from behind Evaine. "This is actually part of what I wanted to talk to you about. This is Rú he just saved you, well, us," he said looking nervously from Evaine to Rú.

"I had it covered," she said looking only at Rú, still not convinced he was trustworthy.

"It was an assist then," Rú offered, relaxing his arms and sliding his hands into his pockets. "She could have walked right past it and it wouldn't have been able to touch her," he explained to Arel. "But then, it would've followed you home and possibly hurt someone else and so...I assisted."

Arel was slightly taken aback by Rú's tinge of snarkiness at that tail end, not understanding where it was coming from.

Evaine picked it up too and was none too pleased by his tone of voice. "Mmhmm and how'd you do that exactly?" Rú smiled as he held up his index finger and took a few steps back.

"Wait, wait, hold on. Sidebar," Arel said rushing to Rú, pulling him to the side out of earshot of Evaine. "What are you doing? You're really gonna change in front of her right now? What happened to manipulating her decision, or path or whatever?" Arel asked in hushed tones.

"Her seeing me change was only a matter of time and as there's already been an attempt on her life, her knowing is better done sooner rather than later. Trust me," Rú assured him chapping him on the shoulder and giving him a mischievous smile.

"I don't," Arel stopped himself. "Okay, sure," he said as he made his way back to stand next to Evaine, wiping his sweaty palms on his pants as he walked.

" Alright, try not to freak out, okay?"Arel said once he was beside her again.

"Why? What's he gon-"

In the second it took for Arel and Evaine to glance at each other Rú had transformed into his dragon form with his enormous head inches from their faces. They both jumped back screaming, Evaine holding her protection bag in front of her for defense. Arel pushed Rú's head away and went in on calming Evaine down as Rú emitted a guttural sound that Arel interpreted as a laugh.

"It's ok, he's not going to hurt anyone," Arel said, stepping forward and holding his arms out between Rú and Evaine. He looked away from Evaine to find Rú back in human form bent over laughing.

"You couldn't ease her in by changing into Harrison or something," he hissed furiously.

"And miss the look on your faces? No way," Rú said, still laughing, he looked around Arel to address Evaine. "I swear it doesn't matter what face you're wearing, it's the same look every time," he chuckled, turning away to take a breath.

Evaine's expression shifted from shock to confusion, standing for a moment in silence before turning to sit down on the building's doorstep.

"I don't know dude, you couldn't turn into something a little less jarring?" Arel hissed, as he walked over and knelt to Evaine's level. "Are you ok?" he asked calmly, trying to position his face to meet her line of sight.

"I just need a minute," she whispered and held up her hand for some space.

Arel stood up and stepped back, both he and Rú waited patiently in silence.

"Ok," Evaine said abruptly after a moment, breaking their collective silence. "So what exactly is happening right now and how am I involved?" Evaine's voice was low and she articulated every word, understood by both Arel and Rú to mean she hit her limit in being out of the loop.

"Th-that's a valid question," Arel said nervously, shifting his weight.

"Solid question," Rú echoed.

"Well," Arel started as Rú took a small step forward. "He's a drag-on," he blurted, pointing to Rú who raised his hand and gave her a short wave.

"Yeah, saw that. We're gonna come back to that. Why was I almost attacked by a creepy demon child?" Her strained voice brought out more of her southern accent and she spoke with her hands that accentuated almost every word.

"Why did your friend give you a protection bag? What do you know?" Rú countered. Both Arel and Evaine looked at him like he'd grown another head.

"What? She had a run-in with something paranormal and has been into the craft ever since. How is this relevant to what's happening right now?" Evaines question was less of an inquiry and more of a demand as she was getting tired of Rú's perceived flippantness. Arel interjected.

"We're assuming this has to do with the Brothers project," Arel interjected, ignoring the line of questioning aimed at Rú.

"I FUCKING KNEW IT!" she crowed, shooting to her feet.

"Knew what?"

Dylan had walked up without alerting anyone to his approach, they'd been distracted by Evaine's excited outburst. Arel was about to disclose what he'd just shared but was cut off by the sound of a scream echoing from the parking lot.

The Parking Lot

"What do you think is taking them so long? I didn't think they were going to tell her the whole story here," Dylan complained, looking at the time on his phone. Music droned in the background, serving as the baseline that accentuated the cry that disrupted its rhythm.

"Did you hear that?" he asked, reaching for the stereo touchscreen to turn the music down.

"I don't hear anything," Eugene said, after a few seconds of silence.

"I'm gonna go see if everything is alright," Dylan said already halfway out of the SUV.

"Famous last words," Eugene joked. "I'll keep it running."

Dylan flipped him the bird as he walked in front of the headlights and started into a jog to round the trees to get and the sidewalk.

Eugene watched until Dylan was out of sight, scanning the trees and the rest of the parking lot. He checked his mirrors, a habit whenever he was in his car alone. Through his rearview mirror he thought he'd seen a small figure but when he did a double take the figure had disappeared. He tapped mute twice to bring up the rearview camera for confirmation and was put at ease that nothing was there. This frightening moment lasting a good thirty seconds, left his entire body tense. Eugene turned the music back up to a reasonable volume and let his shoulders settle back down to where they were meant to be. He looked around one more time before he was satisfied enough to close his eyes. He drifted into his thoughts and went over everything that happened earlier that day, for a moment forgetting where he was and why he was there. He let his optimism take over allowing the warm feeling of home to fill him up like it had talking in the office with Dylan, no longer afraid to keep his eyes closed.

A knock on the passenger window shook him from his thoughts, he looked over expecting to see an annoyed locked-out Dylan. Instead, he was only able to see the top of what he assumed was a black hoodie.

"What's a kid doing out this late?" he mumbled to himself as he muted the music and hit the button to roll down the window a few inches. "Hey, buddy are you ok?"

From the driver's seat, he couldn't make out what the small voice was saying. Eugene unbuckled his seatbelt and opened his door. "Hold on bud, I can't hear you," he said rounding the front of the car and stopping short in front of the passenger side headlight. The moment he had eyes on the small hooded figure a wave of nausea and dread flooded his insides, feeling exposed and isolated.

"Can you help me? My ride isn't coming." The child didn't lift its head as it spoke and as the words hit Eugene's ears a fog fell over his mind, holding on to a train of thought became difficult.

"Yeah, I don't thi-" he slurred, turning to stumble back to his car door as fast as his limbs would allow. He couldn't tell where the child was or if it had even moved, his only concern was getting in the SUV and locking the door. Reaching the driver's seat didn't bring the relief he was hoping for as blinding pain began to build over his eyes. Eugene wasn't looking as he extended his arm out to grab the door handle and before he could pull it shut a small hand caught his wrist.

His dread slid into a panic as the touch of its frigid hand began to burn his skin. Frozen in fear, he did his best to focus his sight and get a good look at this child as it tightened its grip around his waist. The child seemed to glide out of the darkness as if it were an extension of it.

Eugene's mind was in overload trying to will himself to move, kick it, anything, but found himself powerless as he watched the monstrous child reach his other hand out to touch Eugene's face. The child lifted its head revealing cold black orbs that took the place of eyes, they were the only things Eugene could see clearly as they bore into his. Eyes, there's always understanding to be found in the eyes and Eugene had always taken comfort in being able to make sense of someone by looking into their eyes. As he fell into the black-eyed child's all-encompassing gaze, he felt himself go numb. His limbs flashed frozen by a paralyzing sensation that was working its way to his chest. Breathing in as deep as his lungs would allow, he released the loudest scream he could muster until he felt his vocal cords go still. Eugene hoped his scream would at least alert the rest of the group to the threat that lay in wait for them. He could do nothing but observe the stillness as it steadily moved slowly through his face, painful as it moved up his nose like the sting of inhaling water. Eugene felt himself being pulled from the sight of his eyes, watching the picture get smaller as he was dragged away. More and more, the figure distorted to the point that all he could make out was the light from the street lamps, fading the farther he fell into a plunging abyss.

Eugene felt himself sinking, drowning, and the cold was quickly becoming a comfort now. The surrounding pressure acted as a strange security faintly reminiscent of the warmth he reveled in earlier, a small consolation as he watched the light around him consumed by black.

Rú was the first to the Jeep, appearing behind the black-eyed child. He uncurled his fist to reveal extended claws and thrust his open hand through the back of the childlike creature looming over an unresponsive Eugene. He was careful not to break through its sternum, scratching the bone as he wound his fingers around what should have been the creature's heart only to realize there was no heart to be found. Rú could feel no discernable organs to grab onto. He proceeded to wrap his fingers around its sternum and pulled its body away from Eugene then launched it over the roof of the SUV. The momentum in which Rú pulled on the sternum dislodged it and when he sent the black-eyed child flying over the car, the sternum and a good portion of the sediment that filled its chest remained in his hand. He glanced down to review the contents half expecting to see something reminiscent of ground beef, observing instead a putrid black muck sticking to his fingers. Rú walked around the SUV to witness the creature crawling back toward him. He glanced back to see Arel and the others getting to Eugene then turned back at the monstrosity now only a few yards from him, its relentless gaze on the SUV behind him. Rú took a deep breath and let his skin fall away feeling the heat of fire rise through his throat and release its devastation on his crawling target. He watched as the creature continued to crawl until it was completely consumed by fire. Only satisfied enough to walk away when its charred limbs crumbled to ash.

Arel pulled Eugene's body from the driver's seat with the help of a panicked Dylan.

"Gene? Can you hear me, buddy?" Arel's voice was clinical as he checked his pulse and breathing.

"Should we have moved him?" Dylan asked frantically, his hand still gripping the back of Eugene's head so it wouldn't be resting on the cold ground.

"That would only be the case if he were physically injured," Arel explained, now checking Eugene's open eyes for a response. "RÚ!" he called out, his voice beginning to shake. He looked over his shoulder to find him immediately by his side. Rú gently pushed Arel aside to examine Eugene, placing an open hand on Eugene's cold torso. He could sense Eugene's energy still emanating from his body and was relieved to feel the light of his soul, as dim as it was.

"He's still here," Rú said calmly, though the look on his face expressed a grim reality to everyone around him. He proceeded to re-examine Eugene's eyes and put an ear to his chest. "He's stuck," Rú breathed, almost inaudibly.

"What do you mean, 'stuck'? Like he's in a type of coma? Can't you use some healing dragon magic?" Dylan fired off, his panic shaking his already unsteady voice.

Arel placed his hand on Dylan's shoulder, a comforting gesture that also served the purpose of staving off another outburst.

"Is there something you can do?" Arel asked, looking from Dylan to Rú.

"This is something I haven't encountered. These creatures aren't natural, they have to be engineered. I can't fix what it's done," Rú confessed bleakly.

"He is still in his body but he's no longer connected to it, so even if I dove into his mind I wouldn't be able to draw him out. He doesn't have a hold on it anymore," he explained regretfully. Dylan released a defeated sigh that slid into a sob, allowing his head to land on Eugene's chest.

"I might know something we could try." Evaine's voice rang from behind them.

Dylan's head snapped up to attention "What? Wait-how?"

"There's a woman that used to live in New Orleans and had a shop near my Father's first restaurant. A mystic, the real deal. She moved to the city 'bout ten years ago. Brooklyn, if I'm not mistaken." Evaine said, looking at all three as she spoke, landing last on Arel's now hopeful face.

"Can you get us the address?" Arel asked without another thought.

"Yes," she said, already busy searching through her phone. "Got it."

Arel just nodded in thanks then looked over to see Dylan already working on lifting Eugene. Rú, with the creature's sternum in hand, wrapped it in an old t-shirt he found in the back of Eugene's SUV and put it safely under the driver's seat, just in case. He then ran over to the three struggling to carry Eugene and lifted him from their grip. Rú carefully placed Eugene in the center of the back seat then got in holding his head up till Dylan ran around to get in on the other side. Dylan wrapped his arm around Eugene's shoulders and held him against his chest to keep Eugene propped up in a position that wouldn't strain his neck.

The car ride was quiet aside from the occasional chime of the nav system, Evaine sat up front with Arel. She looked over to see both his hands wrapped tight around the steering wheel and a look of restless worry on his face. She reached across the center console and wrapped her hand gently over his, she watched his brow unfurrow and his jaw unclench, his eyes still on the road in front of him. He released his grip and flipped his hand to interlace his fingers with hers.

Chapter Eleven

THE JAR

They pulled up to a small storefront on a surprisingly quiet street in Brooklyn. Three people were making their way down the sidewalk as they parked. They waited for the trio to turn the corner before turning off the engine, not willing to take any chances.

"Are you sure this is it?" Dylan asked, skeptically looking up at the sign reading 'Wine and Tonics'.

"I'm sure, my Dad still gets his wine supply from her," Evaine assured him, though unsure herself.

Arel and Rú were out of the SUV before another word was said. Rú quickly made his way around the car to get Eugene, Arel looked up at the floors above the store for any sign of life, only seeing dark shades drawn without a hint of light.

"Does she know we're coming?" Arel asked as he put his face to the glass door to view the contents of the store and see the walls lined with wine bottles. As he stepped back he heard the faint slide of the lock.

"My Dad hasn't texted me back…" Evaines' words trailed off as she watched Arel pull the door open.

Dylan was the last to funnel through the door, "Normally I'd say this lady is asking for trouble," he heard the lock begin to slide. "Never mind," he said, looking over his shoulder just in time to see it stop in the locked position.

Arel led the way through the store walking toward the back where he saw a light from under a door. Rú stopped in his tracks and sent Dylan clamoring into him, he'd been focused on the items throughout the room instead of what was happening in front of him.

"Why'd you stop?" he asked in an aggravated huff.

"I know who she is, I know where we are." Rú's voice was low and cautioned on defense.

"Oh, don't sound so bothered, Lóng Rú," rang the voice ascending the stairs. "Or is it Harrison now," mused the woman now standing in the doorway, the light from behind her kept her face in shadow.

"Still Rú, Leila," he affirmed flatly.

"Well, you never know, things change over time," Leila said, a smile dancing on her voice as she flipped the store lights on.

"But not you I see," he uttered, a bit taken aback by her appearance, she looked the same as he remembered, not a day over thirty. Leila's smile widened, she shrugged and crossed her arms.

"What is happening here?" Arel, losing patience, looking from Rú to Leila. "Can you help him?"

"Always the firecracker," Leila said through a proud smile. "Bring him down, let's see what we're working with," she said gesturing for them to follow her down the stairs. Rú was right behind her with Dylan close behind him, Arel stopped on the landing and looked back to see Evaine standing on the customer side of the counter, unmoving.

He walked up to the counter and leaned across. "Are you alright?" he asked softly.

"I -uh... I don't know, I feel strange. Like I've been here before but not here," she said pointing to the floor, then continued to nervously rub her thumb against her palm. Arel took notice of her nervous hands, walked around the counter, and stood in front of her. "Is it like deja vu?" he asked carefully, glancing down at her now trembling hands, her jitters were getting worse. She let out a deep breath, shook out her hands, and began to pace.

"Did you have this reaction at any time your Dad did business with her?" he asked, keeping a calm level tone.

"I never saw her, he just spoke of her," she said quickly between breaths. Arel stepped in front of her, "If you feel like you can't be here, I can take you home and come back. I know nothing will happen to Gene while Rú is with him," he offered, ducking his head so his line of sight met hers.

"No, no I feel like...I have to be here. It just threw me, is all, I just needed a minute," she said, shaking her arms out and releasing a deep breath to steady her. "Ok, I'm good." She pushed passed Arel determined to overcome the anxiety that had left her temporarily immobilized and took a quick pace down the steps. Arel followed and almost ran her over when she stopped short at the base of the stairs. Eugene was laid out on a burgundy velvet couch set against the wall across from the staircase, Dylan was sitting next to Eugene checking his pulse. Rú was standing at a kitchen island across from Leila to the left of the landing, they were speaking in hushed tones that stopped when Evaine hit the last step. Leila glanced over at Evaine, smiled, and walked over to her. Leila reached out to touch Evaine's face, she flinched away as Leila raised her hand to her cheek, stopping before the tips of her fingers reached her skin.

"Still so beautiful," Leila crooned, searching Evaine's face finding only confusion and defiance. "Oh, I see, still not over that jar incident are we," she said with a pout.

"Jar? What are you ta-," Evaine was cut off by Leila thrusting her palm to Evaine's forehead, instantly putting her to sleep and collapsing into Arel's arms behind her. Arel stood speechless looking from Evaine to Leila with a combination of anger and shock.

"THE FUCK DID YOU DO?" Arel exclaimed after finding his voice again.

"LEILA!" Rú roared, rushing toward her. She held out her hand lazily, stopping Rú in his tracks.

"She's fine," she assured both Rú and Arel with a roll of her eyes.

✷✷✷✷

Evaine had shut her eyes and opened them to a scene different from the one she was in just a second ago. She was standing in a dimly lit room in front of a shelf of containers of all shapes and sizes. Her hand was gripping one of the smaller bottles. As she focused her attention on the hand around the glass bottle she realized it was not only larger than her actual hands, it was about seven shades lighter than her skin tone.

'Oh ok, this is a dream,' she thought to herself. She began to relax, this wasn't the first time she'd dreamt of being in a man's body. It felt familiar to her like what she was experiencing was an extension of a previous dream. The body stepped back and she felt the heavy weight of his step as it hit the floor with a thud, louder than it was intended to. Her instinct was to look around to see if anyone had heard and would come running but the body didn't respond to her commands. She had never been a passenger in her own dreams, but as it was a dream, she didn't panic. Instead, she observed the wave of relief that came over his body as he held the bottle in his hands. Gazing at the bottle, a vision of an older woman clouded her sight, *his mother*? A slew of information came flooding into her mind; why he was there, the cure he was deter-mined to find and his desperation to save the only family he had left. As she received all this information, she felt everything in connection to him as her own feelings. This situation was completely new, Evaine

had never experienced a disconnect between her consciousness and what was taking place in a dream.

'Am I creating this?' There was nothing she could manipulate here, all she could do was watch through different eyes.

He was still reveling in the relief and satisfaction of having the solution to all his worries, security in hand. For Evaine the relief was short-lived, quickly giving way to the urgency to move. She knew something was coming and he needed to run but she couldn't recall from what, exactly.

"Have you changed your mind?"

The voice rang out from the corner of the room, a voice that she'd only just come to recognize. Leila stepped out of the shadow obstructing her. Evaine didn't know how to process what she was seeing, going back and forth between this being a dream and something else entirely. She remembered the strange little remarks Ru made when they arrived at her store and the comment Leila made just before waking up here. Then all of a sudden a thought dropped into her consciousness, she was in memory from a past life. She focused all her attention on Leila. She was surprised to see everything about her was exactly the same as the present day, same curly black hair, her piercing hazel eyes set against the softness of her desert skin, not a day over thirty.

She was slowly walking closer.

"Well?" she asked hopefully.

"I'm all she has." There was a pleading in his gruff voice and it was laid heavy by deliberation, but Leila already knew his answer.

"I wish you would have chosen another way." Leila sounded genuinely apologetic as she spoke, it put him at ease. He had planned to leave the honey and furs she had rejected when he offered a trade but her apologetic tone and warm eyes gave him hope that she had reconsidered.

Evaine, watching Leila through his eyes, knew his assumption to be wrong. She screamed to no avail for him to run, hoping somehow he'd hear her, but it was too late. Leila extended her hand, igniting sparks on the tips of her fingers.

Evaine felt the panic and fear as he clutched his chest in pain as the air was pressed from his lungs. His arms were no longer under his control, mechanically snapping to his sides as his legs gave out from beneath him. The skin on his legs began fusing together and his arms to his torso. The sound of snapping bones was all that Evaine could focus on over the agony of them resetting and changing into something else entirely. She didn't know how much longer he could stand the pain before losing consciousness, trapped in a silent scream with no relief in sight. The sound of his skull cracking thundered in his ears as his eyes shifted to the sides of his head allowing him to watch a giant-sized Leila slowly approach him. Her monstrous hand was the last thing he saw before losing sight entirely.

Evaine remained in the dark for what seemed to be a few minutes before his eyes opened again, she couldn't make out where he was until he began to strain his eyes for a clearer view. He was looking at a large dirty window. He intended to wipe the glass but found his arms couldn't be moved and were no longer arms at all. He frantically began to move with only the space to go in circles.

'*The Jar,*' Evaine realized. She he moved she was able to catch a glimpse of what he transformed into. '*A tail? The bitch turned him into a fucking fish,*' she thought furiously.

As he swam he noticed large figures getting closer to the glass, making him swim faster. With each pass, he inched the glass jar closer to the edge of the shelf. After a few more laps, he sent the jar crashing to the floor. He flopped among the shattered glass, struggling to breathe but was relieved to find it easier with each inhale. The giants he'd seen from inside the jar grew closer but before fear could overcome him the pain of his bones as they began breaking, twisting, and growing devoured his thoughts. As his eyes made their way to the front of his face he was able to focus on the three figures now standing over him. Who they were was not yet clear to him as his sight was still blurry. After what felt like ages, his agony dulled into a burning sensation and then eased into the cool static of waking limbs. When he was able to move his fingers and toes, he did his best to try to drag himself away from the three people he perceived as a threat. One of their party approached him with something hanging from their hands and he flinched as they flung it over his shivering body. The figure wrapped it tightly around his shoulders.

"You're safe, you're safe." The woman spoke softly and her voice soothed his racing heart.

He looked up to see big brown eyes looking down into his. Evaine knew those eyes and looking into them gave him the same feeling she felt looking into Arel's. She felt at ease knowing they were the same.

"Wh- who are you?" he stuttered through chattering teeth.

"My name is Kirana. Can you tell me your name?" she asked gently, swiping the wet hair from his face.

"V-Vor, Halvor."

Chapter Twelve

Wine is the Blood of the Purest Vine

Dylan got up from the coffee table he was seated on and backed away from Leila as she knelt next to the couch to take a look at Eugene. He felt more secure standing next to Rú.

"Leila, why?" Rú demanded, working hard to control his rising anger.

"I'd rather her remember why she hates me, it's better than her being in a time fog not knowing why she's feeling the way she does. That way she can either choose to hold on to it or get past it. Either way, we are going to face it together." There was no emotion in Leila's voice as she spoke while checking Eugene's eyes.

"Couldn't deal with the guilt?" Rú spat.

"I have no guilt," she said, now annoyed, and stood to face Rú. They stared at each other in a silent battle.

"ENOUGH!" Arel roared from the stairs, still cradling the unconscious Evaine. He carefully shifted Evaine in his arms cradling her against him to scoop her up, glad that he'd been hitting the weights lately. As he stomped down the remaining steps and Rú walked up with arms out to help him but Arel gave a quick head tilt to the left.

"Just move," he said gruffly.

Rú obliged and Arel brushed him walking up to Leila, his angry gaze locked on her.

"Will she be alright? Don't lie to me," he demanded through gritted teeth, his eyes bore into her with the promise of retaliation should her claim be false. He hated having to put his trust in her seeing as Rú didn't trust her either, but he didn't have much choice.

"She'll be fine," she repeated, her tone matching his intensity, not pleased by his implied challenge. "Put her here," Leila instructed, snapping her fingers. The seven-foot couch extended into an 'L' shape that expanded another six feet, almost completely cutting off access to the door that led to a small bathroom.

The one amused by Leila's magical dexterity was Dylan, who stood wide-eyed but chose to stay silent due to the lingering tension in the air.

Arel set Evaine down gently, opposite Eugene, and brushed back the locs that fell over her face.

"Alright," Leila sighed. "Let's see what we're working with." She cracked her knuckles as she walked back over to Eugene again and placed her hands over his torso. She stared straight ahead like she was watching an invisible screen.

Dylan, Ru, and Arel hovered behind her in silence, watching her hands move in circular motions until they settled just below Eugene's chest.

"There you are," she said with a confident smile. "Ok, tell me what happened." She turned to face all three of them and made herself comfortable sitting on the edge of the couch next to Eugene. They crossed their arms in unison and exchanged looks unsure of where to start as Eugene was alone when he was attacked.

"None of us were there, I wasn't there," Dylan uttered, his voice laden with guilt.

"Honey, it was never going to attack while there were two of you. Don't feel guilty for what you couldn't control. It'll only poison you, atrophy you from the inside out," Leila spoke firmly so her words wouldn't be taken as mere comfort.

Dylan nodded in acknowledgment and allowed his tense shoulders to relax.

"Ru, you have something for me," she said, her eyes still on Dylan, only looking away from him when it was clear that what she said had been taken to heart. There was a split second Ru had no idea what she was talking about until she held out her hand to him reminding him of the rolled-up sternum under the driver's seat of the SUV.

"Yes," he said, and in a blink the wrapped sternum was in his hand before passing it off to Leila. She unwrapped it as she made her way back to the island to the left of the stairway. She laid the fabric out flat and visually inspected the soiled bone.

"Tell me what happened," she repeated, addressing Rú, lowering her face inches from the bone and sniffing before violently jerking her head back with a grimace.

"Wait, if you knew Rú had that thing then can't you just 'magic' what happened?" Dylan asked, it was a question Arel was also wondering.

"Is watching something on a screen the same as being there? There are other variables to consider and Rú has more than the run-of-the-mill 'five senses.' Sometimes feelings give us answers eyes are incapable of seeing and Rú had the most interaction with it. I'd like to hear his interpretation of what happened. There could be a detail that could shed more light on what it is we're dealing with here." Leila lifted her eyes from the bone and looked toward Eugene then at Rú. His eyes grew wide, something she said clicked.

"I couldn't feel it," he said thoughtfully. "I couldn't feel either of them, the only thing I picked up on was Evaine's fear as we made our way up the walk."

Leila nodded silently, running over the options in her mind.

"It felt like being underwater," Evaine chimed in from the couch, sitting up and putting her feet on the ground. "Looking at it felt like I was being pulled deeper into dark water, alone and surrounded at the same time. I couldn't think of anything, I couldn't feel...me." Evaine finished speaking as she reached the island beside Arel, her eyes locked on Leila.

"Are you alright?" Arel asked, relieved to see her up and walking. She looked into his eyes, the same warm eyes from her vision and she smiled before turning a cold gaze back to Leila.

"Yeah, I'm fine." She and Leila remained locked in their icy stare off only a moment longer before Leila shifted her attention back to the bone in front of her. Her eyes widened and her mouth fell open slightly. She began to whisper to herself as she turned around to the counter behind her, pulled a magnifying glass from one of the drawers, and held it close to the bone. They all stood around her in silence as she stared through the glass waiting for an explanation. She finally picked up the bone and ran her fingers down its surface.

"They did it," she mumbled, putting the bone back down on the sullied fabric.

"Who did what, Leila?" Rú asked impatiently.

"Look at this," she said pushing the fabric across the island to him. See all the little breaks in the bone?" she asked, pointing to a spot with the least amount of matter.

"Yeah, bu-"

"Bone doesn't do that, this sternum is made up of other bones," she proclaimed.

"Like an oriented strand board," Dylan spit out, grabbing everyone's attention. They all took a minute to mentally process his comparison and nodded in acknowledgment of his point. All except Leila, who looked at him and tilted her head in confusion.

"It's compressed layers of wood shards," he explained quickly. "My dad's a contractor."

"Then yes, like that, Dylan," Leila said.

"So someone is grinding people up and what? Remolding them?" Arel theorized, his face twisting with disgust.

"Some assembly required," Dylan mumbled morbidly, thinking out loud.

"Why?" Evaine added, ignoring Dylan's comment.

"For decades I've heard rumors of groups working to create infiltrators," Leila said staring down at the manufactured bone in awe.

"Infiltrators?" Dylan repeated the word as if it left a bad taste in his mouth.

"For what function exactly? I mean, yeah, there are a lot of nefarious possibilities but what are they trying to get to?" Arel finished his question by looking back at the comatose Eugene, drawing everyone to his line of sight.

Leila walked to the middle of the room and crossed her arms looking from Eugene to the fabricated sternum on the island, ignoring the others surrounding it. In her mind, she began arranging the pieces of the puzzle. She walked over to Eugene and again placed her hand over his torso.

"Okay," she said mostly to herself.

"Do you know what to do?" Dylan asked eagerly.

"I have a theory," Leila said, quickly walking past them to a stack of books on the counter in the corner of the room. She pulled a marble composition notebook out from the bottom of the stack, opened it, and began listing everything so she could see her thoughts laid out in front of her. Once she finished writing she leaned over the pages staring at her words.

Her eyes widened. "I know what they're made for," she said, finally lifting her eyes from the pages.

They all watched her walk over and stand over Eugene, eager to hear her answer.

"WELL?" Evaine snapped impatiently, breaking Leila's train of thought.

"He's right here," she said, placing her hand right above his belly button.

"But he's not connected to his physical body and mind," Rú interrupted.

"Yes, but the good news is he's only halfway from where he was intended to be. He's stuck where his will lies and it was not yet broken when you got to him," Leila said with a confident smile the others didn't quite understand.

"So what was it trying to do?" Dylan asked.

"Essentially, break him down to the lowest form of himself so something, another entity, could gain control of his body. Stripping him down to nothing but a shell with a dormant soul as fuel," Leila said not mincing words.

"So it's possession..." Arel tried to specify.

"Yes!" Leila agreed enthusiastically. "But in a fraction of the time. Possession can be a long process depending on the individual, these black-eyed children are a shortcut to that process. I initially thought the black eyes might have been a defect or just lazy engineering. It's difficult to fabricate the complexity of emotion displayed in eyes, but they have a strong hypnotic function to incapacitate its prey."

"Not everyone can be hypnotized," Evaine pointed out.

"I think that's why we know about them at all, the ones whose fight or flight kicked in to shut their doors or run away," Leila postulated.

"Gene wouldn't have opened the door," Arel said adamantly.

They all stood silent, each of them creating scenarios as to what Eugene did or didn't do. Arel took a deep breath and turned away to compose himself. He let all his thoughts move through his mind and tried not to get attached to anything that would send him into doubt or fear. He brought both hands to his face and rubbed his eyes, a subconscious act of clearing the mental fog before returning to the conversation.

"How can we get him back?" Arel said, his voice calm and controlled.

Leila held up one finger and walked through the group, shoving Rú out of the way. She walked over to a corner of the room, just behind them across from the kitchen island they were standing around. Bookcases covered the lower half of the wall but above the books were shelves of wine that lined the wall all the way up to the ceiling. She reached for the second shelf up and lifted the bottle third from the end.

Arel and the others heard a click and watched the back wall reveal a secret door leading to a secluded room. She kept the room unusually dark, Leila looked like a shadow as she made her way down the center aisle. To her left were racks of wine from floor to ceiling, and at her right stood massive oak shelving units holding bottles and jars of all shapes and sizes. Leila looked straight ahead as she walked down the aisle running her fingers along the bottles as she passed. As they watched her, her silhouette grew smaller the longer she walked and they couldn't tell if the room had an end at all. Leila finally came to a stop and to everyone's surprise, she turned to face the wine bottles. She reached up and grabbed a bottle just above her head and started her way back up the aisle. Arel waited for her to stop again to pluck a jar from the other side of the aisle but she never did. He looked over at Rú to read his face to which he saw nothing to gauge his own feelings of confusion and growing impatience. Rú, listening in on his inner chatter, offered a simple *'wait.'*

"Do you know what this is then?" Arel asked him. Dylan and Evaine looked over, curious about his outburst, unaware of his and Rú's mental back and forth.

Leila emerged from the hidden room and allowed the door to disappear into the wall once more. She set the bottle in her hand on the Island for everyone to see it.

"Wine?" Evaine spat in disbelief. "How is wine supposed to help him?"

Leila picked up the bottle again and smiled proudly, "This, my darling, is going to bring him back," she said, wiping the dust off of the label.

"How?" Dylan asked in earnest.

"A lot goes into wine, so many factors come into play to make its flavors and character what it is. The heat of the sun, how much rain that year and what was carried in that rain, what traveled with the wind to settle in the soil, and the soil itself. The magic is in the soil. The life-sustaining minerals we need to survive are found in the soil, of course, not all soil is created equal," Leila stopped herself as she realized she was getting off-topic. "Anyway, because the process of making wine can be quite ceremonial, it's been used in spiritual and healing rituals around the world, as well as celebrations."

"If wine can be used for healing then how do you explain alcoholism?" Evaine challenged.

"We don't have ti-" Leila put up a hand cutting off Rú's interruption, her eyes locked on Evaine.

"Alcohol can liberate you from the restrictions of society, fears, insecurities, and even your troubles for a time but for a troubled mind, it's a means of escape that's often the easiest to access. Some diseases are caused by just that, 'dis'-'ease.'"

"Okay, so, how will this particular wine bring back Eugene?" Dylan asked quickly, hoping to defuse the tension and the energy between Leila and Evaine. His tactic worked, Evaine relaxed her shoulders and sat on the stool next to her and Leila's face softened as she spun the bottle around so they could all see the label.

"This is my 2012 Merlot, planted in limestone clay, as the grapes prefer. It was dry that year and when the clay dries it cracks and allows the roots to burrow deeper to soak up all those delicious molecules and ions that otherwise would not have been accessed. It's a struggle to get there but we're left with more character, there's power in that struggle as well as the limestone clay and the oak it was aged in."

"What's with the limestone?" Dylan asked. Rú rolled his eyes, he wanted to get on with whatever Leila was planning to do but as he looked around the table he noticed Arel and Evaine's interest. By tuning into Arel, Rú could feel that Leila's breakdown was easing his anxiety.

"Limestone is made of shells, sand, and remnants of lost sea creatures compressed over time and cleansed by the salt water. There's a light found in sea creatures, a purity, that's found in no other animals on earth. When their spirit leaves their bodies it's kept by the sea to be returned to remaining life, leaving sparks of light behind, a gift from the waves."

There was a reverence as she spoke about the sea and in her eyes a gleam of sadness Rú couldn't make sense of as he watched her. At that moment, he realized he couldn't read her or hear her thoughts like other human beings, it put him on edge. He had always been conscious of how easy it was to invade the privacy of the human mind and had always focused on tuning out its noise; it became effortless, so her radio silence didn't register. He had encountered his fair share of mystics and practitioners of the elements and as far as he could tell she *was* human but something didn't add up. Humans aren't immortal, not even Nephilim were immortal, she was something else but he couldn't get past her walls to get the story. He was brought back to the conversation with another one of Dylan's questions.

"And the oak?"

"It's charged and blessed under a full moon by Dionysius himself, twice-born and god of wine."

"You just opened up so many questions," Arel said, he shook his head and squeezed the bridge of his nose doing his best to wrap his head around that bit of information just casually dropped into conversation.

"We can discuss in length when this is done," Leila assured him as she pulled a wine glass from the bottom cabinet.

"Are you sure you want to trust her?" Evaine asked Arel. Still on guard from her vision, unwilling to trust the woman who changed her past self into a fish and kept him in a jar for god knows how long.

"She's the only option we have to bring Eugene back," he responded decidedly. Evaine then looked over to Rú, his face reading skepticism unbeknownst to her for another reason entirely.

"Do you believe this will work?" she asked as Rú's eyes met hers, to which he gave a nod.

"Belief and intent are the soul of magic, so have a little faith," Leila said lightly, her face unbothered and confident. "And if you don't trust my word you can always take solace in what the beloved Yeshua used to say 'Blood is the life and wine is the blood of the purest vine.'" Leila quoted casually, smiling fondly as she grabbed the bottle and the glass as she headed to the couch where Eugene was lying. Rú's eyes widened and he stood up straight, just as surprised as the rest.

"Yeshua? As in Jesus?" Evaine called out in disbelief.

"Wait, he existed? How old *are* you?" Dylan asked in a low tone, unconsciously stepping back from her suddenly aware of how little they all knew about her. He looked over at Rú to see his face like stone but in his eyes, he saw uncertainty and alarm.

Leila looked back at Dylan with a look that shot a chill through his body, a look that said all too much and nothing at all.

"Darling, you know better than to ask a woman's age," she said with a sly smile before she turned back around to tend to Eugene.

"What are you?" Rú challenged stepping forward, no longer able to observe in silence.

"You know what I am," she said flatly.

"Impossible, I watched this planet form and no human has ever lived as long as you seem to claim, not in one lifetime," he stated definitively with accusation in his tone.

"You and I both know nothing is impossible," she said setting the bottle and glass down on the coffee table across from the vacant Eugene. "If time has proven anything it's that," she said looking back at him. He didn't need to read her mind to know what she was thinking, this conversation was over.

"Now," she said, clapping her hands together and rubbing them. After a moment her fingers began to emit an amber glow which she held up to her lips and blew into her praying hands. This set her hands ablaze with white light. She took the glass in her hands and began to whisper, keeping her eyes closed as she spoke into the glass. They all stood in silent awe as they watched her, all but Rú, whose expression was more of concern.

Slowly the light from her hands seeped into the glass and the wine itself. As the last of the light left her hands she opened her eyes, stepped toward Eugene, and waved one hand over his face. His eyes snapped open causing everyone to jump in unison. Dylan and Arel rushed over as his body sprang up into a sitting position, his head flopping forward like a ragdoll. Dylan stopped short realizing it wasn't him controlling his body, it was Leila.

Arel continued in hope, a wave of relief came over him as he watched Eugene's head lift from his chest.

"Gene?" he asked softly, walking around Leila to stand in the direction Eugene was facing.

Eugene didn't answer, he stared dead ahead with his mouth agape. Leila held the glass in front of Eugene's face and his hand rose to grab it. The movement sent chills down Arel's spine, they were not fluid but jerky like a marionette.

He watched as Eugene's head fell back, opening his mouth wide and pouring the wine down his gullet. Arel felt his stomach churn as he watched his friend's body move under someone else's control, it was too much. He felt the drop of his heart and didn't know if he was going to burst into hysterics, vomit, or both. To have Eugene in front of him, his body animated, moving, but not able to see life in his eyes was a torture he never could have fathomed.

Once the glass was empty Eugene's body fell back to sleep as if never disturbed. Leila caught the glass before it left his fingertips and positioned his arm back against his body. She looked up and saw the tears welling in Arel's eyes.

"This WILL bring him back, right?" he asked, working to keep his voice steady, his eyes pleading for certainty.

"This will liberate him from his confines, that I have no doubt, but whether he decides to come back to his body or release it altogether will be his choice," Leila explained delicately.

Arel brought his hands to his face to catch the tears running down his cheeks. Leila stood and pulled away the hand that was covering the bottom half of his face and held it in both of her hands.

"The physical absence of a loved one is a pain that can only be intensified by knowing they're not truly gone and accepting that as torture instead of a blessing. Whatever the outcome, he'll be with you," she said, releasing one of her hands to wipe away another tear from his cheek. "Don't give up, let your belief and love be his anchor."

She then turned to face the three across the room, Dylan with eyes full of tears.

"That goes for all of you."

Chapter Thirteen

THE SHACK

Despite Eugene's guarantee of Nalini's thorough nature giving them an extended amount of time, or at least the weekend, she had gone through and signed all necessary forms before 10 AM the morning he dropped off the paperwork. She even went so far as to send them to all the relevant department heads so there were no more hang-ups in going through superfluous channels. Meaning, of course, any information that would have alerted Evaine to the progress of the Brothers Project would bypass her desk completely.

Instructions had come down the line to run a small team to mark off potentially hazardous areas across North Brother in preparation for the Xelas assessment teams arriving Monday morning. The idea to make the run to the Island that afternoon was well-intentioned so they wouldn't have to send a team out on a Sunday, at least that's how they spun it. Instead, they pulled urban rangers from their Saturday posts.

Mal didn't mind, he jumped at the opportunity to change up his Saturday. He wasn't one to believe any of the ghost stories that others had told him and taking an afternoon to walk around a deserted island sounded like the break he needed away from the city, why not get paid for it?

The ride over to the North Brother was quiet. There were four other members on this team and all of them wore the same look of uncertainty on their faces.

"Okay guys, this shouldn't take more than the allotted time of five hours. We already know the areas we need to cover, so be careful and we'll be out of there before you know it," said their team leader, Leona Waite. Yelling to be heard over the wind and splashing water, her voice was stern and commanding, a habit ingrained in her from her time in the military. She kept her eyes on the island as she spoke, scanning the shore left and right. Mal was the only one to look away from the island to look at her, her aviator glasses covered most of her serious face as her short hair danced wildly in the wind. He couldn't help but be reminded of Linda Hamilton in Terminator, Judgement Day. Same badass attitude. The perfect person to keep anyone in line. He once heard a rumor that she shoved her fist in some guy's mouth and pulled out the french fries he'd stolen from her plate then proceeded to beat him with the metal lunch tray he took them from. Whenever he saw her he wondered if it were actually true, but was way too afraid to ask about it.

The boat began to slow as they got closer to shore, pulling up to a stone wall with a small patch of sand just above the water. Mal was the last one to start getting his things together and the last one to leave the boat. Leona led the way up the stone steps and through the opening in the metal fencing. Mal caught a chill as he walked past the rusted post but shook it off without another thought.

Everyone had stopped in a cluster waiting for him to join the group, to his surprise there were no impatient faces, only apprehensive ones.

"Everyone, make sure the volume to your walkie is on high, I don't want anyone missing any calls. They're all set to the correct channel so don't mess with it. You all have copies of the map marked with the area you'll be covering. And don't forget to put on your gloves! Let's get going," Leona instructed, turning away to cover her allotted area.

"Leo, what if we see something?" asked the team member standing directly behind her. She turned around and then looked at each of their faces, all of them thankful someone spoke up, except Mal. He was preoccupied by his map.

"You mark the area and radio me, do your best to ignore it. Stick to your assignment and you'll be fine. If you feel overwhelmed I'll come find you and we'll all meet back right here." This seemed to put those on edge at ease and they began going their own way.

Mal didn't hear half of what was said, only catching the words 'we'll all meet back here,' but that was good enough for him. From what he understood on the map, his assigned area was to the east of him, removed from the main buildings. He walked through the trees and marveled at their leaves as if he'd never seen that shade of green. It seemed to stand brighter against the decrepit buildings they surrounded. The ground beneath his feet crunched as if he were walking over layers of thin ice.

"Strange." He bent down to touch the soil and found it ice cold to the touch. Looking up, he saw the sun blocked by illuminated leaves and concluded it was due to the canopy blocking the heat and left it at that. The path to his destination grew increasingly difficult. As he grabbed a low-hanging branch to steady himself as he stepped over a large log, a shadow appeared off of his left shoulder. He turned quickly and lost his balance, stumbling a few feet before falling and hitting his head on the frozen ground. The shadow appeared again, this time a few yards away and directly in front of him. Mal stared up at the shadow trying to make sense of what he was seeing until it disappeared to reveal a shack in the distance. Half of it was obstructed by brush and trees, if he hadn't fallen he would have walked right past it. As far as the shadow went, he figured it was his imagination, a post-fall hallucination brought on by his budding headache. As he walked toward the shack he kept an eye out for anything he needed to flag, occasionally seeing shadows out of the corner of his eyes or shadows moving quickly from tree to tree. His headache continued to get worse the closer he got to the shack.

By the time he reached his destination his eyesight had begun to blur and he felt dizzy on his feet. The shack was an oasis in the clearing and the only thing he was concerned with was getting out from the sun's rays now that it was beating down on his throbbing head. He, not once, thought of going back to the tree line and sitting down on the ground he knew to be ice cold, instead only listening to the small voice in his mind telling him to take refuge in the crumbling shack. No longer having the use of his eyes, he felt around the rotted wood to find a door. Unable to see the rusting sign prohibiting entry due to unstable conditions. He pulled viciously at the ivy that had wrapped itself around the doorknob so many times he couldn't grip it. It was as if nature was working in defiance of evil to keep whatever was lying within that shack trapped inside of those four walls. Mal persisted in ripping away the remaining vines and pushed the door over the uneven floorboards, warped by the elements and time. Once inside, the strain of pushing the door open left his arms weak and heavy, but the dark room lessened the pain of his headache allowing him to open his eyes. A flash of light caught his attention from a vanity that sat opposite the window at the back of the room. There was a chair that looked as if it had been pulled out in preparation for his arrival. Without another thought he trudged over and collapsed onto its wooden frame, thankful only after the fact that it was strong enough to hold him even after all this time. He closed his eyes and took in a deep breath, inhaling decades of dust that sent him into a coughing fit disrupting the layer of soot covering the vanity, revealing a hand mirror lying face down. He picked it up noting the weight as he held it to wipe the soot off of the porcelain back unveiling delicately hand-painted flowers. It was framed in a gold plated handle, the upper righthand corner seemed to be untouched by time, like that corner alone was kept and polished. He surmised that it must have been this corner of the mirror the light gleaned off of that caught his attention.

He turned the handle around in his hand to see the state of the mirror itself, noting the small brown spots clustered along its edges where the silver fell away from the glass.

He held the mirror up to his face and let out a yelp, it was not just his reflection looking back at him. He turned to look behind him, twisting his neck at a weird angle sending an intense pain up to the base of his head. He didn't realize he had been holding his breath and turned this way and that to be sure there was no one in this shack but him. He released a sigh of relief once he was sure he was absolutely alone. When he looked back at the mirror he was surprised to see the same haunted faces still peering back at him.

"This headache is really messing with me," he said to himself, chuckling lightly as he brought the mirror closer to his face. Through his hazy sight, he squinted to see the foreign faces in more detail. To his left was a woman with her hair swept up into a knot at the top of her head and a firm brow. Her lips were pressed into a thin line and her cheeks were gray and hollow. He didn't dare look into her eyes, he looked away before he met them. He looked to his right, to see a skeletal man waiting to meet his gaze and he couldn't help but look directly into the wide bulging eyes, a pale gray. They would have been beautiful if not for their bloodshot state and the sunken sockets they were protruding from. The man bared his blackened teeth exposing oozing green gums. His purple lips stretched thin by his maddened smile were cracked and bleeding. Mal felt himself getting sick, it was as if he could feel this man's breath wafting into his face and could smell the rot of his gums. It made his stomach lurch. The temperature dropped and he began shivering uncontrollably all the while unable to look away from the mirror. He watched as the faces moved closer to his reflection, feeling their breath in his ears and on his neck. He flinched away without the relief of withdrawal; he could still feel them. In the mirror, he watched as they placed their hands on the shoulders of his reflection and could feel the strength of their grip and the pain of their nails as they dug deeper into his skin as they held him still. He tried to drop the mirror but there was a hand clasped tight around his holding it in place.

Mal did his best to fight against the hold his invisible captors had on him, flailing and trying to kick out the legs of the chair as he couldn't move his arms. He felt his legs caught by invisible hands and held down against the legs of the chairs. The heat of panic and fear rose from his belly to his chest as he let out a scream with no sound, it descended into a quiet sob. He tried multiple times to scream looking in every direction for a sign of life, but he was alone, in the clutches of monsters he couldn't see. He thrashed his head from left to right catching a glimpse from the mirror he still had in hand that made him stop and his blood run cold. His reflection in the mirror was motionless and calm, with its eyes closed. The sight raised every hair on his body, he wanted to look away but he couldn't, mesmerized by disbelief and his desperate desire for it all to be in his mind. He wasn't sure how long he was staring at the mirror before his reflection opened its eyes to reveal milky white where his iris should be. At the same time, he heard the radio in his pocket go off. It was Leona checking in on everyone. Mal tried again to free himself and attempted to force sound from his muted vocal cords in the hope that someone might be close enough to hear his struggle. Looking back at his reflection, he saw that man and woman had disappeared and had been replaced by a shadow. He watched a grotesque smile form over his reflection's face before being completely engulfed by the shadow standing behind it. When his reflection was completely consumed by the darkness a thick black smoke began to flood from the mirror flowing straight into his nose and mouth, forcing its way into his body. The smoke burned as it worked its way down his throat and the pain became too much as it spread to his limbs. He knew after reaching a level of pain he would pass out but his relief never came.

The light from the sun had moved across the room by the time the invisible hands that were holding him down released their grip. His arms fell limp at his sides, the motion felt like being stabbed by thousands of tiny fire pokers. He felt his body begin to slump forward and slide off of the chair and he landed face-first on the ground. It felt like he was laying skin bare on a bed of hot coals. Mal wanted to scream out but his lips remained closed as his arms moved to lift himself off the floor. Every movement made was excruciating, but he was no longer in control.

The radio went off once more as Leona called for everyone to come back to the meet point. He watched his hand reach into his pocket, pull out the walkie, and bring it up to his mouth. He fought hard to gain control of his voice to call for help but what came from his mouth were not his words. Hearing words come out of his mouth that had no connection to his consciousness was a violation beyond comprehension.

"On my way," he heard himself say.

If he could, he'd be sick right now but he could no longer feel a connection to any part of his body, only the intense burning as his limbs moved. He watched his hand pick up the mirror and slide it into his pocket.

Mal did his best to think of something else as his body made its way out of the shack, anything to keep his mind off the pain but it was as if he was being wiped clean. He tried to remember the faces of his mother and father, his girlfriend.

'*Wait, do I have a girlfriend?*' he thought to himself, he couldn't remember.

He tried his hardest to focus on a memory, a happy feeling he could cling to, a song, anything. The intensity of the burning began to build the harder he tried to focus on his memories, it's all been replaced by fire and pain.

Everyone was at the meet point by the time Mal walked out of the tree line, their faces wore looks of relief to be going home. Leona turned to greet him as she saw a few team members look in Mal's direction. Her feelings of relief from a day free of incidents disappeared as Mal walked closer. She noticed all color had been drained from his face, a bluish shade of gray lined his lips and under his eyes. Leona's stomach dropped as she walked to meet him out of earshot of the rest of the team.

"Are you alright? Did something happen?" she asked him, keeping her distance a few feet from him. His eyes were bloodshot and he was sweating enough to tell through two layers of clothes.

"I'm alright," he answered.

There was no fluctuation to Mal's tone which set off a red flag in Leona's mind and as she looked into his eyes she caught a chill that ran down to her bones. She didn't know him that well but enough to know what was looking back at her wasn't right. Every hair on her body was standing up and her muscles tensed as she stepped her left foot back to ground herself.

"You don't look alright, Mal," Leona said cautiously, her voice airing on suspicion. Without another word, Mal moved to walk away from her toward the rest of the group.

"Hold up," she said reaching out to stop him. Barely touching his arm she felt heat through her work gloves, and quickly pulled away, instinctively looking down to his hand and saw he wasn't wearing the gloves as instructed.

"You're burning up, you need to see a doctor as soon as we get back," she insisted, meeting his eyes. The way he looked at her would have struck fear into the heart of whoever was at the other end of it, it was a look with the intent to scare but she wasn't going to give him the satisfaction.

"You hear me?" There was no question in her low, commanding voice. They stood for a few seconds glaring at each other neither one willing to blink. Leona wasn't going to let up and continued to search his gaze for the Mal that walked into the trees four hours ago. Just before he turned away from her, she noticed a shift in the energy around him and a spark of life, just for a moment, before it disappeared again behind lifeless eyes.

Leona watched him like a hawk on the boat ride back. The rest of the team spoke amongst themselves seated as far from Mal as possible, having watched the brief interaction between him and Leona. They could all feel something wasn't right but a confrontation on a notoriously haunted island or in a small confined boat was not the place or time to deal with it.

Everyone but Leona let out a sigh of relief to see Mal get off the boat as soon as it hit the dock. She did her best to gather her things and get off as fast as she could while keeping an eye on him. They all traveled there in one van so she assumed the only reason he'd be rushing away from the group was because he was about to be sick. By the time she set foot on the dock, Mal was out of sight, sending a wave of panic to come over her.

'Shit, how'd he get down the dock so fast,' she thought furiously. As much as she wanted to run after him she waited for the rest of the team to walk to the van together. She figured he'd probably be waiting for them by now but as they walked up to the van she saw him get into an ordered car. Maybe he was ill and if that was the case then not traveling with the group was understandable but she couldn't shake the feeling that she just let something dangerous slip away from her.

Each team member was gripping their seat and thanking their maker for safety belts as Leona screeched to a stop in the Parks and Rec parking lot, she made it back in half the time. There was no need to make an excuse for a quick getaway, everyone got out of the car immediately but took their time walking back to the building to pack up their things and clock out for the day. Leona hoped to catch Mal before he left for the day and went to the main office where everyone checked in and out, but she had missed him again. The woman behind the front desk smiled as she looked up from packing up her bag.

"Hey Leo, how'd things go?" The woman asked brightly.

"Uh, good I guess. Everyone's back in one piece. Hey Jules, did you see Mal come through here at all?" she asked, rushing her words, but doing her best to sound as casual as possible.

"Yeah, I said hi but he just blew me off and went straight into the mailroom. He didn't look like he was feeling so hot, so I let it go," Jules said with a shrug.

"What was he doing in the mail room?" Leona asked as she walked by her to look in the mail room. There was tape on the packing table, it was the only thing in the room out of its place.

"I don't know, he was gone by the time I got back from grabbing my leftovers from the fridge. Is everything ok? Did something happen to him on North?" Jules asked, her eyes wide with concern.

"I don't know, he didn't say anything but he didn't seem right. He was off to you right?" Leona asked, brushing by Jules to take a look at the computer behind the desk.

"Yeah, he kinda gave me the heebie-jeebies, actually," Jules replied thoughtfully, staring dead ahead in thought, Leona took note of her abrupt silence.

"What is it? Did you notice anything else?" Leona asked, looking away from the computer.

"I was talking to Evaine, from Permits a few days ago and we got to talking about just creepy stories and she told me about this one experience her friend had while she was back home in New Orleans. This just reminded me of it," Jules said timidly, now worried about whether or not the story was supposed to be in confidence.

"What happened?" Leona asked eagerly.

"She said she was meeting up with her friend one afternoon and when she walked up, Evaine noticed something was wrong. She said the color was drawn from her friend's face, she was jittery, and she said there was this sadness rolling off of her. When Evaine asked her what happened she said she was just walking and all of a sudden she wasn't feeling well. And all the while she was walking she knew where she was going, but at the same time, it was like seeing everything for the first time. She also said it was getting harder for her friend to focus on her own thoughts. Her mind was being clouded by sad and painful impressions to the point when she tried to think of any memory that made her happy she couldn't remember any. Like, it was being blocked, it was like she couldn't feel who she was. So Evaine asked her if she had walked a different way to meet her and the friend said yes, that she took an ally with a gray house, one that was under construction. It was said to be haunted and then Evaine told me that commotion like renovations can stir up spirit activity," Jules explained.

"Ok, so, what happened to her friend," Leona asked impatiently.

"Evaine took her to see her Mom. She read tarot and tea leaves and stuff! Anyway, she figured out a spirit had attached itself to her, attracted to her 'light'. Then her Mom told them that it happens more often than people realize but most people just aren't that sensitive to the changes in energy. So they're walking around with these spirits tethered to them that could be feeding off their energy and don't even know how to recognize it. The symptoms could be things like mood changes out of nowhere, feeling ill, nose bleeds, but that's only if it's a negative spirit. She did say some spirits have no negative impact, some just like your energy and hang around you for a while. She said those are the ones you won't notice at all unless you're some kind of medium or empath, something like that." Jules stopped speaking and sat across from Leona, she opened her mouth to respond but Jules wasn't done. "Evaine said her friend got into the craft after that, made her a protection bag before she moved up here. Isn't that nice?" Jules finished brightly.

"Yeah, neat. So, you think what happened to her friend is what happened to Mal?" Leona asked her almost absentmindedly, she was running over her interactions with Mal and matching up the similarities.

"I've been around him on bad days, when he's been sick, and I've never seen him like that. He's never once given me the heebie-jeebies before. So yeah, I'm thinking it's a possibility." Jules shook out a jolt of energy moving through her. "You know, saying it out loud somehow makes it more real than just thinking about it," she said, wrapping her arms around herself.

"So how did they get rid of it, the spirit attached to her friend?" Leona asked, determined to remain focused on a solution.

"Oh, um, I think it was just by telling it to leave, that it was *not* welcome and that it had to move on. 'Claiming your space' is what she called it." Jules finished her explanation with a snap of her fingers.

"That's it?" Leona asked in surprise, "No rituals or anything, no burning bones."

"Ok, Dean. They may have burned sage, I'm not sure if I'm making that up, but Evaine said they did pray for assistance from ancestors and angels and the like," Jules added casually.

"So, what happens if you're not religious? What then? You're just screwed?" Leona threw out there not expecting a response. "Can I use your computer real quick i want to check something," she asked, moving so she a Jules could switch places behind the desk.

"Mmm, I don't think it works that way. I think when it comes to things like this and support in general if you believe that support is out there and ask for it, it'll be there. If we're talking higher powers here, I don't think they're playing within the confines of the human divide. Well, I hope it's like that, anyway," Jules said, leaning against the desk as she stared up at the ceiling.

Leona took a few moments to absorb Jules' point of view. "I hope so too, Jules," she remarked as she checked the log information for the day, she noticed Mal never clocked out before he left.

"Hey Jules, can you pull up the security camera footage from earlier? I know we can't see in the mail room but maybe we'll see something," Leona said suddenly optimistic this would help her shed some light as to what was actually happening.

She got up from the desk chair so Jules could find the security camera footage. Jules knew the exact time to start looking as it was the same time she left the room to get her things from the break room. The camera was mounted in the corner just above the mail room, offering a wide view of the office. They watched intently as Mal entered, ignoring Jules and her presence altogether. They saw at the same time as she turned away to walk around the desk that Mal pulled something reflective from his pocket just before disappearing from the frame.

"A mirror?" Jules said, bewildered to see such an object so out of place.

Leona continued to watch the screen without a word, not willing to be distracted by conversation. After a minute and a half, Mal walked out of the mailroom with a box tucked under his right arm, obstructing any view of a label, if any. Leona rushed into the mailroom to check the label maker and found nothing recorded from that day. She gave the room one last look and walked back out to the desk.

"If he did put an address on it, he must have written it by hand," Leona said, she walked over and leaned on the desk, crossing her arms over her chest. They both sat silent for a few moments before Jules broke their silence.

"Hey, maybe we're letting the islands and ghost stories get to us. Maybe he found the mirror, didn't want to hand it in and was nervous about getting caught with it. Guilt can make us behave in weird ways, that could be all it is," Jules rationalized. "He'll probably be back to normal Monday, we can grill him then."

"Yeah, you're probably right," Leona agreed, rubbing her eyes and responding with a humorless chuckle.

✸✸✸✸

Mal stood outside a lush apartment building standing twelve stories high, waiting for the right time to get past the doorman. At least that's what he knew his body to be doing, he remained trapped screaming behind a lifeless expression. Everything he remembered himself being, doing, and feeling was now consumed by the fire eating away at his organs. There was no longer anything he could hold onto, not even the hope that someone would see the fight behind his masked eyes. He wanted nothing more than to let go but the thing controlling his limbs and burning him from the inside was keeping him prisoner, it would not release its hold. He felt the pleasure it derived from burning him alive and his internal screams were like the sweetest song. Every moment was agony, even the smile that formed over the face he could no longer call his.

He watched as the doorman propped open the doors and walked to the curb to help a tenant get out of a cab. He quickly slipped through the doors and made his way over to the elevators. Standing in front of its mirrored doors was the first time Mal was able to see his reflection since the shack. He wanted to weep as he took in the face staring back at him. It was a face he could no longer recognize. His eyes were sunken and empty and his cheeks hollow, all the warmth of humanity gone. All that remained were harsh features only accentuated by the smile that widened in response to his hopelessness.

Chapter Fourteen

THE MIRROR

Nalini stood in front of Arel's apartment door, a bouquet of white lilies and roses in one hand as the other hovered in hesitation inches from the door. She was early even after her last-minute stop at the flower stand. It hadn't felt right showing up with nothing, not after the news of losing one of his patients. As angry as she was in her belief of her brother's attempts to sabotage her biggest project with the city, she was willing to talk. She knew Eugene wouldn't just go along with any jealous plan her brother would come up with. She stood firm in the knowledge that Eugene would never intentionally plan to hurt her or her future no matter what kind of relationship they had, or had left. With that in mind, the flowers in hand were also a peace offering.

'*I can be the bigger person,*' she coached herself as she pulled her shoulders back and stood tall. She knocked on the door twice and waited a moment, no response. She pulled her phone from her jacket pocket and checked the clock, it was now 9:35 PM.

Frustrated and impatient, she pulled her keys from her pocket, Arel's emergency spare had its place as the last key on the ring.

She unlocked the door, slid her hand up the wall just inside of the frame, and flipped the switch. The short hallway remained in the dark, she flipped the switch a few more times in rapid succession; nothing.

'*Of course the bulbs out,*' she thought stepping through the threshold of the apartment.

The living room was cast in a dim glow from the bit of light coming from the building hallway and the street lamps through the windows of Arel's bedroom at the back of the apartment. She released a tired sigh and confidently made her way through the dark. The last time she'd been there was around the time he moved in but, thankfully, Arel wasn't the kind to move furniture around. She crossed the living room and turned on the lamp next to the couch. When the room lit up, she was surprised to see an air mattress with a set of sheets folded over a pillow and the same at the end of the couch. The first thing that came to mind was how strange it was but then she caught her thoughts, she didn't know her brother's life well enough to determine what was strange or not. As her eyes darted around the room, a framed family photo caught her attention. It was a picture taken after they moved her things into her dorm freshman year of university. Arel's face was the only one she could focus on as she was drawn toward the picture. She searched her memory and counted the conversations between her and Arel that didn't involve Eugene in some capacity. Over the last 12 years, she could only remember having eight conversations with her brother. She couldn't recall any details about his life, what his hobbies were, who he dated, his pursuits at work, nothing.

All she could remember was the smile on his face, a smile that asked for nothing. There was something about it that she couldn't stand. It mocked her in a way but, for the life of her, she couldn't understand why. He never spoke about himself or his life, and she never asked.

He'd just ask her questions and would appropriately respond to her answers, but that was it.

As she stared at his face she tried to remember the last time he came to her to talk, for anything at all. Then all of a sudden she was taken back to their teenage years. The memory was clear, he'd woken her from a dead sleep, shining the flashlight from his cell phone in her face. Disoriented and annoyed, she watched him set the phone down, flashlight up, so she could see him, he started frantically moving his hands. From what she understood through groggy eyes, he had a nightmare. She saw the fear in his eyes as he told her about the people in the nightmare reaching for him, attempting to latch on to his limbs from the dark. She remembered instinctively looking around her room expecting to see one in the dark, his descriptions sent chills through her and she remembered feeling goosebumps as she ran a hand up her arm.

The last thing he told her was that the power was out in his dream. She remembered his eyes being so wide. They pleaded for help, for belief in what he was experiencing and to receive some kind of comfort.

"The power is out," he signed through shaking hands.

Looking back, she remembered his fear as well as her own and her stomach sank with guilt. She had called him crazy and told him his dream and the blackout were not related then told him to get out. What he had told her scared her and her only reaction was to shut it down, to shut *him* down.

Nalini shook herself from the memory, she didn't want to fall back into that feeling or question her actions toward her brother that night. A rose petal fell from the bouquet in her hand onto the table, pulling her back to reality. She put the photo back in its place and walked around the breakfast bar to open the refrigerator door. Acutely aware of the the dry lump building in her throat. A bottle of Merlot lay next to a carton of eggs.

'*That'll do*,' she thought, as she pulled out the bottle and proceeded to search for a glass. The cabinet to the right of the fridge was the first place she looked and was happy to see her first guess was the right one. On the first shelf were the glasses and in the back of the cabinet was a two-liter das boot.

'*Perfect*,' Nalini thought proudly, grabbing a wine glass for herself first. She was in no hurry to move all the glasses around to get the boot from the back so she took her time, pouring herself a hearty serving of wine before diving in.

It didn't take as long as she thought to fish out the glass boot and before she knew it she was standing back admiring the white calla lilies and roses protruding from their unconventional vase. Crossing her arms and holding the wine glass to her lips, she tried to picture them in anything but the boot and concluded that anything else would have been out of place. It was perfect in a 'country chic' sort of way. The thought made her smile and she hoped it'd make Arel smile too.

She looked at her phone, it was now five to ten, and still no reply to her previous texts from her brother or Eugene. With a sigh, she set her glass in the empty sink and headed toward the door.

On the way back to her apartment she thought of every scenario that would keep her brother from responding to her messages. She pushed her annoyance to the back of her mind and chose to focus on what he must be dealing with. Probably just caught up with Eugene getting drinks, that MUST have been it, and that was something she could forgive.

Before she knew it she was standing in front of the elevators in her apartment building wondering how she got there, making it home on autopilot. It hit her how tired she was and the elevator was taking longer than usual but, then again, when you're tired anything less than instantaneous feels too long. She stared at her reflection in the elevator doors and zeroed in on the dark circles around her eyes that dulled the color in her irises to a muddy green. As she leaned in closer to inspect the damage her nonstop schedule had inflicted on her skin she caught a glimpse of something black stepping out from behind her. It happened too quickly for her to make out its features. She gave a quick look around the lobby to confirm she was alone aside from the doorman standing just outside the glass doors of the building and jumped as the elevator doors sprang open.

'*I really need some sleep*,' she thought, convinced that must be the reason for seeing shadows and the tension creeping down her neck to her shoulders.

When the doors finally opened on the twelfth floor she found herself moving slowly and absentmindedly looking at her phone, dragging her feet as she walked. Oblivious to the box set in front of her apartment door until she hit it with her foot. She stared down at it for a while and thought through the conversations she'd had recently and if anyone mentioned leaving anything for her at home. The thought of it being a bomb crossed her mind, it was unmarked with no return address or shipping sticker of any kind.

Nalini's next thought was to run back downstairs and get the doorman, but instead, she reached down and picked up the box, it was as if she had no control over her actions. The box was in her hands before she could mentally object, any reservation to the delivery of the box disappeared as she held it. Her eyes stayed glued to its blank surface as she went through the motions of opening the door and setting her things down on the foyer table. She stared at the box for a long time going back and forth between 'Bringing it inside was a mistake and the desire to rip it open.' She felt her mind falling into a different state like she was falling into a dream.

When she dreamt she would often dream of a different time, a different place, and being a different person. It was in those dreams she could hear the delicate sound of wind blowing through the trees and the melody it carried with it, not understanding how her mind was creating the sounds or if it was even right. Standing in front of the box she heard the same faint melody from her dreams floating through her mind. Had she been able to view the events leading up to this moment through a logical lens she'd see the madness and malice behind this box, but she stood hypnotized, lulled into submission. She watched as her hand slowly stripped the tape off and opened the wings of the box. To her surprise and delight, the only item in the box was an antique hand mirror.

Nalini held the mirror up to her face to meet her reflection and wondered who could have left such a curious gift.

As she continued to gaze into the mirror she noticed the color of her eyes began to darken and her features shift and change. First the eyes, then the shape of her nose, until she was no longer looking at her reflection but another woman entirely. She knew her, but not from work or in passing. This was a face that would frequent her dreams. It was the eyes, she knew those eyes. Nalini could never place them on his face, the eyes looking back at her in the mirror were her brother's eyes. In waking life, she never understood the rage they incited, not until now seeing the whole picture of the woman from her dreams with her brother's eyes looking back at her from this mirror.

Her grip on the mirror tightened as the memory flooded into her mind the anger she felt in the field that day. '*A woman didn't belong here.*'

'Wait, what?' she caught that thought, combating the past life memory, trying to shake herself from the vision. As much as she tried to focus all her will on breaking free of the unfolding scene, she found herself being overcome by rage once more.

'*This isn't me,*' she told herself, trying to release the mirror from her hand, but her fingers were no longer obeying her commands, instead tightening into a fist. She felt herself falling into a suspended state, no longer having a grip on her mind and conscious thought. She felt an unnerving sensation in the back of her skull, like the scurrying of insects burrowing through her brain toward her frontal lobe. With this scurrying came feelings and thoughts that had been shrouded by a mind fog coming into form. She began to see a clearer picture. She saw herself as a young man, his anger and resentment toward Kirana vibrated through his every cell. In that moment she acknowledged that this boy's anger had been with her throughout her life and was a part of who she had always been. He was a part of her, dwelling in her shadow keeping her from moving beyond the shroud of his resentment, it had no part in her life but it had become all-encompassing, blinding her.

The memories played back like a film, Kirana favored by the teachers all because of the dragon. '*She had no right,*' he thought.

Nalini felt the bitterness of his thoughts as they ran through her mind. The perversion of his entitlement made her skin crawl yet she couldn't stop it from moving through her body.

In his memories, she saw the praise Kirana received was for, what he believed, no reason other than that she was guarded by a dragon.

The sight of Kirana meditating in the garden that day sent a maddening fury through him. Her still face read smug to him. He could no longer hold himself back from a confrontation and assured himself that there was no way she could best him one on one. He had no intention of actually hurting her, his aim was humiliation and her dragon would most likely interfere, proving her a coward unworthy of the praise she received.

Nalini saw through his eyes Kirana's calm demeanor as he approached her, as he spit the poisonous accusation of her trying to invalidate him and his accomplishments. She watched as Kirana maintained her composure as she addressed his misplaced frustrations and turned them back on him.

There was no conscious thought behind his actions after she finished her rebuttal, he moved quickly to strike her motivated by blind rage. Nalini wanted to look away as she couldn't interfere in this memory of her past life, she wouldn't be able to stand watching him hurt Kirana. She was sure he would be too fast for her to deflect his blow, but to her surprise and his, Kirana veered to the side with ease and grace. It was as if their exchange were choreographed, she danced around him sending him into a downward spiral. Nalini could feel his need to hurt Kirana now and it was his downfall. He moved hastily and without a strategy, sending him tumbling to his knees. He was surprised when she appeared in front of him with her hand out to help him up, but instead of gracefully conceding to the fact that she'd won, he tried once more to strike a blow. His movements were wild now and Kirana's composure began to fade from her face, he took this as a victory and an indication that he was wearing her out. Nalini knew different, she knew Kirana's expression wasn't one of tired frustrations but growing impatience. She stopped dancing and began fighting back, she was guiding him toward the trees. As Nalini was only a third-party observer she was focused on trying to figure out Kirana's strategy to win. They were close to a large oak now, he didn't notice how she was moving him around, too distracted by his rage.

Nalini heard a name called out for the first time but it was the last thing he'd ever hear, Kirana struck a blow sending his head crashing into the base of the oak tree. A deafening ring rang through his mind before everything went black for him, leaving Nalini seeing red.

CHAPTER FIFTEEN

PAST LIVES, PAST LOVES

Slowly the darkness that enveloped Eugene began to lift. First, he only saw shapes moving in shadow, he assumed these shapes were his friends and a wave of relief fell over him, they'd gotten to him in time. As his sight cleared he realized he wasn't in his SUV or anywhere he recognized and had no recollection of how he got there and how he was standing at all.

He stood frozen, working hard to control his breathing in his panic. He didn't want to draw the attention of others. He was amongst a group he didn't recognize and began to look around slowly observing each person. Thankfully he was standing in the back of the group. There was one whose face he could make out, a tall man to his left. It was Rú, Eugene felt all his muscles relax at once. He stepped closer to him and pulled him a few feet away from the group.

"Rú, where are we? Where's Rel?" Eugene asked in a frantic whisper.

Rú just stared at Eugene for what seemed like ten minutes to him but in reality might have only been about thirty seconds. Rú's gaze darted wildly between Eugene's eyes as if he were speed-reading a particularly difficult word problem. Before he could ask what he was doing Rú put his hand up to stop him from speaking then walked over to the woman at the head of the group. This woman was speaking to someone he couldn't see, his view being obstructed by a tall blond man with long braided hair who glanced back at him.

He heard Rú tell her he was going to walk the perimeter and take Bówēn with him, the woman nodded and resumed her conversation. Rú walked quickly back to Eugene, grabbed his arm, and started walking faster toward the trees at the edge of the clearing.

Once Rú was sure the others could no longer see or hear them he turned back to Eugene and crossed his arms.

"When are you from?" Rú whispered.

"What? What do you mean when?" he asked through gritted teeth, working hard to conceal his panic. Frustration was building a lump in his throat, "Do you mean the year?" he asked with eyes closed and clenched fists.

"Yes," Rú answered bluntly.

"2028. Rú, what the fuck is happening right now?" Eugene urged, worry shaking his voice.

"What's your name?" Rú asked, crossing his arms and turning away from him.

"Eugene," he said in a disheartened tone, recoiling from Rú. Rú turned around and walked back up to him, stopping not a foot from him.

"You are out of time, Eugene," he said coldly. His delivery was so curt it almost sounded like a threat. Eugene's eyes widened with fear and Rú saw that he was about to fall into hysterics.

"No, no, no," he said quickly, realizing how it sounded.

"You are out of *your* time, Eugene, your consciousness has traveled back to this point in your soul's collective history," Rú clarified.

Eugene stared at him for a few moments. "Ok," he sighed, pinching the bridge of his nose between his thumb and index finger. "Can you tell me how this could happen?" he asked, beginning to pace.

"For humans, there are very few ways without training and divine intervention. As all this has taken you by surprise I assume this was not your intention."

"No, it wasn't," Eugene seethed.

"What do you remember before waking up here? Rú asked thoughtfully, beckoning Eugene to walk with him.

"I was," Eugene paused, frozen with fear by the memory of the black-eyed child grabbing his wrist, "Attacked," he finished, nearly choking on the word. Rú not only saw the fear in Eugene's eyes but felt the fear he experienced as the memory moved through his mind, it was suffocating and without any hope of release.

He saw the creature as Eugene did, its immeasurable darkness masquerading behind the innocent features of a child, an unnatural perversion.

Although Rú didn't intend to oversee Eugene's memory, it did answer his question of how Eugene found himself out of time. Whatever this thing was, it wasn't something he was familiar with at this present time.

"Eugene, had you ever seen what attacked you before then?" Rú asked cautiously, treading lightly so as not to aggravate him further, worried he'd shut down.

Eugene shook his head, staring blankly past Rú's head. There was nothing more to gain by pushing forward in that line of questioning.

Rú took a few steps back and began thinking of different solutions, he drummed his fingers against his chin mindlessly.

'Could there be something he needs to learn about this life to move forward in his present?' he thought.

"Eugene, the good news is you're not dead in your time," Rú said brightly.

Eugene breathed a sigh of relief, "Are you sure?"

"Yeah, pretty sure." Rú shrugged and the relief from Eugene's face fell.

"You didn't end up here by accident, most likely there's something here you need to see or learn," Rú explained.

"Are you fu-," Eugene stopped himself for fear of being too loud. "Learn what?" he snapped.

"Calm down, I don't know and if I did know telling you would defeat the purpose," Rú said.

"Fuck off," Eugene mumbled. "How is it defeating the purpose if I'm here to learn something?" He did his best to keep the annoyance from painting his voice any further.

"Being told what you should know pales in comparison to discovering a lesson and learning it firsthand. I'd be cheating you," Rú answered patiently, fully aware of Eugene's irritation.

Eugene couldn't argue with that logic, as frustrating as it was.

"This is infuriating," he whispered. "Fine, what do I do?" he asked flinging his arms out.

Rú looked around and spotted a puddle at the base of a large oak tree. He grabbed Eugene's arm and led him over to it, together they stared down at the reflection in the still water.

"You start by being here. This is," he started, placing a hand on Eugene's shoulder, "Bówēn."

Eugene was so focused on the bizarre circumstances that he hadn't noticed he wasn't himself or the fact that he was now in robes as opposed to the dress pants he was in before. He ran his fingers over his face, feeling the alien features, and shifted his weight from his left to right foot registering the slight difference in build. The only thing he could think to relate this situation to would be wearing some kind of full-body costume or suit. He couldn't wrap his mind around the reality that this was him or even a version of him.

"If I'm him then why don't I remember anything from his life up until now?" he asked curiously.

"There are seas that collide but do not become one the moment they meet, although the water contains the same minerals it takes time to come to an equilibrium and become one. His history is there; you just have to release the idea that there is a separation between you," Rú explained.

Eugene nodded, recalling Rú saying something along those same lines to Dylan this morning. If it was still even Saturday.

"Right, let's get this going. What can I do to get to my equilibrium?" Eugene asked, eagerly rubbing his hands together.

Rú stepped back from him again, spread his arms wide, closed his eyes, and took a deep breath in.

"Be here," he answered on the exhale and dropped his arms back to his sides. "You have to clear your mind, just be, and observe the thoughts that come to you. It cannot be forced, it will come in time. So, for now, just be still and observe."

That wasn't what Eugene wanted to hear but he closed his eyes and took a deep breath. He released the tension he was holding in his shoulders and did his best to clear his mind.

"Good," Rú said when Eugene opened his eyes again. "Come on, I said we were checking the perimeter, should give us some more time to get you centered," he called over his shoulder as he began walking away, gesturing to the wide clearing.

"Great," Eugene grumbled as he started into a jog to catch up with Rú. "What are we keeping an eye out for?" he asked, now scanning the trees for movement.

"Smokeless fire," Rú responded seriously.

"Smo-" Eugene's train of thought was abruptly halted. They had walked around and were just outside of the clearing directly across from where the group remained talking. Eugene could now see the face of the woman he and the rest were standing behind, the woman leading their group. There was something so familiar about the expressions on her face as she spoke to another woman who was facing away from him. Even the way she moved her hands as she spoke, he couldn't put his finger on it.

"I know her," he spoke aloud without thinking, without expecting a response.

"Good. Let's go," Rú chirped as he began his trek through the line of trees into the clearing

"Wait!" Eugene called out after him. "What do I do? I don't know anything about Bówēn yet, they're gonna know something's up," he stressed, pointing to the face he could not yet call his.

"Don't say anything, it wouldn't be out of character. They're an important part of your life in this time, they could be the key to your lesson," Rú said calmly.

"Okay," he agreed nervously. Rú had already started walking away and he, once again, had to run to catch up to him.

The tall blonde man and the woman Eugene found familiar glanced in their direction once they stepped out of the trees but returned their attention to the other woman they were speaking to when they left. Eugene relaxed as he took comfort in the fact that something was happening that didn't seem to involve him directly. As he walked closer, the features of the familiar woman became clear and he could now see her eyes. She glanced over to him again, he knew those eyes as well as his own.

"Rel?" he whispered to himself. It was like looking at a friend wearing a mask or when someone you've known forever walks into a room and you don't have to turn around to confirm it's them, you just know.

"What?" Rú asked, intrigued by the surprise in Eugene's voice. Eugene's mind shot back to the conversation with Rú over coffee about how he and his father were connected in different ways through their lifetimes but didn't think that extended beyond family. Then he realized Rú had answered that question too, he just hadn't been paying attention.

"That's Arel, well, she's Arel in my time," Eugene whispered, subtly gesturing toward the woman leading their group so he wouldn't draw her attention

Rú's eyes dashed from Eugene to Kirana, and then he turned away from him and walked past the group back to the tree line as far away from them as he could get. Once satisfied with the distance, he turned around and beckoned Eugene to join him. Rú quickly leaving Eugene behind attracted the tall blond man's attention. He cocked his head to the side and squinted his eyes, non-verbally asking him what was happening. Eugene panicked, he smiled nervously and shrugged before quickly looking away, making a beeline for Rú standing comfortably out of earshot.

"Thanks for leaving me there!" he hissed through his teeth.

"I assumed you'd follow me. Anyway, the woman you recognize is Kirana, how can you tell she is your 'Arel'?" Rú asked, once again crossing his arms and studying Eugene's face.

"They have the same eyes somehow, they're different but the same. Her mannerisms are the same as his. This is so weird, I just know," Eugene explained, staring intently at Kirana.

"The reason the eyes seem the same and different at the same time is because you're not only seeing with your eyes, but with this." Rú pointed to the space between Eugene's eyes. "This is what is helping you see beyond what your eyes show you. Not your mind, but the consciousness and the soul working as one to see the truth. Who you are extends past your physical body in space and time. It's how you are able to recognize Kirana, you know her soul and it's been long enough that you know it even in another body."

Eugene stood quiet for a moment. "How does that happen? How can I figure this out with other people in my life then?" Eugene asked, his mind was racing and the only subject of his focus was Dylan and if this was the reason he was so drawn to him. Arel had been in his life for so long that there was no question about why he felt like he'd known him forever but he barely knew Dylan in comparison.

"Well you're in the throws of a rare opportunity, you got the chance to come back and see the beginning and you can relate the feelings of familiarity to its origin. In the future, you can be confident in knowing that those feelings have a place and time and are meant to be explored or they would not have entered your life again." Rú finished speaking and Eugene remained quiet, an excitement built in his chest. It clicked all of a sudden and it hit him, the tremendous opportunity he had.

"Are you ready to observe up close?" Rú asked, nodding toward the rest of the group.

Eugene shook out his hands at his sides. "Yeah," he squeaked, the sound of his voice going up at the end. Rú began walking toward the group.

"Wait!" he called, grabbing Rú's arm before he got away. "Wait! Do they speak English? Does Bówēn speak English?" he asked frantically.

"I've taught you many languages, as I have Kirana, that includes English. And to my surprise, Vor knows English as well as a few other languages. But you don't have to worry." Rú assured Eugene.

"Vor, the tall Viking guy." Eugene clarified.

"His name is Halvor, we call him Vor. We all caught up?" Rú asked impatiently.

"Mhmm." Eugene nodded.

"Good!" he exclaimed, as he playfully punched Eugene's arm and started to walk away, this time Eugene followed.

As they made their way to the rest of the group, it was clear they were walking into an emotional ordeal. The woman Kirana had been speaking to was now standing with her forehead pressed against Vor's. He had to bend over quite a bit to meet hers.

Eugene did his best to look like he knew what was happening.

'She's his sister, this is their first time meeting.' Rú's words popped into his mind, answering what he imagined was the confused look he must have had on his face, despite his efforts.

'Is this a cultural thing?' Eugene thought.

'Kirana and Vor told her why he'd been away and Vor was just told their mother passed on not long ago. They are sharing a moment in honor of her,' Rú summarized as much as he needed to know at that moment.

Vor and his sister broke away from each other and it was the first time Eugene was able to see her face. She gave Vor a comforting smile and wiped a tear from his cheek.

Witnessing that nurturing action sent electricity through him, a dizzying fog swam through his mind and he wasn't able to grasp onto one thought.

'*Déjá vu,*' he thought, trying to figure out whether it was from his time or if this was just an effect of being in the past. There was a glow about her, an allure that extended beyond the lively green of her eyes or the perfect shape of her full lips. Her magnetism was undeniable, but her beautiful familiar features weren't the reason he felt he knew her. She was the melody above his baseline. It was the song his heart sang when he felt the comfort of home. In that same moment, a name ran through his mind and she looked at him as if he called hers aloud. His eyes locked with hers and there was no doubt.

'*Dylan.*'

Chapter Sixteen

OLD WOUNDS

Arel found himself, once again, alone in the dark. The moon, partially hidden by clouds, cast eerie shadows within the trees he was facing. There was no question in his mind, he knew exactly where he was. The island came calling again, this time he wouldn't run, he couldn't run.

The wind rolling off the water whipped against his shirt and pants with a force that sent him stumbling forward as if to urge him on his way. He could tell the ground was freezing and was thankful he had the buffer of grass under his bare feet. He stared into the trees and took three deep breaths before entering by way of a small walking path made by heavy foot traffic. He broke through the barrier of trees and was immediately inundated by the energy of souls that surrounded him, sending his head swimming.

"Get back!" he called out, holding his hands up and visualizing himself encased in light. The pressure in his head began to subside as he watched the shadows retreat.

"You'll have your chance soon enough," he mumbled and he resumed his trek through the trees unsure where exactly he was going but he was being drawn somewhere. The shadows ahead of him stood still patiently waiting for his approach. There were some that just stood and watched him pass and a few that rushed at him before stopping short. Although he did as he was taught and claimed his space so nothing could penetrate the energetic barrier he set, there was a part of him that believed it wouldn't work. Each time another shadow came at him he flinched less and less as they tried one after another to break his defense but none succeeded. Fully relaxed now, he wondered if this would work the same way when he was physically on the island. He continued confidently through the trees and came to an opening where a small shack stood away from all the other buildings. In the window stood a figure, it was facing away from him but he could tell it was a woman. The moment he stepped out of the trees the shadows began to line up just outside of the clearing, from them came a hum that built with every step he took toward the door of the shack. The hum built into what sounded like a symphony of out of tune woodwinds, pushing him to quicken his pace to get indoors.

When he reached the door it was open, prepared for his arrival. He didn't think about it as he ran inside and shut it tight behind him. Catching his breath, he noticed none of the noise from the shadows standing in the tree line could be heard inside. Aside from the ringing in his ears, it was pleasantly quiet with only the low pings of a music box from the far end of the shack where the woman from the window sat in front of a vanity. The tune from the music box sounded so familiar but he couldn't place it, his memory of it was too dim. It was like the melody was a remnant from a dream he had years ago.

Swept up in the song of the music box, he was aware he was being drawn closer. The woman facing away from him was humming the tune, her voice familiar now. It had been years since he heard her voice but it was unmistakable now as he listened to her attempt to hit the right notes.

"Lin?" he asked as he reached out to touch her shoulder, but before his hand met her she caught his hand in a grip that could break bone. This may not be real but the pain was and he couldn't help but scream out. She turned to face him and the eyes that glared into his struck a fear that broke every defense he had set. They were his sister's eyes but in them was *his* malice, the boy Kirana fought had taken hold of her. Arel began to panic. Worry, guilt, and fear created an ache in his chest that hollowed the foundation he had built his strength and courage. As his strength was failing, so were the barriers that kept the shadows at bay, with the force of a tidal wave they burst through the windows and the door, chasing the air from the room.

Arel's body lurched forward gasping for air, launching a sleeping Evaine from his chest.

"What's wrong?" she asked frantically, bypassing her grogginess and shifting straight to sober concern. She took his face in her hands and waited for his wild eyes to focus on hers. His breathing was erratic and he shot up off the couch and started pacing, working hard to bring his breathing under control and his consciousness back to waking reality. His fists bawled tight at his sides with his wrists tensely twisted upward in an unnatural fashion. He began to hum and sing low to himself.

"What's-" Evaine started.

"He's having a panic attack, give him a minute," Rú explained calmly. "Singing helps him to control his breathing and the lyrics give him something to focus on.

Everyone, now awake, stood patiently with enough distance that he could pace comfortably without them being in his way.

"I'm gonna grab you a glass of water," Dylan said reassuringly and ran back to the kitchenette. Arel nodded and uncurled his fist, flattened his hand, and waved it in acknowledgment.

After another few minutes, they watched as he relaxed his wrists and the song became a hum again. He took a few deep breaths as he walked toward them.

"Thank you," he said calmly, taking the water from Dylan's extended hand and looking at each of them.

"Yeah, no worries, buddy," Dylan said empathetically. Evaine took Arel's hand.

"I have to go see my sister, something's wrong," Arel said, sure that what he saw in his dream was real.

"Let's go," Rú said, knowing better than to ask him what he had seen. It would only waste time.

"No, you should stay with Eugene," Arel said, unconsciously glancing at Leila, there was something he still didn't trust about her.

"No, Dylan will hang back," Rú said firmly.

"Yeah, I'm good with that," Dylan chirped.

"Rú, If I can't help my sister alone how can I face what's on that island alone?" Arel declared, ignoring Dylan completely.

Rú knew he was right, he wasn't going to be there to fight the battle he was facing.

"Fine," he agreed reluctantly. "I'll be here," he said, tapping his finger against his temple.

"Ok," Evaine said walking to the stairs. "Let's go."

"Did you not-" Arel began to protest.

"Try, go ahead. Try and tell me no," she cautioned him, "I need to know you can do this too, and at least with this I can be back up." Evaine shot a look at Rú that screamed 'DON'T YOU DARE' to which he threw his hands up in surrender.

With that Evaine disappeared up the stairs without another word, leaving Arel to trail behind her grabbing the keys from Rú.

Evaine finally broke their silence when they reached the third stop light into their drive.

"Do you know what we're walking into?" she asked, the severity of before now gone replaced by focus.

"I can't say for sure," he answered, his voice heavy. She could tell his mind was elsewhere but she couldn't keep her thoughts to herself anymore.

"I know a lot has happened in the last few hours but we still haven't talked about how or why you're involved with this or why it has to be you," she said looking down at at her hands as she picked at her nails.

"Yeah, I'm sorry. Not the first date I had in mind," he said willing his voice into a lighter tone but was unable to hide his latent guilt.

"Going to check on your sister after your friend was attacked by a demon child? No, not what I envisioned either," she smiled, looking over at him. "But I'm glad I'm here, is that weird?"

"Yes, you're an absolute freakshow," Arel said with a smile.

Evaine playfully punched his arm as they shared a laugh. "Can we talk about it though? Why is this on you? You some kind of savior?" she was only half joking on that last question.

Arel chuckled, "God no, the way I understand it, it's because of my relation to my sister and her direct involvement in reviving the islands. My role is more of a specialist, my profession is helping people heal themselves and I think I might be able to do that for the people still stuck there. That's my best guess, but I really won't know till I get there," he finished with a sigh.

His answer added another level of apprehension but she maintained her composure and kept her expression from being too serious, masking the fear of what waited for him.

She felt a bit guilty, she believed Arel and had hope that he could do whatever he needed to do to neutralize the threats on the island but still grappled with all of this madness coming down to one person. She sat silently, her mind moving so fast through scenarios that she barely noticed Arel when he finally said something to break the silence.

"Hmm?" she finally responded.

"You have your protection bag?" Arel asked.

"Yes," she answered looking over at him to observe his pensive face. Arel nodded in response but said nothing, his eyes focused on the traffic ahead.

"We should have a plan," Evaine said, as they pulled into the garage around the corner from Nalini's apartment. Arel pulled into the first spot he saw so quickly Evaine instinctively closed her eyes expecting to hear the car sliding against the one parked beside it. Arel had it parked and shut off before she opened them again.

"You're right. I want you to stay in the hall after I go in," Arel started.

"What?" Evaine objected.

"Only to give her, or whatever else is there, a false sense of security. I think if something comes up I want to have the element of surprise, and nothing can touch you as long as you have that," Arel finished, pointing to the protection bag lying just inside her purse.

Arel then turned to open his door but turned back to face Evaine fast enough to give her pause.

"Can you box?" he asked.

"Judo."

"Oh, good," Arel quipped, he was genuinely delighted to hear it. The way he answered lightened her mood, intentionally or not.

"Why?" she asked, she couldn't help the smile that formed across her face.

"In case you need to save me," he shrugged. "My sister has a serious right hook and she can be wily," he said stepping out of the SUV. He watched her do the same before he shut his door and walked around to meet her. The sound of her chuckle as he made his way around the SUV gave him a sense of achievement. He felt her apprehension the entire ride over and the weight of her worry struck him. He didn't want her to worry; as impractical as it was, he wanted to see her smile. For whatever was ahead of him, he needed the comfort of her smile.

"And what will you do when I'm not there to save you?" she asked, her tone was playful but her eyes displayed the truth of her concern. The playfulness fell from his eyes but his smile remained.

"I'll deal with it when I have to," he said holding his hand out to her. She didn't respond, she just took his hand and they began their walk around the corner to Nalini's building.

They didn't say a word to each other, too busy working through individual scenarios in their heads. Everything was normal up front, the doorman recognized Arel and let him through without incident and the elevator was waiting for them when Evaine pressed the button. The moment they stepped into the elevator Arel's head began to swim and his stomach felt uneasy.

"Woah," he whispered, shaking his head to clear the fog.

"What is it?"

"I just got really lightheaded, I'll be ok," Arel assured her. He knew the feeling was a sensory overload, so much energy hitting him at once. He took deep slow breaths until they reached Nalini's floor. The moment he stepped out of the elevator his mind cleared enough for the rolling in his stomach to subside. He could still feel the energy and his eyesight was drawn down the hall to his sister's apartment door.

"Something is here, that's what hit me in the Elevator," he said as he slowly started walking toward the door.

"Do you know what it is?" Evaine whispered as they were close to the door now.

"No, it just feels like I have something looming over me. Something domineering and it's in there," he confirmed. Negative energy has a way of sucking the air out of a room and it leaves a trail wherever it grows. He stood in front of the door now, her apartment key in hand trying to think of his approach, experiencing a touch of analysis paralysis. Evaine watched his face as he worked through his thoughts for a few moments before she stepped in front of him and took his face in her hands. She gently pulled it down to hers. He took a moment to admire the amber in her eyes and followed the soft lines of her face to her lips just inches from his. He moved the rest of the way to meet her lips and pulled her into him holding her tight. He couldn't think of anything other than the softness of her lips and the warmth of her body against his, loosening the tension he was holding in his back and shoulders. He realized then what she was doing and pulled away from her, unable to stop himself from laughing.

"Nice job, getting me out of my head," he said, his arms still wrapped around her. "Good move."

"Gave me an excuse, I've been wanting to do that since you came into the office," she confessed through a smile.

"Terribly cliché though," he quipped as he loosened his hold around her waist. Evaine laughed and stepped back.

"What's cliché?" she snarked, crossing her arms.

"You just kissed me before I have to walk into a dangerous situation, well, possibly dangerous. It's a plot device used in, like, every action-adventure movie," he laughed.

"Uh huh, you in your head right now?" she asked, playfully pushing him away. Cliché or not her antics were successful, aside from being self-serving. "And *you* kissed me," she said stepping to the side and leaning on the door frame.

"Fair enough," he conceded. His eyes then drifted from Evaine to the door and he once again was back in the reality of what he had to face and couldn't waste any more time.

"Alright, let's do this." he sighed, turning the key in the lock.

"Wait! Should we have a code word if you need me?" she whispered, putting her hand over his, stopping him from turning the doorknob.

"I'll just call your name, did I not tell you my sister is legally deaf? I'm sorry this has been a lot in such a short amount of time," he said, glancing at her apologetically.

"I know," she squeezed his hand before letting hers fall back to her side. "I'll be right outside the door," she reassured him. Arel nodded and opened the door, slipped in, and quickly shut it behind him.

Walking into Nalini's Foyer he couldn't see much of anything. The only light was coming from her living room to the right of him. It illuminated the table against the foyer wall where she kept her keys. Sitting on that table was an open box, he walked right to the box momentarily forgetting his sister. Drawn to it, he could feel the remnants of its contents, it was the same magnetic draw he felt in his dream.

"I thought I'd have to go to you."

The words came from behind him and the sound chilled him to his core. It was one thing to hear his sister's voice in his dreams and another to hear it in waking life. Nalini hadn't said a word since her freshman year of high school, but it was different. The voice coming from her now wasn't hers alone, it was two-toned joined with another voice he'd become familiar with only a few days ago, the boy's voice.

He turned to face his sister in the living room not knowing what he would see, what state she would be in. He was afraid he'd turn around and be faced with a different version of her but was relieved to see it was only her voice that had changed. She was still there for him to fight for. Although the eyes peering into him from across the room were full of pain and vengeance, it was still her.

"Lin? Can you hear me?" Arel asked calmly. Nalini didn't speak, only nodded in response. The way she moved kept him on edge, although she was across the room he felt as if she could strike or charge him at any moment. He quickly looked around the room, not sure of what he was looking for, only that he would know it when he saw it. A vintage hand mirror lay in front of her on the coffee table. *'That must be it,'* he thought to himself.

"Lin, where did you get that mirror?" Although he knew she could somehow hear him, he signed his words as he spoke and slowly stepped down into the living room, careful to stay close to the wall farthest from her. Nalini picked up the mirror and held it in front of her face.

"This?" She held the 'S' as she gazed in the mirror and adjusted the hair that had fallen over her eyes.

"Yes," Before he could get out another word she whipped the mirror at his face. He was able to dodge it and shield his face as it hit the wall behind him breaking free shards of mirrored glass. At the same time Arel had ducked to avoid being hit, Nalini rushed him and tackled him to the ground, quickly grabbing a large shard of glass next to his head.

"Let's try this again," she said, as she looked over his face holding the tip of the mirrored shard to his eye. "Brother..." she said the word under her breath like a curse.

"What should I take from you now? Your eyes? Your tongue?" There was a satisfaction in the voice that came from her, It broke his heart. He'd caught her forearm when she lunged at him pinning his hands between his throat and her arm. Her skin was hot to the touch and it began to burn the palms of his hands. The hold she had on him was abnormally strong. He ran over his options in his mind about what he was able to do in that moment and at the same time his muscles took over. A surge of adrenaline allowed him to push her up far enough that he could swing his leg over her head, hook it around her shoulders, and send her flying backward. It gave him enough time to roll over his shoulder into a crouch.

"Lin, if you know what happened you know I was defending myself," he explained. "Don't make his anger yours."

Evaine ran into the room after hearing the commotion from outside, Arel held his arm out to stop her from coming any further. Nalini kept her eyes on her brother, her limbs twitched and lurched forward as if she was fighting for control.

"Nalini, he was plagued by his inability to see his own worth. He blamed others, me, for what he could not give himself." Arel began to walk slowly toward her as he spoke. "Your understanding is stronger than his anger. Show him, Lin, that his lessons made you strong." He wanted Nalini to hear her name as much as possible in hopes that it would keep her from falling into the boy's reality. A voice that would keep her victim to the illusion of external validation and the domination of others.

"Only you can give him peace," he signed his words, standing in front of her now. This was her language, her world.

Her clenched fists were shaking as she fought for control, blood dripping from her left hand that still held the shard of mirror. She screamed as she swung it at Arel's face which he gracefully avoided. She continued to swing at him, and Evaine moved to help him.

"No!" he yelled, "She can do this!" He believed she could gain control again and dropped his arms and stood still. She continued her assault, stopping herself just before puncturing his eye with the glass.

Nalini stood frozen for a moment before forcing her fingers to release the shard. The boy was fighting to hold on to his anger, unwilling to release the strength it gave him. In her mind, she saw him before her, writhing in pain, confined by the chains he placed around himself from the anger and resentment he allowed to fester. The weight of the chains had dug into his skin and embedded into his muscles. She went to him, in the prison he created in her mind. She knew his loneliness, its depth and his need to be seen, to feel worthy of love. It was hers, he was a piece of her so deep in her subconscious still holding on to the suffering from a life she had no part in, and yet, it had shaped so much of who she was. She held his face while he cried and held her forehead against his silently thanking him for all he'd gone through, for his strength that helped her become who she was. A woman unafraid to fight for a life she wanted and now a woman able to feel worthy of the love she deserves from herself. The love she had been investing in was that of condition and external validation, now they could both let go and heal. As she held his weary head in her hands she felt his chains begin to fall away. As he released the last chain, the boy allowed himself to fall into her, becoming one.

Arel and Evaine watched as Nalini collapsed to the floor and began to cry. She was crying not in sadness, her body was releasing all the pain her spirit had carried through the lifetimes, leaving it for good. Arel and Evaine wasted no time joining her on the floor, Arel wrapped his arms around his sister and could feel the shift in her energy. As her sobs subsided she looked up into his eyes and smiled.

Chapter Seventeen

THE ILL-FATED

TW: BM

Nalini, exhausted by all that had happened, retired to her room to lie down. Leaving Arel and Evaine to deal with what was left of the mirror and to question who it was that left it for her. Arel only had to think of Rú for him to show up moments later in Nalini's living room.

"How is she?" he asked, looking around the room.

"Alright, I think. She's lying down," Arel answered from the floor where he was picking up the glass.

"I'll check on her when she wakes up." Rú then looked to Evaine. "How'd he do? Did you have to save him? Lin's a wild one."

Evaine chuckled and looked at Arel with pride. "He was amazing, it was like he knew exactly what to say to draw her out."

Arel looked down with a bashful smile as he picked up the larger mirror pieces with his hand. "What actually happened to her?" Arel asked, looking back up at Rú, now standing over him.

"May I?" Rú asked with his hand already out to him. Arel handed him the pieces along with the handle they had been encased in then ran to the kitchen to throw the smaller pieces away.

Rú turned the pieces over in his hand. "The woman who owned this mirror was a very angry, bitter person. It was the perfect tool to turn Nalini against you. She spent a lot of time gazing into this mirror in doing so pouring all her energy into it."

"Can you tell who it belonged to?" Evaine called from the kitchen helping Alrel discard the rest of the shattered bits. "And is it still...contagious?" she asked cautiously, stopping at the sink to wash her hands before walking back out to the living room.

"Contagious, is definitely the appropriate word when referring to the person who owned this mirror," Rú mused as he turned it over in his hand. "It belonged to Mary Mallon but no it's no longer 'contagious,'" he said, making air quotes with his fingers as he said the word.

"Mary Mallon? Wanna remind the class?" Evaine asked back in the room and plopped herself on the couch, exhausted but still invested.

"Typhoid Mary," Arel answered. "But why wouldn't Lin just get sick? How would it have affected her like that?" Arel asked as he walked into the living room from the kitchen and took a seat next to Evaine.

"Like I mentioned, she was very angry, forcibly locked up against her will and she died alone. A pain like that can stick to anything possessed by its owner, but mirrors are very powerful. They show you the reality of who you are, a portal of truth. They can work both ways that's why so many cultures have superstitions about them. A few being, that the soul can travel through mirrors or be trapped in one but there's another truth to a mirror. When you gaze upon a mirror there is the ability to leave a part of yourself, an essence. The reflection acts as an open door for the essence remaining in the mirror and can attach to the person looking into it." Rú brought the shard very close to his face as he finished explaining and looked up sharply.

Nalini stood frozen in her tracks the moment she stepped out from the hallway to the foyer, her eyes locked on Rú. He knew she recognized him from the boy's memories, that's the only way she could have known him, and she was frightened but not surprised. He could see the pictures forming in her mind, they were all so far away. Nalini remembered the boy feeling so undeserving when Rú was around, intimidated, but he was happy to see she was having a hard time understanding what the boy found so intimidating. He smiled at her.

'*You know me.*' He spoke to her not with words but with impressions and feelings. Nalini nodded and finished making her way into the room. He showed himself to her as Harrison in her mind, her expression softened and her eyes grew wide.

"This whole time?" she signed, then turned her attention to Arel with a look that read 'why am I the last to know?'

It was as if he had heard her mind scream the question, "You wouldn't have believed me!" He burst out laughing as his hands moved quickly with excitement. She then turned to Rú for an answer and, so the others wouldn't feel left out, signed his response as well. "You weren't ready."

"BULLSHIT!" Nalini exploded, before falling back onto her couch next to her brother. "What else don't I know?" she signed. She looked over and finally noticed Evaine sitting quietly, not looking to interfere with the family argument happening in front of her. Nalini held up her finger to her, got up quickly and ran to the foyer where she left her bracelets. They chimed to life as she slid them over her hands and she ran back in to introduce herself. When she walked back into the room from the hall both Arel and Evaine were standing. Arel wanted to introduce Evaine to his sister properly.

"This is Evaine, she has been helping us," he signed, looking from Nalini to Evaine, relieved to see Evaine so at ease. He wasn't comfortable calling her a friend and it was too soon to put a title on their relationship without talking to her about it.

"Hello, it's nice to meet you. Sorry about before." Nalini's bracelets sang out as quickly as she was moving.

"Don't worry about it," Evaine said with a wave of her hand. "You've got some moves," she said lightly.

Nalini Laughed and signed her thanks, relieved and feeling more relaxed.

She looked around the room and then at her brother and Evaine. "Thank you for taking care of the mess," Nalini's bracelets chimed. Arel felt warm as she thanked them both, he could see a change in her and it was one he'd always hoped to see. He smiled and nodded, though he felt no thanks were needed.

Getting right back to business Nalini turned back to Rú. "Do you know who did this? Who sent me the mirror?"

"I was just looking into it," Rú answered, Gazing back down at the mirror in his hand. He was quiet for a moment, trying to work through the energy attached to the mirror. He closed his eyes and focused on every face that popped into his mind, settling on one.

"Malory, Mal." His eyes flew open.

"I know a Mal, he's an urban ranger," Evaine blurted out in concern.

"He was on the island, he went with a group of other rangers," Rú said apologetically, the expression he wore indicated Mal faced a grim fate. Nalini's eyes widened in fear, she stood up and began pacing the room.

"I sent the order to do a walk-through so our team could get out there Monday, tomorrow." She walked back over to the couch and sat back down. "I did this." she lamented before allowing her head to fall into her hands. Rú walked over, knelt in front of her, and pulled her hands away from her weeping eyes.

"You didn't know, this is not your fault," he declared firmly. "They did this to hurt you and Arel."

Nalini nodded and wiped away the tears streaming down her face.

Evaine, tense, shot up from her chair. "I have to see if he's ok," quickly gathering her things. She and Rú locked eyes, he gave her a grave look.

"I'm going with you," Arel added standing quickly to follow her.

"Me too." Chimed Nalini's bracelets. All three turned at the same time to see her already standing.

"Do you know where he lives?" Arel asked, signing as he looked back at Evaine and glanced over at Rú waiting for either of them to answer his question.

"Yeah, the PR portal has all the rangers' contact info and addresses," Evaine said as she pulled her phone out and got to work pulling up the portal. She held her hand out to Arel, "I'll start the car." He dropped them in her hand and she disappeared out the front door leaving everyone to trail behind her.

"I'll meet you there," Rú said before disappearing. Nalini did a double take then looked at her brother and mouthed the words 'what the-'.

Arel shrugged. There was too much to talk about and he didn't even know where to start, he just landed on the words, "Let's go."

Evaine was waiting in the SUV with the engine running. "Where's Rú?" she called out the window.

"He went ahead," Arel said, hopping into the back as Nalini sat in the front seat. Evaine took off as soon as she heard the click of their seat belts. They sat in silence as Evaine weaved through the New York traffic, an air of dread hung over them as they wondered what they'd find when they got to Mal's apartment. Arel couldn't help but have questions, it was completely normal to feel concern for a colleague but he wondered about how Evaine knew the 'Mal' that delivered the package and the type of guy he was.

'Am I jealous?' Arel shook the question from his mind. It wasn't the time or the climate to have such thoughts, but it came to mind nonetheless.

Evaine was parking the SUV when he came back to reality and realized they were at their destination. It was an older building not far from his apartment building. Evaine was out of the car and up the stairs to the door before either he or Nalini closed their doors.

"Third floor!" she called over her shoulder holding up three fingers as she disappeared through the doors leaving them to run after her.

There was no lobby, no doorman, just a staircase flanked by two apartment doors. It was quiet, aside from the sound of Evaines' steps echoing off the walls as she ran up the stairs. The closer Arel got to the third floor the heavier he felt the hollow feeling of hopelessness. He did his best to keep up with Nalini who was a flight ahead of him already making her way through the third-floor door after Evaine.

The air was thick when he pulled open the door Nalini let close behind her, a scent in the air that he found to be out of place.

'A little early for a roast,' he thought as he looked at his phone, it was only 10 AM. He didn't think much of it, being a Sunday, lots of people gather with family.

Mal's apartment door was left partially open for him, the smell he noticed as he entered the third-floor hallway was stronger now but with the added scent of burnt hair. The door opened up to a living room with a small kitchen off to the right where Rú and Nalini stood, their eyes transfixed on the recliner facing away from the front door.

Nalini's hands were over her mouth and in her eyes was a look of horror. She turned and disappeared into the kitchen at the same time a sobbing Evaine emerged. He ran to her and wrapped his arms around as she buried her face in his chest. It was a second before he turned his attention to what they were all staring at.

Mal sat melded to the recliner where he rested, smoke still rising from his carcass. Arel cursed himself for the image of a perfectly baked turkey popping into his head. His eyes were drawn to Mal's shoes first, the plastic fused to the foot. The baked muscle of his thighs showed through crisp broken skin and was oozing liquid fat. It would seem in an attempt to cool himself down, he shed all items of clothing other than his boxers, now melted in place. Mal's agape mouth exposed a shriveled tongue and his dried lips pulled unnaturally from his teeth. They were curiously charred, the thin skin split and curled in different directions.

'*What could have done this?*' Arel thought, as he finally brought himself to look at Mal's bulging eyes, now lidless due to shrinkage as the skin dried out. His timing was regrettable as Mal's right eye exploded the moment it became Arel's focus. The jarring event was then followed by the subtle sound of fizzing as ocular fluid streamed down the skin of Mal's torrid face. Arel's stomach lurched and he willed his body not to projectile vomit all over the poor man's corpse. He turned to Rú and reiterated his question aloud, to try and take his mind off the gruesome scene in front of him.

"Rú, what did this?" he murmured, trying to keep his gag reflex in check.

Rú walked over to Mal's body, pulling a handkerchief from his jacket pocket and holding it over his nose as he knelt next to it. "A Shaitan did this, a type of Djinn," he said thoughtfully, placing his hand on top of Mal's.

"Djinn?" Evaine asked quietly.

"A being of smokeless fire. I haven't seen a possession like this in centuries. Djinn can't be in human bodies long or…" he trailed off and gestured to the body in the chair. "Shaitan are the only kind known to do something like this."

"I thought Djinn could shapeshift, why wouldn't it just take his place? Why do this?" Arel asked but had a feeling he already knew the answer.

"Shaitan can't shapeshift as well as others, there's always something off about their appearance. She wanted to do this to him," Rú answered, bluntly turning to look at Arel.

"She?" Arel interrupted.

"Yes, she, and you've crossed paths before."

Arel searched his memories and he found no recollection of a situation in which he was face to face with a Djinn. When he exhausted his options within his current lifetime a clear picture came to mind.

"The Djinn in the woods," Arel mumbled to himself. Rú pointed at him in confirmation.

"How? Why?" Arel asked frustrated, his eyes widened with concern.

"Djinn don't like to be challenged and they have a long memory, they live for thousands of years and when you took yourself to the island in that first dream it put you on everything's radar. A beacon," Rú said, to remind Arel of their first conversation and the type of soul he is.

Arel inhaled a deep breath. "Great," he exhaled. "So she's coming for blood."

"More like she wants to make you a carrier. She wants to poison your energy and slowly torture your soul. You're a healer, the energy you generate has a strong reach, to taint that is a big win." Rú's attention was drawn quickly to the front door. "Someone's coming."

"Can you tell who it is?" Nalini's bracelets chimed out from the back of the room.

"It's someone who knows him," Rú answered, looking from Nalini to Mal.

Evaine and Arel turned sharply as three knocks hit the door. As Rú started walking to the door, Evaine caught his arm and shook her head. He smiled weakly and whispered the words, "Trust me," before disappearing from the room altogether.

Rú reappeared in the hall behind Leona, now knocking frantically on the door.

"Leo Waite?" Rú asked softly, careful not to startle her. She was tense as it was.

"Yeah?" Her tone was defensive.

"You were on the island with Mal..."

"How did you know that?" she cut him off and stepped toward him, on edge now. He saw images of Mal as they ran through her mind and how she suspected something was wrong on the way back from North Brother. She was fighting her logical mind as she tried to push away the supernatural as a reason for Mal's behavior.

Rú's next words were telepathic. '*You were right, it was something from the Island.*'

Leona's eyes widened and she stepped back from him. He held up his hands to express he was not a threat.

"How do you know? Is he Alright? Who are you?" Her last question was a demand. Rú's face fell somber as he thought of the grim reality beyond the door they stood in front of.

"No, Leo, Mal didn't make it," he told her gently. She fought to keep her resolve.

"Who are you?" she demanded through clenched teeth.

"I'm sorry, we didn't get to him in time," Rú apologized. She walked up to him and stood close craning her neck up toward his face.

"Answer my question, who are you?" she enunciated each word in a way that insinuated she wasn't going to let anything slip by her and she would stand her ground if need be.

Leona was losing patience, her concern and sadness shifted to rage. She didn't like not knowing what she was dealing with, or people talking in circles. Rú knew he was never going to get her to walk away. She was invested from the moment she saw Mal walk out of the trees when she saw him and knew something wasn't right.

"This isn't going to be easy to face, Leo," he warned her.

"Cut the shit, you're going to tell me what's going on, now." Her tone was flat and her face cold, all emotion gone, she wanted the truth.

Rú didn't want a fight, so he opened the door and gestured to her to enter. Without hesitation, she walked through the threshold and stopped just past the doorway, hit hard by the smell of baked flesh and burned hair. Unlike the others, she was familiar with the smell. She looked around the apartment expecting to see charred walls and furniture. Surprised to find everything in working order and three other people standing in the room.

"Leona?" Evaine sniffled from the back of the room.

"Evaine? What are you-" Leona's voice trailed off as she walked far enough into the room to see Mal's smoking corpse. She stood frozen, her eyes unmoving and her expression blank as she tried to make sense of what she was looking at. Evaine could see she was fighting to hold her composure and quickly went to her, gently touching her arm, a subtle gesture to show she was with a friend and could take comfort in that. Leona didn't look at her right away, she couldn't bring herself to look away from Mal. She felt like doing so would be denying the pain he endured, it needed to be seen, he needed to be seen. She couldn't help but feel responsible.

"There's nothing you could have done," Rú said from behind her, snapping her out of the rabbit hole she was falling into.

Leona placed her hand over Evaine's and held it for a few seconds silently thanking her before releasing it and turning to Rú, wiping the tears from her eyes.

"What did this?" her voice was steady and urgent.

"A Djinn, they're-" Rú began.

"I know what they are," she snapped, it was unintentional and she looked at Rú with tired eyes. "Sorry, I spent a lot of time in the Middle East and Northern Africa, I've heard stories." Leona's eyes jumped over the word 'stories.' "Jesus, Malory," she whispered as she rubbed her forehead, shutting her eyes tight.

"I didn't know that was his full name till today," Evaine said quietly.

"Malory Dearil," Leona confirmed. Rú slid his hands into his pockets and shook his head, silently drawing Arel's attention. "What is it?"

"Names have power, a good name given at birth can benefit its owner but poor Mallory's worked against him. His name literally means 'unfortunate call of death.'"

"Could that be why it chose him?" Nalini's artificial voice rang out.

"Most likely, a cruel joke in her eyes," Rú answered thoughtfully.

Leona looked back at Nalini, she knew exactly who she was. A heat rose to her chest, her anger and sadness having found their target. As far as she was concerned, Nalini was the reason Mal was dead.

"This is your fault," Leona hissed, pointing at Nalini, she moved to advance on her but Rú was quick to intercept.

"If it wasn't her it would have been someone else and it would prove to be much worse. She's not responsible, a catalyst yes, but not the villain here. This is a chance to heal the pain trapped on North and South brother," he said calmly.

"How is that supposed to happen? I think this is beyond sprinkling holy water and sending thoughts and prayers! If this is what happened to him, what will happen to the boats of people heading to North Brother tomorrow?" Leona exploded, suddenly panicked by the time restrictions they were facing.

"Nothing will happen," Arel declared, stepping forward. "I'm going in tonight."

"Who the fuck are you? What are you going to do?" There was a condescending tinge to Leona's words as she looked him up and down.

"He's the best shot you've got at the moment. The islands need to be healed, he's a healer," Rú vouched, walking over to stand beside Arel.

"So you're a doctor, what's that going to do?" Leona challenged.

"Psychiatrist." Arel's specification did nothing to ease Leona's doubt, she did a double take in disbelief.

"Right, so you're going to water the grounds with antipsychotics and antidepressants?" She was just taking a piss now, afraid and they all knew it, no offense was taken. Even in the tense climate Rú couldn't help but smile not only at her jab, it was funny, but he knew Arel. He waited for Leona to look back at him to flash his orange eyes.

"It's a little deeper than that, trust me," he said flatly. Leona didn't know how to react in the moment and stared at Rú with wide cautious eyes, debating to herself if she imagined what she just saw.

To answer that question he closed his eyes and opened them slowly to reveal his fiery orange eyes again this time allowing them to remain. Leona continued to stare into Rú's eyes thinking of all the questions she was afraid to ask out loud, and he was about to answer her when she decided maybe it was best not to know. She was exhausted and had already had so much of the world she knew turned upside down, it was enough for now.

"Fine," she conceded, walking away from him to stand on the far side of the room. "What's your plan?" she asked, looking around the room meeting all of their eyes and ending on Rú's.

"I go in tonight and do what I can, with what I've learned these last few days that will weaken whatever entities or malicious spirits that have found their way there. Heal what I can." Arel knew he was oversimplifying, he didn't know what exactly to expect but there was no room for doubt.

"Wait, are you serious? Just you? I thought you were speaking for everyone?! Alone? Why can't you go with him? You're, like, magic or something right?" Leona urged, taken aback that Rú would let him go alone.

"He's a dragon," Arel said, leaving Leona without words to respond.

"Yeah, did I miss the explanation of why he has to do this alone?" Evaine interjected, looking from Arel to Rú as if this was a secret they were attempting to keep to themselves.

"Anyone else there would be a liability and it would be too easy to use us against each other, she'd prey on any doubt or fear that would arise," Arel explained to Evaine with pleading eyes.

Evaine then looked to Rú "Then why can't you be there with him?" she asked him angrily, to which Arel stepped into her line of sight so she could hear the answer from him.

"The islands have been steeped in dark energy so long that beings of light energy, like Rú, can't reside within dark energy only alongside it. Human beings are the only creatures that exist as both light and dark energy with the freedom to travel back and forth. This is the result of human energy and has to be healed by human energy." Arel took

Evaines hands in his and stared down at their interlaced fingers. "I can do this," He assured her, kissing her hands before releasing them.

She exhaled a long breath and nodded reluctantly.

"Ok, let's do this. It's afternoon already. I have something to do alone. I'll meet you guys back at Leila's, to see how Eugene is doing and regroup."

"What's wrong with Eugene?" Nalini's bracelets chimed, the sound in stark contrast to the panic in her eyes. "What happened?" she asked, looking from Rú to Arel.

"He was attacked but he's going to be ok," Arel assured her. "Rú will take you to see him."

Rú nodded from behind him and she immediately started toward the door.

"What should we do for Mal?" Evaine asked, looking over at Mal's desecrated body.

"I'll take care of him, call it in," Leona offered, as she walked over to stand next to him. Evaine walked over and hugged her and Leona welcomed the comfort.

"Is it ok if I call you later?" Evaine asked her. Leo nodded and smiled weakly in agreement.

"Thank you, Leo," Arel said, walking past her.

"Just finish it." Leona's response was cold, not how she intended, but there was no warmth left in her.

"I will."

Chapter Eighteen

MOTHER KNOWS BEST

Arel stood on the stairs of his parents' stoup and thought about all the things he wanted to say to them. He'd been standing there for a good five minutes when the front door opened to reveal his father with a large smile. The same smile plastered to the back of his book currently lying in the same spot Arel tossed it the night he had his dream, waiting to be finished.

"What are you doing just standing out there, Beta?" his father said, waving him inside. "Ayra! Your son is here!" he called over his shoulder. Arel stopped a step from the top, bent over, and touched the tips of his fingers to his father's feet. His father laid his hands on his head then lifted him by the shoulders and wrapped him in a bear hug. "You don't come home enough, Beta," he said before planting a kiss on his cheek causing them to break into a laugh.

"Let him in, Vida," Ayra demanded playfully as she walked down the hallway. Bahuvida released his son and looked around Arel's legs and down the stairs.

"Where's Harrison?" he asked curiously. Arel froze for a moment trying to think of a mundane reason why his partner in crime wouldn't be by his side, it was harder to think of than he thought.

"He's with Eugene. He wasn't feeling well, Eugene, not Harrison. He just wouldn't leave him," Arel shrugged, it wasn't a lie.

"Nalini told us what happened," Ayra said, finally in front of Arel. "Enta wahashtini," she crooned as she reached up to Arel's face and pulled it down so she could kiss both cheeks. She held it in front of hers and stared at him with her big green eyes and smiled. "My beautiful boy," she gushed as she brushed his hair away from his face.

"Hi, Mom," he smiled, it didn't matter what mood he was in, when he was around her it was like trouble couldn't touch him. He always thought that if there ever existed a physical embodiment of an angelic being, she was it.

Ayra's smile widened, "Come, I made Ta'ameya." She said pulling him through the door before disappearing down the hall to the kitchen in the back of the house.

"It's past noon," Arel jabbed, closing the front door behind him.

"So?" Bahuvida shot back, throwing his hand up in dismissal as Arel followed behind them. He never appreciated how free his parents were and felt guilty not seeing it before, not seeing them. They reached the kitchen and his mother went to work.

"Grab a plate, Bebah," Ayra instructed, as she quickly put together his Ta'ameya "So what brings you home? Have you seen your sister?"

Arel set his plate down in front of him. "Yeah, I just saw her actually."

"Oh good, how is she? Is she taking the break up ok? When we saw her, she was starting a big project, I hope that's keeping her mind off things," Ayra finished, as she set the food on his plate.

"Yeah, it's, uh, gonna be challenging," Arel said, stumbling to find the right words for the present situation.

"Oh, and Eugene, we love him. When you pick up Harrison please give him our love. That poor boy, he's been crazy about your sister since grade school," Ayra went on.

"Ayra, he doesn't want to talk about his sister's breakup," Bahuvida nagged playfully. "He wants to tell me what he thought of the book." He nudged Arel lightly and winked at Ayra.

Arel's first bite went down the wrong way and he began to cough while trying to think up excuses as to why he hadn't finished his father's book but ultimately came up with nothing, he'd feel guilty lying anyway.

"I'm sorry, things have been crazy with work. I haven't had a chance to finish it," he admitted, looking at his father with apologetic eyes.

"That's ok, Beta, that just means you have to come back again soon," Bahuvida said with his large unrelenting smile. It hit Arel, how fast time goes and how little time he spent with them. He smiled weakly and stared down at his Ta'ameya.

"What's wrong, Bebah?" Ayra asked, her tone taking a serious turn. She searched his face hoping to find the answer to the sadness in his eyes.

He didn't know where to start. He didn't want to scare them with the truth and weigh them down with worry. It would only lower their vibration and put them in danger.

"Is everything ok at work?" Ayra pressed, determined to get a real answer and Arel knew she wouldn't give up, it would continue to bother her. He'd have to give her something.

"I have a new patient, I'm worried their problems are beyond me, that they'll overtake me," he responded, trying to be as vague as possible. As much as he wanted to believe wholeheartedly that he could face whatever was on that island, he couldn't look at his mother and lie. He became a little boy again.

"Is there another doctor you can refer them to?" Bahuvida asked as he shoveled a hummus-covered cucumber into his mouth.

Arel shook his head. "I'm their last shot," he said, looking into his glass of water like he was going to find his strength there.

Ayra leaned over the counter and ran her fingers down his cheek. "Arel, when you were about a year old I was visiting your Dad for lunch at his office. There was this professor he kind of shared an office with. Do you remember this?" she asked, looking over at Bahuvida.

"Ah, Tristan Valdis, I remember this," he confirmed while scooping more food on his plate.

"Yes, anyway," she continued, "He was a miserable man, walking by him was like walking over someone's grave. There was nothing to make that man smile and he made everyone around him miserable, except your father," she said, glancing at him with a smile. So I take you and Nalini to have lunch with him and I forget what it was but Lin started having a meltdown and I had to set you down. In my mind it was seconds but I looked down and you were gone. I frantically searched the room and then I looked through the door of the other office and there you were. You were in this man's arms laughing and touching his face. At first, he looked at you like you were green and had three heads. I quickly got up to get you but I was shocked to see him begin to smile and laugh as you laughed. When I walked into his office to apologize, it was the first time that man did more than grunt in my direction. He even offered to watch you while we ate lunch. It was then I knew I chose your name well. You have a way of leading people out of their darkness to bring out their light and you've never needed a medical degree to do it." She cupped his chin in her hand and squeezed it tight.

"You can face anything, my Arel," she assured him in a tone that left no room for objection or debate.

Her story worked and he began to feel lighter than he has since this all began.

Arel took a deep breath, "Thanks, Mom," he exhaled, offering her a grateful smile. She walked around the island and wrapped him in a hug to which his father couldn't help but join in, causing them all to break into laughter and release their hold on each other.

"Ok, eat your food," Ayra instructed as she walked back to the other side of the island to stand across from him. "How long do we have you with us today?"

CHAPTER NINETEEN

FAMILY

Nalini stared up at the Wine and Tonics sign as she and Evaine waited for Rú to unlock the door from inside. Neither of them bothered to contact Leila to let them in. Nalini liked this new Harrison, his ability to communicate telepathically meant there was no reason to wear her caption contacts, but she had them with her just in case. He worked as a type of antenna for her, picking up all communication around her and feeding it to her mentally with the option of responding or not. She knew the moment he had the door unlocked and where Eugene was. As soon as the door was wide enough she was through it and on her way to the back of the store, leaving Evaine and Rú to follow her. She was practically jogging when she reached the door to the basement. She flew down the steps but stopped abruptly when she saw Dylan lying on the floor along the couch where Eugene was. Eugene's arm was hanging off the side, his fingers interlaced with Dylan's hand resting on his chest. It seemed like they were both sleeping but only Dylan woke up from the noise of her clamoring down the stairs. She walked the rest of the way down the stairs, her eyes on their intertwined hands until Dylan released his grip and positioned Eugene's arm to rest across his torso. Dylan then offered her a tired smile and he worked to smooth the wrinkles in his t-shirt, she returned his greeting. He couldn't tell if the look on her face was sadness, confusion, or both.

"I should introduce myself properly, I'm Dylan, I work for your brother," he signed slowly.

"Is that how you know Eugene?" Nalini asked, looking from him to Eugene. She felt Dylan's energy drop off, something she noticed happens when there's something someone doesn't want to talk about. He was doing a good job of hiding it behind his welcoming smile.

"Yes," he answered overenthusiastically. She could feel his unease rolling off of him, his fear, his love. She wasn't paying attention when they first met at the office but it was there too. An undeniable connection, an invisible cord between them. She felt a pang in her stomach, it was a bittersweet feeling. Although they weren't together anymore, she loved Eugene but was glad to know there was someone to love him like he deserved.

Nalini gave him a smile, "Have you been with him the whole time?"

Dylan nervously raked his fingers over the top of his head and nodded before he looked back at the unconscious Eugene. Nalini slid past him and knelt next to Eugene's head, she couldn't help herself from running her fingers down his face.

'*It's like he's only sleeping,*' she thought, brushing her hand over his mahogany hair.

She looked back at Dylan and signed her thanks.

"We think what Leila did worked, he's got more color now and is a lot warmer than he was." Dylan moved quickly through his statement, and Nalini was impressed more than before. If Eugene felt the same way about Dylan then she could understand it, he had an infectious airiness.

"It looks like he's only sleeping, doesn't it?" Dylan asked, before returning his gaze to Eugene.

Nalini was slightly surprised to see him express the same thing she had been thinking not a moment ago, she nodded in agreement.

She turned her attention to Rú now standing next to Dylan.

'*What happened?*' she thought and signed the rest. "You never told me."

Rú replayed for her all that he witnessed, faster than if he were to sign it and made it as if she were there for it all. Her eyes opened wide with fear as she saw the creature that attacked Eugene then turned back to look at Rú in disbelief.

"A child did this?" Nalini asked in disbelief.

'*It wasn't a child.*' This answer didn't come from Rú, it came from across the room and the way the answer came to her was different. It wasn't impressions, feelings, or pictures. The information just appeared in her mind, like words on a screen.

Leila walked out of her wine room with a bottle in one hand and a small jar full of tan powder in the other.

Nalini watched her in wonder. '*How?*' she thought as she made her way over to the kitchen island where Leila set her wine bottle and jar.

'*That's not important, Lin.*' Leila answered in thought as she turned around to grab a glass pitcher from one of the cabinets.

"Rú walked into Nalini's line of sight, "What did she say?" He spoke verbally even though there wasn't a need.

Nalini looked at him with wide eyes, '*I can understand her in my mind but the way she communicates is different from yours.*' she thought to him. "I can't explain it," she signed as she moved around him to take a seat at the island.

'*Has this ever happened before?*' he asked, his eyes darted back and forth as he turned the information around in his mind.

"Forgiveness, it's good for the mind, body, and soul," Leila remarked aloud, her voice monotone. Her mind was far away, focused on measuring out the right amount of the tan powder she pulled from the back room.

"Wait, What's happening right now?" Dylan interjected, leaving Eugene's side to join the rest standing around the kitchen island. All except Evaine, she decided to hang back and stay on the couch and listen.

"Healing and forgiveness raise your vibration and sometimes that healing unlocks channels within the consciousness, Nalini seemed to open a pathway in her mind that allows information to travel through certain frequencies," Rú explained, he stared at Nalini but it was as if he was looking through her like he was working out a fascinating new puzzle.

"So she can READ MINDS NOW?" Dylan exclaimed, lifting his arms and miming his head exploding.

"No, she'll be able to understand me and Rú because we're intentionally sending her information. For others, it'd take practice. It's easier if people are on a similar frequency. It's something she can work on strengthening if that's what she wishes," Leila said, finally looking away from her preparations to focus her gaze past the group to Evaine on the couch toward the back of the room. Evaine looked up to meet Leila's eyes like she called out her name.

"No," Evaine said, though her response was quiet, it caught the attention of Dylan and Rú standing around the island. Dylan turned a curious gaze to Evaine as Rú looked from Evaine to Leila.

"You can't force her forgiveness," Rú stated firmly, growing impatient with Leila.

"I'm not forcing anything, she can hold on to whatever she wants for as long as she wants." There was a taunting amusement in Leila's voice that made Evaines' skin crawl. She saw the corner of Leila's mouth lift into a smirk and saw red.

"YOU TRAPPED ME IN A FUCKING JAR!" Evaine exploded off the couch. "FOR HOW LONG?" she screamed with tears of rage in her eyes.

"As long as you needed to be," Leila said calmly, as Evaine flew past the others and grabbed her by the throat. Dylan moved to intervene but was stopped by Rú.

"You're seriously not going to stop this?" Dylan scolded.

"Leila doesn't need to be saved and I saw what she did," Rú replied, unconcerned on Leila's behalf, but if the situation turned against Evaine he was ready to defend her. He had a feeling Leila wasn't going to do anything to hurt Evaine.

"I LOST THE ONLY FAMILY I HAD LEFT!" Evaine growled as she grabbed Leila around the throat and shoved her hard against the counter.

"I gave you a family," Leila cooed, reaching up to touch Evaine's cheek. Rú could feel Evaine about to lose it, the tears that pooled in her eyes began to stream down her cheeks. Leila's answer threw her off, and Evaine loosened the grip around her neck.

"What are you talking about?" she asked through clenched teeth.

"Look around you and remember, you know them. Their faces have changed but they remain the same," Leila said softly, lifting her hands to wrap them around the hand that still gripped her neck. "They needed you then like they need you now."

"That's not what I meant, I was all she had. You not only kept me from my family, you took hers! SHE DIED ALONE!" Evaine screamed, her face inches from Leila's.

"She didn't die alone," Dylan said, suddenly next to her. In her rage toward Leila, she didn't notice his approach. He placed his hand gently on her arm, a silent plea for her to release Leila from her grip.

"What?" she snapped as she turned to look at him, keeping a firm grip on Leila.

"She wasn't alone, she had me...and my father." Dylan's voice weakened with guilt at the mention of him and his father.

Evaine looked from Dylan to Leila with shock and confusion, released Leila, and stepped back.

Her eyes bore into Leila's, demanding an answer.

"After I put you in the jar I sent a man with the remedies your mother needed and more, that man never came back," Leila said looking to Dylan.

"That man was my father, if she hadn't sent him I would have never been born," Dylan said, before turning back to look at Eugene.

"You knew? How long?" Rú cut in as he got up from his stool and walked around the island to stand on the other side of Evaine so that he could speak to Dylan face to face, disappointed in himself that hadn't picked up on the subtle changes in Dylan's energy.

"Since the morning Eugene freaked out about me speaking Tibetan," Dylan answered cautiously. "I've been getting flashes of visions and more information has been bleeding into my dreams."

"Tibetan?" Nalini's bracelets chimed before sitting back down at the island. During the commotion, she had slipped away to put her caption contacts in as she was only getting bits of what was happening. Rú had been too preoccupied to relay what everyone was saying.

"Eugene taught me in that life, once I learned it was the only language we spoke to each other?" Dylan signed, smiling as he recalled the memories.

"Why didn't you say anything?" Rú asked Dylan, then looking quickly to Nalini and signing his apology for not keeping her in the loop before returning his attention to Dylan.

"The first things I saw and felt were a lot to process and I wasn't up for an audience," Dylan answered, shrugging unapologetically.

"That's fair." Rú could understand his apprehension about coming forward, there was a lot of information that he'd need time to integrate and understand about his past life dynamics.

"Never seemed to be a right time, there were more important things to worry about," Dylan added.

"This is affecting all of us, so what's happening to you is important," Rú expressed, as he gestured to Nalini, Evaine, and Leila then shot a look from him to Eugene.

Dylan's eyes grew wide, he knew Rú was aware of his feelings for Eugene. The first emotion to rise was fear and then came a sense of peace, he realized this was not new information to him.

"You've been waiting for this to play out?" Dylan asked, releasing the tension in his shoulders.

"Like a RomCom plot," Rú joked as Dylan rolled his eyes. The only one that didn't catch on to what was happening was Evaine. She looked between Dylan and Rú, at a loss for what this situation had become in the span of a couple of minutes.

"What's happening right now?" Evaine's words were tense, she was angry and confused as to where that anger needed to be directed. "It's a pretty picture now but that doesn't change the fact that you took time from me, him! Time he couldn't get back!"

"Not in that life, but now you have this one," Leila responded softly. "You've connected through lifetimes long before me and will continue to do so until you've learned all you can from the lessons while on this planet. It was a moment, a painful one yes, but it has passed."

Evaine stood quiet, there was a storm still raging in her heart, she wanted destruction but she also knew that it wasn't the time. The acceptance of it all was physically painful. It happened in the past, but the resurfacing of these memories has brought it to the present. It was far from removed, it was as if it just happened all over again. Seeing the bigger picture felt arduous and she hated being in the dark especially now. She looked over at Dylan and stared at him for a bit, trying to find a memory that would put some pieces together but the rage she felt for Leila kept her mind in a fog. As she looked into his eyes she felt the angry storm begin to calm.

"Brother, huh?" Evaine remarked flatly, conceding her fight for now.

"Sister, actually," Dylan corrected lightly. "I was hoping I'd get to talk to you at some point about it. I have these flashes of memories of us talking and laughing, I've wanted to get to know you more but with everything..." His thought trailed off as he looked at her with wide pleading eyes and an expression that hoped she'd want the same.

Evaine nodded and gave Dylan a weary smile, sighing as she pushed herself off the counter she was leaning against. She shot another look at Leila that would have struck fear in anyone on the receiving end of it. It was murderous, on the edge of monstrous as she stepped closer to Leila and leaned in so her face was again inches from hers.

"We'll pick this up another time," Evaine whispered.

Leila gave her no response and simply nodded slightly. Evaine turned away from Leila and followed Dylan to the couch to start their journey into their past relationship as siblings. Rú released a sigh of relief. Looking into Evaine's mind was so cluttered with pain and different scenarios and plans of attack. What she could use to slit

Leila's throat, wondering if she could do it before Rú could stop her. In her mind, he saw her breaking the wine glass right behind her and shoving the stem through Leila's neck, visualizing it over and over. Walking away was at the back of her mind and he was glad she took the high road, at least for now.

Everyone turned at the sound of footsteps barreling down the stairs and Nalini followed suit, It was Arel. He was wearing a confident smile.

"Alright, Le-" He stopped mid-sentence as he was hit with the heavy tension that remained in the air. "What happened?"

Chapter Twenty

Human Magic

Arel got the play-by-play courtesy of Nalini, signing her rendition of everything that had taken place. No one else had it in them to rehash what had just gone down. Although nothing about the sequence of events was comical, Nalini's enthusiasm made it so. As serious as all this was, it was difficult for him not to enjoy seeing his sister animated and willing to contribute. It may not have been new to others but it was to him, he was seeing a new side of her. He was grateful, but as he looked over at Evaine he saw a completely different reality. Just looking at her was sobering. He excused himself and walked over to the couch where she sat looking at her phone. As he sat down he noticed she had her mother's contact information up.

She looked at him and gave him a smile that read of relief. He pulled one hand away and kissed it.

"I'm sorry," he said simply. "I'm sorry that the memories that were so painful for him are the ones you're reliving now."

"I'm not thinking about it," Evaine said, as she looked down at her phone and hit the power button, turning the screen black. "I still have my Mom here, but I was thinking about something else. There's something good that I remember."

"Yeah?" a hopeful smile spread across his face. "What's that?"

"You. You were the first person I saw." she turned her body so they were sitting face to face and stared into the warm dark eyes she saw in her vision. "They're exactly the same and when you look at me it feels the same."

"Like coming home," he said, finishing her thought.

"Do you remember it?" her voice rose with excitement.

"Uh, no, the memory hasn't come back to me yet. It's just what it felt like when I saw you for the first time, but I remember what you looked like. I had this weird break in reality when I first saw you at the permit office. You were, like, this super tall buff Viking. You kind of reminded me of that one actor, the one that played King Arthur a while back."

"I know exactly who you're talking about and, yes, I agree!" she exclaimed. Arel was glad to hear the enthusiasm in her voice and a smile on her face as she laughed. "It's crazy remembering being him." She released his hand and leaned forward, resting her elbows on her knees. She stared blankly ahead, returning to her memories.

"I remember being so glad you were the first thing I saw. He, I, thought you were so beautiful."

Arel intended to make a joke feigning offense to her use of past tense, instead, she triggered a memory. A glimpse back to that life. Arel was struck by a vision of that exact moment. He saw himself as Kirana covering the man he knew to be Evaine. The moment Kirana brushed the hair from his face, he felt the same flutter she did as she looked into his eyes. The feeling had caught her off guard, it was unfamiliar, the draw to this man and not knowing why. First, Kirana's mind swam with confusion, her mind working to rationalize the feeling. When there was no answer, she allowed herself to surrender to its warmth, to the same feeling he felt looking at Evaine, like coming home.

Not a second had gone by and he had received, what felt like, a world of emotion falling over him. Information and a thought process that didn't belong to him. It was the first time he'd taken notice of the difference between him and Kirana.

Evaine noticed his expression blank, "Where y'at?" she asked, running her fingernails over his back.

"I think I just saw what you did, you triggered the memory," he said, as a smile formed over his face. "It's strange, the apprehension when Kirana looked at you. It threw her," he said with a laugh.

"I don't blame her, I was so fine," she joked. "Even as a gooey mess previously inhabiting a jar." Evaine's light-hearted energy quickly shifted as she looked back up to see Leila working on what she assumed was a potion or spell.

Her face fell back into a murderous glare. Arel followed her line of sight and put his arm around her shoulder. "Whenever you want to talk about it, I'm here," he assured her.

"Sure thing, Doc." Her words dripped with sarcasm. Arel knew not to get defensive, this wasn't something she was going to talk about or want to forgive right away. She was reliving a trauma, one he guessed, she was never able to heal from in that lifetime.

Looking at Leila was sobering for him as well. The weight she held for him was not one of the past, it was his present, his near future. Looking at her was a reminder of what he had to face. He pulled his phone out of his pocket, blinking twice when he saw the time. It was half past six already, and the plan was to finish this tonight and head over to the dock after the sun started setting. His thoughts started to speed up, his day had gone by so fast. There was so much more he wanted to do.

"Rel!" Rú called from across the room and waved him over to where he stood next to Leila at the kitchen island.

"Actually, all of you stand to benefit from this," Leila added, turning around to grab more glasses from the cabinet.

They all made their way over and found their place around the marble island, Evaine was the last to join. Leila had prepared a pitcher and was pouring its contents into glasses, being meticulous as to how much each received.

"What's this now?" Dylan asked, watching Leila gently place a glass in front of everyone.

Nalini picked up her glass and inhaled deeply. *'Sauvignon Blanc...'*

"With Angelica root and Mullein flower," Leila said, answering Nalini's thoughts out loud for all to hear. Leila smiled at her like as if a proud teacher to a student.

To everyone else not privy to the information floating through the mental airwaves, they were left looking from Leila to Nalini with blank expressions.

"For the rest of us?" Dylan droned, his lack of sleep catching up to his mood.

"Lin simply called the type of grape, she was correct," Leila answered.

"There's more than one type of white wine? Why do they all taste like battery acid then?" Dylan asked flatly. Leila looked at him like he just slapped her across the face as Arel and Evaine choked back their laughter. Evaine more so than Arel, enjoyed seeing Leila visibly bothered.

Dylan grimaced, lifted his glass to his nose, and inhaled like he saw Nalini do, he recoiled violently.

"I'm the only one going to the island, do they really need it?" Arel asked, regretting it right away.

"You may be the only one going to the island but we're not just going to wait here, we're going to be waiting on the dock until you get back," Evaine proclaimed for herself and everyone else.

"I'm actually good with hanging back," Dylan chirped, glancing back at Eugene.

"We kinda figured that Dyl," Rú cut in.

"Cool," Dylan said, looking over at Arel.

"You're good, buddy. I didn't want Gene left alone anyway," Arel reassured Dylan.

"Well that's cleared up, so how is this working?" Arel asked. Lifting his glass and taking a whiff himself. As he swirled the wine around the glass he picked up its floral and earthy notes. As far as potions go, this wasn't one he was going to complain about.

Dylan began to walk away from the table. "Oh no, Dylan we're still gonna need you for this," Leila said quickly. He stopped in his tracks and returned to his place around the island.

"As you saw with Eugene it doesn't take much to activate magic, it takes intention and attunement to the energy you're trying to extract." Leila grabbed her glass and began walking around the island as she spoke. "In your glasses is my 2020 Sauvignon Blanc; its components vibrate in the light of companionship, love, and peace. A base to strengthen the Angelica root, a powerful guardian and healer to strengthen courage. And last but not least, the Mullein flower to center the spirit, for clarity and to limit negative thought patterns." She stopped next to Rú. "We won't be needing you, darling."

"Why did you pour me a glass then?" Rú asked, he picked up his glass and looked at it suspiciously. Wondering if she added something to his when he wasn't looking.

"I was being polite, it won't do anything for you but it's still damn good." She raised her glass and gazed at it proudly for a moment. "And I don't believe in exclusion," she said pulling herself back to the task at hand.

Rú stared down at his glass as if he were analyzing its contents. He glanced up to see Arel watching him, his eyes wide with caution. They kept eye contact as Rú lifted the glass to his lips and took a sip. If anything, it would have been a warning to the rest if something were to happen.

They all waited with bated breath for some response from Rú.

He pursed his lips as he let it sit on his tongue and then smacked his lips. "Not bad Leila, Dylan you're still gonna hate it."

"You don't happen to make whiskey do you?" Dylan whined.

"Thank you," Leila said as she nodded her head toward Rú, "Dylan darling, it's on my list. Let's get back to it, we're losing time," she said, taking her place again in the circle around the Island once more. Rú stepped back pulling a stool with him to sit down and enjoy the rest of his wine.

"So why can't we use him for this? He's actual magic, wouldn't he strengthen the magic you're using?" Arel questioned, gesturing to Rú.

"Because his magic is cosmic, we need magic of this realm, human magic." Leila breathed, as she worked to center herself, holding her hands out. "Take hands, close your eyes, and focus on the glass in front of each of you. Clear your mind and focus on the attributes we're activating, search your memories for those feelings. Feelings build your reality. They can be your greatest strength or your greatest weakness, focus on your strength. Sit in those memories, you'll know you've chosen the right memories when you feel the energy begin to build in your chest. Love is light energy, it does not weaken or wane, it is a constant source of energy to be called upon." Although her eyes were closed, she was fully aware of everyone on their journey to find their memories. She felt the energy building in each of them, flowing between them and strengthening each other. Gently, Rú got up quietly to walk around the group.

"Release each other's hands, now," Leila instructed calmly, her voice low and smooth, it kept them all in a trance-like state. The outside world didn't exist, the only thing filtering into each of their inner worlds was the sound of Leila's voice.

"Once you feel this energy begin to build, pick up your glass and hold it with both hands. Visualize the energy in your chest flowing down through your arms, into your hands, and into your glass. Now see the particles fuse with the light energy."

Dylan was the first to pick up his glass, then Nalini, Evaine, and finally Arel.

"How do we know if it's doing anything?" Dylan asked, he sounded half asleep.

"It is," Rú answered. "It's subtle but the atoms making up the wine are moving faster," he said, staring intently at Nalini's glass as he took another sip of his own.

A low hum came about the room as if someone struck a low chord, all of them working together, a harmony. Leila lifted her arms like a conductor to an orchestra and waited a moment longer.

"Now, all of you open your eyes and drink from your glasses."

They followed her instructions in unison. Nalini, taken by the mixture of its floral and fruity notes, was the first to finish her glass. Arel watched her through the corner of his eyes as she guzzled down the contents of her glass.

"Don't judge me, it's been a long day," she signed, as soon as she put down her glass.

"Not judging," he signed, his mouth still full of wine.

Dylan had a hard time finishing his glass, he cringed with every mouth full and gagged periodically. None of them were sure if he was faking or if he was actually in danger of losing the contents of his stomach.

"Do I have to finish it?" Dylan struggled to ask. Nalini shot her hand in the air, an offer to finish his glass.

"Yes, all of it," Leila answered, grabbing Nalini's empty glass to serve her another glass of the Sauvignon Blanc. Nalini's smile stretched ear to ear.

"BLECH!" Dylan exclaimed, as he finished the last of his wine he turned on his heels and fell into a full body shake. "Now what?"

"That's all I've got for you, the rest is up to you?" Leila said, looking over to Arel. He looked at his watch, it was now quarter to 8 PM. The sun was setting and Arel's heart began to beat faster.

"No I mean, what exactly did this do?" Dylan specified, a bit more snappy than he intended.

"Reinforce your natural defenses to spiritual attack and enhance the energetic bonds that exist between you. Your connection is a barrier and a source of strength any of you can draw from even when you're not together. Set it and forget it," Leila said, lifting her hands and flicking her palms out to indicate it was finished.

"How long do we have before the defense wears off?" Evaine asked, there were scattered looks of disbelief in response to the calm tone of her voice.

"It doesn't, it was built by your collective energy. It is now a part of the energetic bond that exists between you. It will never cease to be, it will remain as a source to be called upon."

"Yeah, but what happens if sometime down the line we're no longer together or..." Dylan's voice trailed off, he was intentionally stopping himself from looking in Arel's direction. "...if one of us dies."

"Energetic bonds are not so easily broken, you forget you've followed each other through lifetimes. If a death were to occur it'd only be a layover until you'd meet again. Nonetheless, the connection would remain."

"It doesn't go away, the law of conservation," Dylan said thoughtfully.

"Exactly," she agreed brightly.

Arel sucked in a deep breath and stood from his seat. "We better get going." He turned to Dylan and pulled him into a hug. "I'll see you guys when I get back." Arel tried his best to keep his voice as normal as possible, the same way he said goodbye every day. "If Gene wakes up before I get back, tell him he's a bitch for fainting," he joked, his attempt to lighten the mood worked as Dylan began to laugh as he released him.

Rú and Nalini were already on their way up the stairs but Evaine hung back to wait on the landing.

Arel looked back at Leila and nodded.

"They'll be fine here," she said, to calm his worrying mind of another attack happening while he was away.

"Thank you, Leila."

Leila bowed her head, turned, and made her way to the side of the couch opposite Eugene.

"I'll see you later, bud," he whispered, as he squeezed Eugene's shoulder. He turned around quickly before he let the idea of not seeing his best friend again cloud his mind. He found relief in Evaine, waiting for him with a warm smile.

As he followed Evaine up the stairs he heard Dylan, "Please tell me you have something other than wine, I'm not waiting this out sober."

Arel couldn't keep the smile from stretching across his face.

CHAPTER TWENTY-ONE

NORTH BROTHER

TW:BM, S

They were going to be in the car together for quite some time, geographically the docks weren't too far away but with city traffic, they were looking at a half-hour ride. There was an awkward energy floating around the SUV's cabin, no one knew what to say or if they should say anything at all. Arel didn't feel like talking but he also didn't want to be in his head either.

"Rú, can you put on some music?" he asked, breaking the silence to everyone's relief. The radio wasn't ideal, he hated the commercials but he didn't feel like going through the process of syncing his phone to the SUV's Bluetooth. And this way no one could complain about his choice of music.

Rú hit the power button and surprise, surprise, it was on a commercial break. The entire car, aside from Nalini, was hit with a wave of annoyance. It wasn't long before the music began to play, the first song off the break was a song Arel hadn't heard in over a decade.

His freshman homecoming dance flashed through his mind. It was a popular song at the time with him and his friends, the perfect anti-party song he bribed the DJ to play. It ended up being a huge hit that night, the memory made him smile. The chorus hit and he heard Evaine singing the words quietly as she looked out the window and he wondered if she even realized she was doing it. He watched her for a few seconds, recording the sound of her voice in his mind as she sang but he couldn't stop himself from joining in. The words were perfect at this moment, contradictory to the dancy beat that compelled them to move.

They began to sing the lyrics to each other, their own over-the-top version of carpool karaoke. Watching them through the rearview mirror, Rú turned the music up higher and adjusted the bass to make it more prominent, catching Nalini's attention to the commotion happening in the back seat. Nalini joined in dancing as she could now feel the beat through the surround sound. As long as the song played none of them thought of what was coming, what Arel would have to face and it didn't matter. At that moment, it was just them living in that song, together, and it was perfect.

Arel couldn't believe their luck, every song after that was one he and Evaine knew well and could sing to. He chalked it up as a gift from the universe as a type of pump-up playlist of all the songs he loved when he was younger. By the time they arrived at the docks, they were in various fits of laughter that died out as soon as Rú put the SUV in park and reality set in again. Nalini and Evaine turned to look at Arel, both of their gazes saying more than words would be able to capture in the time they had. A mixture of hope, love, and concern lingered in the air. He gave each of them the most confident smile he could muster, surprised by how calm he was. He was truly beginning to feel like he wasn't going into this alone and as soon as that feeling came over him, his mind chimed in with the question, '*You feel this way now, but will you still when you're standing alone on that island?*'

Arel knew that was going to be his biggest challenge, keeping his thoughts in check through all of this. Arel shook his head slightly, symbolically shaking off the idea offered by the survival portion of his brain. Nalini, still in the front seat, adjusted her turn as held his hands out to both her and Evaine to take, he looked from one to the other and smiled. He didn't need to verbalize his message, it was loud as he looked into their eyes. Nalini nodded with tears pooling at her lashes but Evaine simply nodded and offered a guarded smile. She wanted to be strong and he knew she didn't want him to see her worry. Arel kissed Nalini's hand and released it to cup Evaine's cheek in his hand. She leaned into it and closed her eyes as he traced his thumb along her cheekbone. Arel let his hand fall away when she opened her eyes again and nodded, it was time for him to take his leave.

Rú was already out of the SUV waiting for him at the foot of the dock. Arel was surprised as he opened the door to see Rú talking to Leona. She saw his curious expression and waved slightly.

"Leona, hi. What are you doing here?" he asked as he closed the distance between them.

"After doing what I could for Mal, I couldn't just sit at home. You guys mentioned you were going over tonight and I took a guess that you'd be leaving from here. I was responsible for Mal while he was there and I don't want to keep doing things to help only after the fact, I want to do something now, in any way I can," she said, looking at the boat at the end of the dock, dangling the keys she had in her hand.

Rú smiled at her, he admired her willingness to be on the front lines for no other reason than to keep others out of harm's way.

"Thank you, Leo, but since I'm going to be dropping Arel on the island, I'd ask you to hang back on the docks with Nalini and Evaine while I keep an eye from the sky. I don't know what's in the water and I don't know what Arel being on the island might trigger. I'd feel more comfortable if the three of you kept an eye on things down here."

Leona reluctantly nodded, she was used to being in the thick of a mission but she understood that she didn't know exactly what they were facing, and being unprepared could easily make her a liability. At the same time, she felt she was there for a reason, everything that had happened leading up until now, everywhere she had been stationed overseas, the people she'd met, the jobs at the parks department, it all led her to be here now. As terrifying as this all was, she wasn't going to walk away.

"Okay, we'll hold things down on the ground from here then. What about him? What's his contingency?" she asked, nodding toward Arel.

Rú crossed his arms and rolled back onto the heels of his feet. "Him? He'll be fine," he breezed.

"Thanks," Arel remarked sarcastically.

"You're good, buddy, full faith," Rú said, slapping him on the back. "We gotta get going."

Evaine and Nalini had joined them, and Arel turned to them again. "Okay," he said after inhaling a deep breath. "I'll see you guys in the morning," he said through a nervous smile.

Nalini pulled him into a hug and squeezed him tight. When she released him she stepped back "Be seeing you," she signed quickly before turning away from him to hide worried tears.

He then turned to Evaine, and she smiled, "No clichés."

Without another word, he was in front of her in two strides. He took her face in his hands and leaned into her, pausing just before his lips touched hers. She giggled, he was using her move on her, it was her turn to meet his lips and she did, This kiss was different from the first, deep and slow like he had nowhere to be. She let herself melt into him.

"Guys!" Rú yelled, impatiently rubbing his forehead, "Not the time."

Arel pulled himself away from Evaine, his eyes still closed. "FINE!" he called over his shoulder before looking back at Evaine. "Pick this up later?" he asked, in an attempt to lighten the mood.

"You better," she demanded, playfully pushing him away toward Rú.

Rú glanced around one more time before shifting into his dragon form. Leona stifled a scream, the shift happened so fast and she wasn't ready for it. Nalini's reaction was similar in the way that she was taken aback, but as she stared at him in his full dragon form, she began to see the similarities between the dragon Rú and dog Harrison. She smiled and walked over to touch the horn on his nose. It reminded Rú of Arel's reaction the first time he saw him.

Arel climbed onto his back and settled himself between Rú's shoulder blades. He didn't even ask Arel if he was ready, he just launched himself into the air and took off toward the Islands. Probably for the best, there had been enough delays, it was time to face the music.

It was a warm night, Arel couldn't help but think this would be amazing if they weren't flying into impending doom.

"You're not gonna die," Rú said, interrupting Arel's internal monolog.

Arel tried not to think about the doubt but it persisted. "You don't know that."

'*But I know you better than you do, so get out of your head and trust me.*' It sounded more like instruction than comfort, but it seemed to do the trick. He felt less nauseous as they flew closer to the ground of North Brother. He could see the letters that read Riverside across the main building. Rú circled the island once and the second time around he headed for a clearing on the edge of the island where the energy felt less dense. Even being so high up, Arel could feel the heaviness, it was like the island was trying to pull him down while at the same time pushing Rú up away from it, Arel felt like he was being smushed.

Rú landed quickly knowing the pressure Arel was feeling being in between opposing forces. Arel slid off his back and, almost immediately, Rú was off the ground again.

'I'll be in the air, just remember everything we went over. You're not alone.' Arel watched Rú float up from the ground; he didn't need his wings, he was being pushed up by the opposing force that inhabited the island. He nodded and took another deep breath before turning around to face the tree line. He was in the same place his last dream began, and like his dream, as he looked into the darkness between the trees people stood awaiting his approach. His anxiety began to build in his chest and his body involuntarily started shaking. He closed his eyes and did his best to be calm, it wasn't working. He watched as more shadows took shape to watch him, he wanted nothing more than to run and take his chances swimming back to shore. In his panic, there was a voice under all the chatter. It was so faint that it communicated in the way of impressions more than words, like a faint sound behind plated glass. He focused on it, it was reminding him this was what he was here for and that he would not have opened this door if he couldn't handle this. He looked once more at the shadows waiting for him.

'Look at them, see them. What are they?' the voice asked louder now but still just a whisper. There was nothing defining about it, it wasn't anything he'd ever heard, and he wasn't sure he could even call it a voice.

'What are they, Arel?' it repeated when Arel didn't answer.

"People, they're people," he answered out loud, and as the words left his mouth his body began to relax. They were just people stuck on a plain of existence they could no longer claim as their own. As he looked into the trees, he began to see their faces, some were angry and tired, others sad and lost. The same type of people he worked with on a regular basis, people twisted by the pain of trauma and manipulation.

This revelation created a shift in his body, the pain in his chest subsided and he took a relieved breath as he looked up from his feet, no longer afraid.

Like in his dream, he walked up to the tree line to see the same footpath that led him to the shack in the clearing, it was as good as any place to start. The moment he broke through the line, the air became thicker, like he was in a room packed with bodies. He was surrounded, but unlike his dream, he could not see the forms so clearly, some manifested as shadows and others had no form at all, but he felt them. As he walked he felt the grip of hands, as they touched him he got flashes of the moments that created the prison each of them was living in. He felt and saw everything that led up to their end, the things they said and what they did. Arel ran once before when others had reached out to him many years ago, and maybe they didn't need him as Rú had told him, but these people did. He vowed that he would not walk away from their cries to be heard and seen. These were not people who stayed behind by choice, their pain and mistakes were weaponized against them.

He stopped walking and allowed the invisible hands to latch onto his arms, back, and chest. His mind swam in images, the sensations were overwhelming like being pulled through a series of nightmares. He felt everything they felt, their fear, their sadness, their loneliness. He stood with them in these moments, no words needed to be spoken in exchange, he opened himself to their stories and held space for their pain to know they were no longer alone and that they could be free of their burdens. For some, it was difficult to convince them they were worthy of self-forgiveness after being convinced they needed permission to move on.

Arel didn't know how long he stood there breaking through the walls these people had built around themselves. He found himself tired as the weight lifted and when he opened his eyes he was surprised to see one more shadow standing in his way, towering over him. He couldn't see its features but he felt its eyes peer down at him. The shadow moved quickly to grab hold of his shoulders, keeping him in place with tremendous strength. Arel could do nothing but stare into voids where its eyes would be, he waited. Slowly the obscurity of shadow gave way to reveal piercing blue eyes, wide with shock and filling with tears. The rest of his face was dirty and blood ran from gashes above his eye and across the bridge of his nose. The scene around them changed; they were now standing in a war zone. A bomb landed not far from where they stood, and along with the sound of explosions came the echoes of screams from the injured soldiers. Arel turned around to see the memory this soldier was reliving in death and saw what he was staring at in such horror. In front of him lay another man, his left leg blown from his body, lying close to his broken arm. His other leg was attached only by skin and the little muscle that remained.

"Shoot me, p-please," the injured soldier begged, blood spilling over his lips. "Please, Hank," he choked.

Arel's stomach churned as he turned to look at the blue-eyed soldier as he made the impossible decision to end his friend's suffering quickly. The soldier said nothing, he raised his weapon and through the haze of his tears shot him once, it's all that was needed. The man's eyes remained open, the soldier couldn't tear his gaze from them and he could never forget the emptiness that was left in place.

The scenery around the soldier changed once again, he was sitting looking out the window of his riverside room trapped by the images of war. He hanged himself that day and was buried on South Brother, his burial attended only by a priest and three nurses in formality, he was alone in death as he was in life.

Arel looked back at the soldier, he had been trapped there wandering in the fog of these memories unable to escape. The fog of loneliness made thick by the collective suffering on this island. The soldier's eyes pleaded for release. Arel laid a sympathetic hand on the soldier's shoulder. "I can't release you," he whispered, "Only you can. Your guilt holds you here."

The soldier's eyes welled with angry tears, he didn't know where to begin, this has been his truth for so long.

"You've shown me what has kept you," Arel said quickly, as he saw the soldier beginning to unravel. "You don't deserve this pain and there is nothing but more suffering for you here. Don't stay."

Arel began to think about all he learned in the last few days, about the lives he's lived, the soldiers' faces softened as he shared in his thoughts. Arel watched as relief and hope came over his face.

"There's more for you, people waiting for you." The soldier nodded and lingered a little longer. As his image faded Arel witnessed his brows soften and his eyes lighten before disappearing completely leaving Arel standing again in the woods, alone. He looked up at the dense canopy barely being able to see the sky through the trees, he felt a little dizzy. He wasn't sure how many spirits aside from the soldier he just came into contact with but they had taken their toll. Not only did he feel mentally tired but his body felt heavy like he could fall asleep then and there.

He closed his eyes and took in three deep breaths.

'*Rú?*' he thought.

'I'm here,' Rú responded right away, Arel looked up and saw Rú's shadow fly over the trees.

"Just checking in. I'm a little wiped," Arel said aloud as he shook his head and opened his eyes wide to force them to stay open.

'Take a minute and remember the energy around you, like before.'

He recalled exactly what Rú meant, he closed his eyes again and envisioned a network of energy beneath where he stood and silently asked for a boost. He envisioned the energy moving through his feet, up his legs, and through his chest. He visualized the energy reaching his mind and felt the build of energy urging his limbs to move.

Chapter Twenty-Two

SIDEBAR

"How do you think he's doing?" Leona asked, disrupting the rhythmic sound of the waves lapping against the pillars of the dock.

"I think Rú would have flown back to tell us if anything was wrong at this point," Evaine answered, her voice low and strained. She was laser-focused on the island, mentally going back and forth on whether or not she'd want an update, it had only been a little over two hours. Perhaps it's best to be in the dark right now or at least that was what she was trying to convince herself.

Nalini's eyes scanned the surface of the water, unsure exactly what she was looking out for but, stare long enough and you'll definitely start seeing things that aren't there. For a split second, she thought she saw eyes staring back at her over the waves. Staring without blinking for some time now, the sting of the wind drying out her caption contacts pulled Nalini away from her thoughts and back into her body. Her eyes had begun watering, blurring her vision, she quickly rubbed the water from her eyes and resumed her attention to the spot on the water. Satisfied to find nothing.

'*Trick of the mind,*' she thought.

✸✸✸✸

Dylan kept his arm over his eyes, trying hard to will himself to fall back to sleep. The blissful warmth from his dream still lingered in his stomach. His mind did not oblige, instead, it began to replay the events of the last seventy-two hours. He inhaled deeply and on the exhale he let his arm fall and his eyes open, surprised to find the room darker. It was lit only by the single lamp at the end of the couch where Eugene rested, the light illuminating his sleeping face. Dylan observed him, searching for the slightest movement to indicate he was coming back. Nothing, not a twitch or eye movement, just the shallow rise and fall of his abdomen.

'*At least there's that,*' he assured himself.

What he overheard Leila telling Arel earlier began devouring his thoughts; it would be Eugene's choice whether he came back or not. He felt the warmth from his dream cramp into a dull ache.

The questions in the back of his mind intensified his pain. '*What if he doesn't want to come back?*' Or worse, '*What if Eugene wakes up and doesn't want me?*'

He let his pain shift to anger, he had been fine not knowing why he was drawn to Eugene. Happy to believe his need to connect was due to admiration, just a stupid crush and nothing more. If it hadn't been for that dream, that terrible dream, he would have remained blissfully unaware of his true feelings.

'*But would I be happy not knowing?*' he asked himself, shaking his head. There was no point in thinking about this now, he'd only drive himself crazy. He sat up and looked around the room and, to his relief, Leila was nowhere to be seen. He swung his legs off the couch and set his feet on the floor, rested his elbows on his knees, and let his head fall into his hands, applying a calming pressure to his eyes. When he lifted his head different shapes were swirling over Eugene. Ethereal lines accentuating the curves of his tranquil face, Dylan's thoughts slipped back to his dream. It was a beautiful distraction, where he wanted to be, a perfect moment he didn't want to forget. He sprang from his seat and ran over to the kitchen island and its surrounding cabinets, furiously opening and shutting drawers looking for paper and anything to write with. Words flooded his mind free and fast, he had to get them down on paper. It had been so long since he'd been inspired to write, he had given up and turned to the sciences. It was something he enjoyed well enough to distract him from his detachment to creativity. After rummaging through several drawers, he finally found a small notepad and pen. There's always a junk drawer, always. Excited by his discovery, he grabbed what he needed and slammed the drawer shut by accident, the bang made him wince. Dylan looked around the room apologetically for a split second before he remembered the state Eugene was in, if only that was the thing to wake him up. He flipped through the notepad looking for a blank page as he walked back to the couch and began writing before he sat down. The rhythm of the words flowed effortlessly as he did his best to relive the dream fading from his conscious mind.

Chapter Twenty-Three

She Is An Angel

Even with the benefit of the flashlight on his phone Arel still found himself tripping over roots and fallen branches. The sound of footsteps that trailed behind no longer had the shudder-inducing effect they did when he began his course through the woods. It was a kind of comfort now, if it had been a threat he figured he would have been attacked by now, so it wasn't something he was going to bring himself to worry about. At ease for the most part, aside from the occasional shadow that moved into his peripheral vision too quickly, making him jump. He let his mind wander a bit, chuckling to himself thinking about the horror games he played as a kid. The ones that took place in dark creepy woods and your character would be armed with nothing but a flashlight. Those games used to scare the living daylights out of him and here he was walking through real haunted woods, armed with nothing but a flashlight. He felt okay, airing on confidence, happy to think that what he's yet to experience couldn't be worse than the horde of spirits he had just encountered. It was a lie he was happy to hold onto.

Just as he wondered to himself how much longer he'd have to walk, a figure appeared a few yards in front of him as if to answer his question. It was different from the rest of the shadow figures, its silhouette wasn't smooth and opaque, and its edges flickered like fire.

"Smokeless fire," he said under his breath remembering Kirana's experience in the woods.

He began to feel the rush of adrenaline move through his veins as he watched it move through the trees drawing his attention off his intended path. When the figure stopped moving, Arel could feel it smiling at him, a mixture of delight and malice wafting from it in waves. Behind it was the clearing from his dream, he could just make out the shape of the shack about thirty yards from the specter. The figure disappeared the moment he brought his attention back to it. Like his dream, it was leading him there.

"This is definitely a trap," he thought aloud, but he had a gnawing feeling that there was something in that shack he needed to know. In his dream Nalini was in that shack, there had to be something that was of some significance. With his mind made up, Arel began his careful trek toward the edge of the woods, hyper-aware of every sound as he broke through the trees into the clearing. From what he could see through its windows, there was nothing but shadows of furniture until a figure appeared in the frame. It appeared solid against the dark and it beckoned him forward.

Arel heard the sound of heavy wings above him, Rú swooped down low a few feet above his head. Not a thought or word was said, it wasn't necessary. He remembered Kirana's memory of Rú standing leaning on the tree, *'I'll be here if you need me.'* Things were vastly different this time, there wasn't the option of a safety net, but he wasn't going to allow that to scare him.

Arel confidently closed the gap between himself and the shack. He stood for a moment observing the way the vines positioned themselves across the door, the same way they appeared in his dream. He noticed the door was ajar when he reached for the handle.

"That's not foreboding at all," he mumbled to himself before giving the door a good push. The door made the classic horror movie squeak until it hit the wall with a soft thud and he couldn't help but cringe. He stood within the door frame peering into the room, giving it a thorough inspection before entering. Feeling himself being watched from the far right corner, he let his eyes drift to where they were drawn. The longer he looked the more the figure took shape. He remained still and didn't blink, wondering if it was his mind playing tricks. This was one of the hardest lessons to grasp, the fact that his mind wanted so much to make sense of what the eyes see and convince him that it was not real. It was real, the figure began to move out from the wall as if it had been fixed to it. There wasn't that much light coming through the window but the light from the doorway where he stood helped illuminate a good portion of the room. He could tell it was situated just outside of the light's limit drawing his attention to the small bed under the window to the right. Shooting a look to the left corner he saw the same vanity from his last dream. Looking back at the figure still standing in the shadows, it clicked, where he was and who lived there.

"Mary," he said quietly, "Typhoid Mary?"

A blood-curdling scream exploded from the figure, chilling Arel to the bone.

In a blink she was out of shadow, standing in front of him. Now he could see her eyes boring into his, wide and wild. Her demeanor was that of an animal backed into a corner, hurt and defending what was hers, what she had left. There was no malicious intent as she looked at him, he relaxed his stance and lifted his arms slowly in surrender.

"I'm sorry, Mary," he corrected himself. Her gaze softened and she turned away from him. Her movements were not smooth as she made her way back into the shadows, they were glitchy and it put him on edge. There was an unpredictable air about the room, he felt a sharp pang just above his right ear that grew into a dull pain behind his eye.

"Mary, why are you still here?" he asked her, struggling to stay focused.

"It's where I must stay." There was conviction in her voice that gave her answer an unsettling weight. "For what I've done, I must remain."

Arel's sight began to go hazy. "No, Mary, there's nothing left but to move on."

"No," she replied firmly. "The guard said I must remain, only when she releases me will I be able to see the face of God."

"Guard?" he echoed. His legs, shaking, threatened to give out from under him. He stumbled forward. "Mary, there's no..." He was having trouble holding on to his thoughts as the pain that began in his head spread to his stomach.

He did his best to steady his voice, "What did this guard look like?"

"She appears as fire, she is an angel," she answered reverently.

Arel began to panic as his symptoms worsened, he wondered how this was possible.

Mary was a quiet deception, her affliction worked as it did in life, with no warning to take preventative measures and it was easy to move past defenses weakened by sympathy.

She looked at him with worry as she watched him crumble to the floor, it was then he knew it wasn't her intention.

Everything hurt and the pain behind his eyes was making it harder to see, but off to the corner by the vanity, he saw fire. A hallucination he would have chalked up to the rapidly advancing fever if he hadn't known the truth.

Chapter Twenty-Four

HOUSES AND NEIGHBORHOODS

Eugene kept his eyes shut as he wiggled his toes and stretched his legs. They were stiff and ached from remaining in the same position for too long. It was quiet with only the sound of deep low breaths of someone sleeping. With eyes still closed, he pulled himself up into a seated position not ready for the sting of light just yet. Feeling too weak to stand, he did his best to stretch some more while seated, slow to finally open his eyes. He looked around to see if there was anything vaguely shaped like his glasses. Shifting his foot he felt a bag leaning against the couch near his right leg. He knew it wasn't his but, he could tell the small front pocket was unzipped with something sticking out of it. His glasses.

As he slid them up the bridge of his nose and the body lying on the extended end of the couch became clear, it was Dylan. He was positioned away from him facing the backrest of the couch, he assumed to avoid the light as much as possible. On the table across from Dylan was a notepad and a pen set along its edge. There was quite a bit written, and thinking it might be just a note or directions, he reached over and grabbed the pad. Surprised to see it wasn't a note and not what he expected at all, it was a poem, a love poem.

I rarely have dreams I want to get back to,
The one thing they all have in common is you,
Your weight in my arms, your head on my chest, my fingers in your hair,
Just let me stay,
Me right here, you right there,
It's torture, not fair,
To have you, hold you, one minute,
Then to open my eyes and you disappear,
I hold my eyes shut tight praying I can fall back to sleep,
Fall back into the dream of you and me.

Eugene read the poem over and over. Each time hoping the words would reveal more of the person Dylan saw in his mind. It both thrilled and scared him that this poem could be written with him in mind.

'*Wishful thinking,*' he thought to himself feeling a twinge of guilt reading something so personal but he couldn't tear himself away, caught up in the dream of them together. He didn't hear or notice Leila appearing out of the dark from her back room and walking toward him. She placed her hand gently on his shoulder, Eugene flinched away from her touch and opened his mouth to protest. Leila quickly put a finger to her lips, a gesture in consideration for the sleeping Dylan. She beckoned Eugene to follow her and there was nothing he observed about her that set off any alarm bells as to why he shouldn't follow, so he slowly stood tucking the small notepad in his back pocket.

Leila stopped in her tracks and quickly walked back over to Dylan. She closed her eyes and held her hand over his ears. After a few seconds, she exhaled a loud audible breath as she let her arms fall back to her sides.

"There, we won't wake him now, poor baby, he's been so stressed," she said, walking toward Eugene. "So glad you've decided to come back to us, Gene," she remarked, leaving him in speechless confusion. He had so many questions but stifled the urge to let them come flooding out all at once. He didn't want to ask any of the overtly obvious questions like 'Where am I?' and 'What happened?' He figured he'd get all that information anyway.

He finally settled on, "Are you a friend of Rú? " to get the ball rolling.

"'Friend' might be a bit optimistic on my end, ally would be more apt. That will change in time." Her last words were weighted by certainty.

"Are you human? I'm sorry, is that a rude question?" he asked.

Leila laughed, "Yes, very, and no I wouldn't consider that rude given the circumstances," she answered and turned away, pulling a small coffee maker from one of the bottom cabinets.

"Are you a witch or something?" he pressed.

"Or something," she answered with a teasing smile that told him he'd never get that full story, so he decided to drop it.

"So, where did you go?" she asked, as they waited for the coffee to brew, she noticed him tense slightly. "Your consciousness wasn't where it should be," she said, reaching across the island and putting her index finger to his head. Eugene grabbed her finger before she could pull it away and held it tight.

"Me first, I'm assuming you used some kind of magic to fix me, do you know what happened to me? What that thing was that took me out?" His request for information was more of a demand. He was determined to get as clear of an answer as possible.

"From what we know, they're called black-eyed children, they're manufactured." As Leila said the word 'manufactured' the face of the creature flashed through Eugene's mind. He thought back to focus on its doll-like face and how was unusually smooth, like porcelain. He had been so focused on its eyes at the time and the paralyzing cold. Leila observed Eugene's face as he re-lived his attack.

"I've read about those, I thought they had to be invited in, like vampires," he said releasing her finger, recalling his research at the office with Dylan, shaking his head. He wanted to shift the conversation, to change the imagery in his head.

"Like vampires?" Leila snorted a laugh. "Those poor things never evolved beyond the leech brain. No, some poor soul encountered a shifter way back and wires were crossed."

"Okay, so what are they then?" Eugene pressed, trying not to sound impatient.

"The working theory is that they were designed by a type of Djinn. Djinn, love a misdirect. If people don't know what they're dealing with it is harder to find a solution to the problem. It works in their favor. At the same time, there are a lot of powerful entities out there capable of something like this, can't rule anything out."

"What are Djinn, exactly?" Eugene asked.

"They were created before man, smo-" Leila stopped speaking as she watched Eugene's eyes narrow and he sat up straight.

"Smokeless fire," he finished.

"Did you see it?" There was an urgency to her question.

"No, Rú had only mentioned it when..." Eugene quickly glances over at the sleeping Dylan. "When I noticed something."

It was only a glance but it was enough for Leila to quickly unravel the reason for his journey into the past. "I see," she said, turning away from him to grab two glass mugs and placing one in front of him.

"See what?" he breezed, as if he had no idea of what she was imply-ing. He reached over and grabbed the coffee pot, pouring coffee into her mug before his own.

"Thank you," she chirped, grabbing the mug and holding it just under her lips as she blew into the scalding liquid. She kept her eyes on Eugene as he squeezed the honey sitting in the middle of the island into the coffee, he was avoiding her gaze and she knew it.

"You're only hurting yourself trying to hide it, you know." Leila's words were quiet as, now looking down as she made the coffee swirl like a tiny whirlpool in her mug.

Eugene let out an audible sigh as he set down his mug and rubbed his eyes. "I don't know where to begin."

"You've already seen your beginning." Leila glanced over at Dylan as she said the word 'your'.

"Stop thinking you have to begin anything and just be, do what feels right from one moment to the next, and everything will fall into place. What falls away from you wasn't meant to remain in your life and what stays was always meant to be yours." Leila spoke as if it was the simplest concept to grasp, it frustrated him until he caught himself falling into a pattern, and he realized it was his resistance to this change causing his mental conflict.

Eugene looked over at Dylan again, he was now in a different po-sition, he turned over as he slept and was now facing them. His mind wandered back to the scene he experienced in the past, he felt a tinge of guilt in his stomach as his thoughts came back to the present and the threat that loomed over them all.

"That can't only be it, though, right? Why I was sent back to see what I saw? I feel like there are more important things," he sighed into his coffee. Leila set her coffee down and crossed her arms.

"Honey, there will always be problems to be solved, but there isn't a problem important enough to let love fall by the wayside. It's our greatest teacher, you lose love, you lose your way. You found your way to the past to make sure you wouldn't get lost in the present."

"But Arel is out there dealing with real monsters and I'm worried about my relationship status? Come on."

"Okay, let me frame it this way, if you were meant to be in this fight, don't you think you'd be in it? You were taken off the board, it's not your game to play. You have your own battles to fight and you may think this is small in comparison to everything else at the moment but you have no idea how your choices now will affect you in the future. This has been put in front of you to deal with now, so address it now, then deal with the rest after. At the moment, your path and Arel's have separated, it will continue to meet and split well into the next life, but his path is not yours to walk and his battles are not yours to fight." Leila had lost her patience by the time she finished her argument. "So curb the guilt, it's useless."

Eugene sat quiet, he couldn't argue and he didn't want to. He nodded and the stern expression on Leila's face softened. She held her mug out and waited for him to raise his to meet it, sharing in silent cheers to put his internal conflict to rest.

Dylan slowly opened his eyes, still in the space between sleep and awake. He looked over to the other end of the couch expecting to see an unconscious Eugene. It took a second for his mind to realize he was no longer there. He sprang to his feet so fast it made him dizzy. It was sudden enough to draw Eugene and Leila's attention, Eugene stifled a laugh.

"You're awake!" Dylan exclaimed. He crossed the room at such a speed neither Eugene nor Leila could tell if his feet touched the ground. "I'm so glad you're awake," he said, throwing his arms around

Eugene. He returned his embrace and allowed himself to sink into Dylan. Eugene lifted his eyes and met Leila's gaze, she smiled and nodded once before turning away to disappear up the stairs. Dylan didn't seem to notice, or care.

Eugene loosened his arms expecting Dylan to do the same but he didn't, instead, he held him tighter.

"I'm sorry, this would have never happened if I had stayed in the SUV," Dylan explained frantically.

"Hey, I'm ok, I'm right here. I'm, actually, better than ok."

Dylan released him and stepped back to look at Eugene's face. "Okay?" His tone spelled confusion.

"Yeah, you know how Rel has been experiencing..." Eugene paused to find the right word. "Uh, vision quests?"

"Yeah?" Dylan answered with a knowing smile.

"Wait, what was that face? What happened? What do you know?" Eugene asked, he couldn't mask the excitement in his voice.

"Everyone's been experiencing 'vision quests,' you missed a lot while you were out."

"So what did I miss?" he asked eagerly.

Dylan half-heartedly chuckled as he walked over to the cabinets to grab a glass mug to join Eugene in a cup of coffee.

"I'll catch you up later. Tell me what happened." He sat down facing Eugene, settling himself in, and taking a sip of the steaming coffee.

Eugene looked down nervously into his own mug. Everything in him wanted to tell him how he felt when he saw Dylan as his past self and how it was the same as he looks at him now. Tell him that he recognized him right away and how sure it made him feel that he was supposed to be with Dylan, through any time, in any form. He wanted to tell him that loving him came as a second nature.

"You okay?" Dylan asked, concerned by his pause. "You know what? You don't have to talk about it, it's your business."

"No, I want to tell you, it was just a little crazy. Like, Rú was there and he looked exactly the same as he is now. It was just so strange talking to him as a different person, kinda hard to wrap my head around."

"Yeah," Dylan chimed in, his eyebrow jumped as he nodded in agreement.

"Right," Eugene started again, rubbing his hand up and down his thigh. Willing his sweaty palms to remain dry. "At first I recognized Rel and Evaine, that was wild," he paused, "and, uh, then I recognized you." His voice rose an octave when he said the word 'you'.

It was quick but he noticed Dylan tense a bit. He wasn't sure what to make of it or how to read him. Did Dylan remember him too? Did his love in that life go unrequited? Was he just psyching himself out? Maybe Dylan was just as unsure as he was, that was the best-case scenario to explain his response. He decided that was the option he was going to put his faith in.

"You remember me too, I know you do. What do you remember?" Eugene asked, he waited for Dylan to look at him but he remained staring down into his coffee.

"I do remember you, I just don't wanna think about what I saw," he said, his words heavy.

Eugene's heart sank into his stomach and a sharp sting rose to his chest. He looked away as Dylan looked back at him. Dylan saw the worry weighing on his brows.

"Oh no no, it was just shocking and everything was going by so fast. That's what I meant," Dylan offered quickly.

"DID I DIE?" Eugene exclaimed.

"I'm not sure," Dylan winced as he answered him, like his not knowing was bad news in itself. There was a comical air to his delivery that eased the sting in Eugene's chest. Dylan was trying hard to hide the frustration he was feeling and let his head fall into his hands, his palms over his eyes. Eugene grabbed onto the hand closest to him and pulled it away so Dylan would look at him.

"I'm right here," he said, placing his hand on his chest. "What happened then won't happen again," Eugene assured him.

"It literally just did," Dylan said flatly.

"Yeah, but I didn't die," Eugene smiled confidently, releasing Dylan's hand.

Dylan laughed in relief but he wanted to shift the conversation back to its intended subject. "Did you see anything else?" he asked.

Eugene grew nervous again, "Uh no, but it did clear some things up."

"Oh? What things?" Dylan chirped before taking a gulp of his coffee.

Eugene took a deep breath as he pulled the small notebook from his back pocket. "Something to do with this maybe?" He set it down in front of Dylan. Eugene didn't breathe and sat frozen, his heart beating wildly, waiting for some reaction from Dylan.

Dylan sat wide-eyed looking down at his words. Eugene started to dread his actions and began to panic.

"I'm sorry, I misunderstood," he uttered and reached to grab the notebook, Dylan caught his hand and held it quietly before releasing it. Immediately picking up the notebook as he turned to stand, he walked a few steps and stood still facing away from him, Eugene readied himself for rejection. Torturing himself with the idea that he had read everything wrong, that what he felt from the past was not meant to be in this life.

"You didn't misunderstand," Dylan finally said, turning back to face him. He walked back over and tossed the notebook back onto the counter.

Eugene let out a sigh of relief and put his hand over his heart nearly beating out of his chest. "You just scared the shit out of me, Jesus."

"I'm sorry, it's just," Dylan paused and Eugene braced himself again. "I was hoping you'd never see this utterly embarrassing poem," Dylan joked and cringed away from it.

"Well, I like it," Eugene declared confidently. "Can I keep it?" he asked, holding the notebook to his chest. Dylan nodded his head and he sat back down with a bashful smile that lit up his eyes.

"So, that conversation in your office, with the houses and neighborhoods..." Dylan mused.

Eugene just nodded, his eyes shut and cringing in embarrassment. "Caught that, did you?" he spoke as if he was in pain. "I didn't think-" Eugene began but didn't have a chance to finish his thought. Dylan had already crossed the space between them and had his hands on Eugene's collar, pulling him in to meet his lips. It didn't feel like a first kiss to either of them, wild and deep, a passion built from lost time.

Chapter Twenty-Five

YOUR CHOICE

Arel opened his eyes and found himself back where it all started. This time he was glad to see he was wearing shoes. There was a figure waiting for him in the doorway to the hall. The same fiery figure he glimpsed before losing consciousness in the shack. She had no defining features, only an intensity, a malice that bore into him as he watched her move from the doorway into the hall, beckoning him to follow her. He wasn't afraid, at this point, he was just annoyed and angry. Done being patient and fighting hate with compassion, he was exhausted and the only fuel he had left was anger. Arel felt the heat of rage rise through his torso up into his chest, giving him the adrenalin he believed he needed to snuff her out.

The Djinn stopped at the window's edge and turned to face him just before disappearing behind the wall. Accepting her challenge, Arel lifted his foot to start into a run, and just like in his first dream he was pulled back. It had him by the arm, a hand with a grip that felt like hot coals on his skin. It only had a hold on him for a few seconds but it was enough to burn the skin, he was sure of it.

"Jesus! Fuck!" Arel called out as he yanked his arm away.

"No, afraid not."

Arel could hear the smile in The Being's voice although he couldn't clearly see their face.

"If you're wondering what I am, that's not important right now. All you need to know is that I'm here to help you," The Being spoke, as they circled Arel like a lion stalking its prey. They moved like they were floating, it put Arel on edge.

"How do I know this isn't one of her tricks?" he asked defensively, turning to watch this thing's movement. It felt different from the Djinn and from Rú, looking at them was like looking into the vast expanse of space. It made him feel small, like standing on the edge of a cliff unable to see the bottom.

"I suppose you don't. I can only offer you my help, whether you take advantage of it or not that's up to you," The Being spoke patiently and with compassion as if they were talking to a young child.

"Ok well, Rú said that light beings can't set foot on the island, so what does that make you?" Arel challenged.

"In your mind." The Being's smile widened as they walked under a ray of moonlight that added a navy hue to their dark skin. "She was going to lead you into a labyrinth deep within your consciousness, putting you in a coma."

"Then wake me up," Arel demanded.

"Not yet," The Being lifted their finger to their lips. "You were going to run after her and do what exactly?"

The smile was gone now.

Arel opened his mouth and then closed it again. He didn't have a plan. He was so angry he could have ripped her apart with his bare hands and then he realized his error. He let his anger blind him, it was what she was counting on, so he calmed himself down and crossed his arms.

"Are you ready to listen?" The Being's voice was firm. Arel nodded, still on guard.

"Djinn are master manipulators, as you just witnessed. She can read your mind and knows your history back to the beginning and she is hell-bent on destroying you."

"How come she hasn't just killed me then, it'd be easy for her," Arel spat, frustrated and annoyed with the games.

"It's one thing to kill you, another thing entirely to destroy you. She wants to break your righteous soul and darken your light. Defeating her will not be easy and it will take sacrifice."

"Sacrifice? Rú didn't tell me about a sacrifice?" Arel fumed, taken aback by this new information.

"There are some things even Rú doesn't know," The Being answered, their words heavy over Ru's name.

Arel was losing patience and began his advance toward The Being that claimed to want to help him.

"And I'm just supposed to believe that I have to make this sacrifice, one that Rú knows nothing about? Get the fuck outta here! You have no right to be in my head, wake me the fuck up!" Arel roared.

The Being looked at Arel like a toddler, having a tantrum. Amused by his brashness and assumptions.

"Arel," they began softly. "Information is presented when you are ready and willing to receive it. Given too soon, we risk fear conquering courage. There are rules, we cannot intervene before you are ready."

"You can't intervene," Arel mumbled to himself putting the pieces together. "You're an Angel?"

The Being smiled and bowed his head, "So I am considered by some, to others a muse or a guide, and to many, I am one they can call upon for protection. What I am does not matter for I am many things to many people. Does this ease your mind?" The smile had come back to their voice. "I'm not here to bring your end, only to inspire its prevention."

Arel said nothing and simply nodded.

"The weapon you will use against her will be your strength of will. She will do whatever she can to weaken that," The Being explained.

Arel, confident in all that he had learned, straightened his shoulders. "I'm ready for that."

"Good, because to destroy her you have to let her in," The Being said bluntly.

"Let her in. What do you mean, let her in my head?" Arel asked.

"The battle must take place in the body," they clarified.

"You want her to possess me? I've seen the aftermath of that, that's suicide!" Arel snapped.

He nervously raked his fingers through his hair and turned away from The Being. The sight of Mal's cooked corpse flashed through his mind and he remembered the unsettling smell of his roasted flesh, it churned his stomach.

"There is a way to walk away unscathed, a way poor Mal knew nothing of, or how simple it is to execute," The Being explained, laden with empathy. "But I assure you he is at peace with this life and is preparing for the next."

Hearing this did bring Arel comfort, something he'll be happy to share when he sees Evaine and Leona again. As soon as that wave of relief came, it left. There was still a chance he wouldn't walk away from this.

"What do you mean simple to execute?" he asked hopefully.

"Intention is the most powerful tool at this moment, it will activate the natural iron and salt in your blood to act as a prison. If trapped behind barriers of iron and salt, Djinn can not break free of their own will. Once she's trapped it will be your light, your fire, that will defeat her."

"What fire?" Arel asked.

The Being closed the space between them and placed their hand over Arel's chest, careful not to make physical contact. "The human soul, made of both light and dark but when in harmony, creates Divine Fire. The purest light activated by your will," they said, a wide smile spreading across their face.

Arel looked down skeptically at The Being's hand and then back to their face.

"Easier said than done," Arel sighed.

"Yes," The Being chuckled. "But I have faith."

"So lamps are a no-go for the Djinn?" Arel joked dryly.

"Did you bring one?" their face was serious and they had Arel going before a joking smile returned to their face. As they turned to walk away but stopped abruptly. "One more thing, Djinn may be master manipulators but they honor their word and they love a deal."

"Why do I feel like you know how this will play out?" Arel asked, hoping to gain more information.

"I know all the possibilities but the outcome will be your choice."

At the snap of The Being's fingers, Arel was back in the shack where he collapsed. He coughed and breathed deep as if he'd been deprived of air, which he may have been for a time. He decided he wasn't going to focus on that, he was back in Mary's shack and he needed to deal with her first. He was surprised at how spry his limbs felt, no longer heavy from exhaustion. He sprang to his feet and brushed the dirt from his shirt and pants. The only discomfort came from his arm, he lifted his sleeve to reveal three red fingerprints where The Being had grabbed him to pull him back from running into trouble. He ran his own fingers over the forming welts, they were still hot to the touch.

He didn't see her at first, she sat so still at her decrepit vanity, staring at her spectral reflection. She looked away only to glance at him.

"I didn't think you'd be back." There was no surprise in Mary's voice.

Arel walked over and knelt beside her, choosing his words carefully. "Mary, the angel you told me about, she is not what she claims to be. As long as you stay here you will continue to spread a sickness similar to the one you spread in life and she will amplify it to make it worse," he told her softly.

He wondered if she was just ignoring him as she remained staring at her reflection, seemingly unmoved.

He tilted his head silently pleading for her to hear him. "Mary, you can only make what happened in the past right by moving forward, moving on." There was an urgency to his voice now. "Don't let her use your pain, your fate is your choice."

Mary finally looked away from the mirror and as her dark eyes met his, it was like floodgates opening. The depth of her sadness, pain, and regret ran through him. It was like a weight dropped on his chest that sharpened into claws tearing their way down to his stomach. It was her guilt, her embarrassment. The pain ripping through his stomach began to subside at the same time he watched the sorrow lift from her eyes, with it, all she had been holding on to. It wasn't a look of peace or happiness, it was a look of acceptance but he could see there was a bit of fear that remained.

"Mary, I can't promise you your next journey will be easier than this one, but it's a chance to make things right. Give yourself that chance."

She said nothing and only nodded once, her furrowed brows found new meaning over the blaze of determination in her eyes. If there was one thing that would carry Mary through her next journey it would be her iron resolve to do the work.

She closed her eyes and Arel remained by her side. He waited and wondered what would happen next. Would she dissolve gracefully into specks of light? Disintegrate into dust? But no, nothing. No grand exit, no lights, he blinked and she was gone. He waited a few minutes in case she hadn't really moved on, but there was a shift in the room, he was completely alone.

'*Was it really that easy?*' he thought, taking another look around the shack. "Yup, I guess," Arel sighed and rose to his feet. "On to the real fight," he said to himself, clapping his hands together to get the dust off.

Before reaching for the door, he took a minute to stretch out his arms and shake out his legs. When he felt he was substantially limber, he opened the door with enough force for it to slam against the wall. He didn't expect it to make such a commotion, the sound made him jump.

"Okay," he said, looking out to the wooded path to the main buildings. "Let's go." He stepped out into the clearing knowing exactly where he was going, he'd been there before.

The Dock

It had been hours. Nalini, Evaine, and Leona sat in silence passing the time in their individual worlds. Nalini sat at the end of the dock watching her feet dangle over the glassy surface of the river. She watched her face on the water focusing only on the way the current distorted her otherwise perfect reflection, careful to keep her mind clear from worry. She let her thoughts flow by like the water beneath her, but one rang out like a scream. If there was anything nefarious waiting beneath the surface she'd never see it coming. Her body shook out the thought only to lead into another. Olivia. How she died and whatever it was that came from the depths of the river. She quickly lifted her legs away from the water onto the safety of the dock. She stood quickly and began to pace back and forth, breaking the other two out of their concentration.

Evaine got up and stepped in front of her, "Are you ok? Did you see something?" Glancing down to see Nalini's bracelets picking up the sound and relaying the message to her contacts. "I'm sorry," she said realizing there was no reason to step in front of her so abruptly.

"It's fine, I just creeped myself out," Nalini's bracelets chimed as she signed, mustering Evaine a reassuring smile. Leona also took this opportunity to stand and stretch her legs, giving Nalini the side eye before turning her back to her. A gesture not lost on Nalini.

"I'm sorry about your friend." The voice that rang out from her bracelet did not convey the sympathy she felt. Leona rocked on her heels and sucked in a deep breath before turning back to look Nalini in the eyes, the expression she wore was a mixture of disbelief and anger. She walked to the end of the dock to give herself a minute and walked back when she had herself in check.

When she looked Nalini in the eyes again she saw the pain therein. Conflicted, the only response she could utter was "This isn't the time," she said through clenched teeth.

"I know you want someone to blame, Leo, but she's not the one," Evaine said carefully, stepping between the two.

Leona's reserve crumbled with tears welling in her eyes, she cried. "If you just had waited."

Nalini couldn't stop the onslaught of her own tears. Knowing the part she played was indirect yet she was still responsible.

She wiped her tears and stood up straight.

"She's right." The clear cold voice rang through the air stopping Evaine and Leona in their tracks.

"I didn't listen," Nalini continued. "I let my insecurity and pride get in the way when my brother tried to warn me. That's something I have to live with, it was my choice that resulted in a life lost."

She stopped moving, searching her mind for the right way to convey what she wanted to say.

"I don't expect forgiveness from you or anyone else..." she paused unsure of how her next words would be taken, "But can you tell me about him?" she finished and wiped tears from her chin.

Leona's sharp gaze softened and settled into sadness again.

She was quiet for a moment as she remembered Mal. "I can only tell you that he was kind and quiet and..." she took another deep breath to steady herself, " ... He was still finding his way."

A harsh reality hit Leona then, she never took the time to know him. She let the sweet kid who didn't make waves fall through the cracks. He was the kind of person she didn't have to keep an eye on, so she never did. The truth of her anger was that she never made an effort to know him when he was alive. It wasn't only that he was part of her team and she couldn't protect him. It was that he was part of her team and she never knew him, that's what broke her heart.

Evaine spoke up to break the silence as she believed Leona to be at a loss for words.

"Mal was a really good cook," she said with a smile as she fell into a memory of one of their conversations, remembering his enthusiasm.

"He walked into the office one day at lunch and we got to talkin' bout food. I was eating stew that day and we got to comparin' recipes. His mom was from Louisiana and had family in New Orleans."

Their smiles fell away at the mention of Mal's family.

"Do you know if he was close to his family?" Nalini asked.

"I know his father died when he was young and his Ma passed a few years ago, never mentioned anyone else," Evaine answered grimly.

Silence overcame them again as they each retreated into their thoughts. A smile broke across Leona's face. "He had a nice voice, he was always humming."

"I heard him rapping once," Evaine added excitedly.

"What?" Leona shrieked with surprise and delight.

"Yeah," Evaine answered with a laugh. "He was grabbing his things out of his locker at the end of the day and was freestyling about what he was gonna do the rest of the day. Aside from the subject matter he wasn't bad, he had a pretty good flow," she finished with a chuckle.

Nalini stood back and smiled, enjoying the moments Leona and Evaine remembered with Mal.

"I wish I'd known him." Nalini's bracelets chimed over their laughter.

"I wish I had taken more time to get to know him," Leona admitted.

Nalini put a tentative hand on Leona's arm and Leona met her gaze through apologetic eyes.

Evaine then jumped as she felt a wind sweep across the back of her neck, like a soft breath, urging her to turn around. A fog had engulfed the dock, she could no longer see the SUV or the parking lot at all. The only thing she could make out was the vague humanoid form illuminated by the hazy street lamp it stood under.

"Hello?" she called out, drawing the attention of the other two.

"Are we expecting anyone else?" Leona asked, her voice now cold and focused. She walked past Evaine and stopped a few feet ahead.

"Who's there?" It was more a demand than a question, there was no fear or uncertainty in Leona's voice. She reached behind her back and pulled her gun from her waistband, holding it at the ready.

The figure didn't respond and remained still. She noticed it was of smaller stature, the frame of a small woman or a child.

Leona turned back to Evaine and Nalini. "I think it's just a kid," she said with a shrug, tucking the gun back where she had it.

"Shit," Evaine spat, grabbing Leona's arm and pulling her back to stand behind her.

"What?" Leona asked, allowing herself to be moved but pulling her gun out again.

"It's another one of those black-eyed bastards," she hissed. "Make sure you stand behind me, it can't get past my protection bag. Bullets won't do anything," she said looking down at Leona's gun.

The figure began to move the moment Evaine started speaking, like the sound of her voice called it forward.

Walking away from the light the creature fought to be seen through the growing thickness of fog.

"Black-eyed what?" Leona asked. She strained to see it more clearly and then she saw them, the piercing black orbs through the fog. Instantly making her feel exposed, alone, like she had been dropped into the open sea. She was frozen, it was fear she had never felt, not even in the heat of battle.

Evaine still had her by the arm, it was the only thing grounding her, keeping her from falling farther into that illusion of fear.

The hooded creature was closer now, close enough to see its porcelain face and the sinister grin distorting its doll-like face. Evaine's heart sank as she heard the sound of rapid footsteps racing down the dock toward them. She expected to be met with another of these black-eyed children and she braced herself.

A baseball bat cut through the fog and made contact with the black-eyed child's head, exploding the soft tissue and knocking it clear off its shoulders into the rushing water.

"WOO!" Eugene crowed, "That felt good," he said through a heavy breath, resting the soiled bat over his shoulder.

Nalini barreled past Evaine and Leona and wrapped her arms around him tight, Eugene let the bat drop to hug her back.

Tears spilled over her lashes as she released him to look around. "Where's Dylan?" she asked, the sing-song voice in contrast to her sniffling. Her question caught him by surprise.

"Right here," Dylan said, stepping out from behind Eugene. "He needed a running start for that hit, thought I'd just take my time," he said, glancing down at the now headless body.

They all took a step back as they realized it was oozing black sludge, deflating its rubbery husk.

"Ugh! Okay, that's enough," Dylan declared, thoroughly grossed out. He did his best to kick the carcass over the side of the dock, finally succeeding with the help of Eugene.

"Any word on Rel yet?"

Chapter Twenty-Six

RUMBLE AT RIVERSIDE

Arel stood at the base of the steps and stared up at the entrance to the Riverside hospital, willing himself to lift his feet. He looked around at the trees that were now so familiar. He took his time walking up each step and through the entrance where he continued to the center of the room and stopped there. Looking down, he almost expected to see bare feet.

Couldn't call it deja vú because he had been there, it wasn't a trick of the mind. Everything in his line of sight was exactly as he remembered from his dream, the shattered glass, the vines along the walls, even the gurney on its side on the floor.

This time Rú wouldn't be there to pull him out of the hands of danger. The image of the black mass of disembodied arms flashed in his mind, momentarily paralyzing his legs. He was in the exact position he was in his dream watching the shadows move in the dark, but he couldn't run this time.

It was weirdly grounding knowing what he was about to face was real, any fear that could be confronted could be overcome. He wasn't afraid of her, he was afraid that he wasn't enough to defeat her.

"Enough," he thought.

He rubbed his sweaty palms against his pants as his whole body shook in anticipation. He knew the moment he'd start moving it'd dissipate and let his feet drag as he walked to the door and through the threshold. The sound echoed off the walls of the hallway. If she didn't know he was there before, she did now. He waited for a moment in the black hallway, he couldn't stop the thought of disembodied arms coming out of the walls to rip him apart. He tensed as he tried to focus on recalling the vision he had in the shack instead of the nightmare scenario he was playing in his mind. She had gone to the right of the door, so that's what he'd do as well. He took slow careful steps as he made his way down the hall but caught his foot on something anyway, sending him stumbling forward. He looked down to see what it was when he felt the breeze of something flying dangerously close to his eye. He didn't want to use the flashlight on his phone but the last thing he needed was to make any more noise tripping on anything else. Holding the phone fairly close to his face, he pulled up the flashlight app. Light exploded, illuminating the arms jutting out of the walls. He yelped and jumped back only to have sharp claws rake across his lower back, others attempting to grasp his shoulders and legs. He let out another scream, contorting himself into a standing pretzel to remain out of their reach. The walls were lined with clawing arms all the way down the hall on both sides, floor to ceiling. The length of the arms was not all the same, some had extended longer than the elbow. He was stuck. Slowly, he allowed his limbs to return to the normal standing position, careful not to get close.

"You wouldn't be 'helping hands' would you?" he joked to himself. A trick he liked to use to loosen his mind from fear, and it worked for the most part. He took a moment to look at the clawed hand reaching desperately for his face. The skin was ashy and charred at the nail beds where long jagged nails protruded. A putrid smell wafted from them as they clawed the air. The smell of infection and the sight of puss made his stomach lurch.

They were real but he had thought of them just before they appeared.

"How real..." he whispered.

He lifted a hesitant hand and waited for the fingers to extend again before quickly placing his hand in its grasp, locking his fingers tight around its thumb, keeping its nails from digging into his skin.

It felt like holding a freeze-dried chicken leg. He waited a moment, but nothing happened. It didn't pull him into the wall or trigger the other arms. Instead, all the arms froze and began to crumble into ash like firewood.

"Confront the illusion and the illusion will fall away," he said to himself, clapping his hands together to get the residue off his hands.

There were still shadows ahead of him but he didn't hesitate to start walking again. He was calm, he didn't know how, but there was a comfort he felt that kept him from falling into dizzying anxiety. Maybe that's what Leila's concoction was supposed to do.

However it was happening, he was thankful and it made him think of the friends he left on the dock and Dylan and Eugene. It sent a warm sensation rising through his chest at the same time he noticed a dim light coming from the stairs at the end of the hall. The warm light of fire blended with the cool light of the moon.

He didn't remember the moon being so bright when he was dropped on the island, or maybe it was cloudy before, but as Arel walked toward the window there wasn't a cloud in sight as he looked out of the window. For a moment he stood bathing in the light of the moon, mesmerized by how close it looked. He'd never taken the time to gaze up at the moon. He was overtaken, suspended for a moment in memory of his mother cradling him as a child and singing as he fell asleep, safe. It felt like a gift delivered to him in the light of the moon, the safety of love.

He could feel her presence at the top of the stairs glaring down at him. The light at the top intensified and a wave of heat made its way down to meet him warming the side of his face.

"Yeah, I'm coming," he responded in a low despondent tone.

Arel took one second longer to gaze into the moonlight before turning to face the raging pyre towering over him.

With every step ascending the stairs the Djinn stepped back, slow and graceful, leading him into the room behind her. When he got to the top of the landing she had moved out of sight, and the light of her fire softened to a warm inviting glow.

He choked a humorless laugh, thinking about the warning he received from The Being in his vision. If this was what she had in her arsenal of manipulation tactics then he had this in the bag. He didn't hesitate to walk into the room but stopped when he saw her across the room, standing next to the metal frame of what used to be a narrow bed. The room was small and familiar but he couldn't remember where he'd seen it, or if it was just something he thought he knew. He reached out to run his hand over the feeble desk next to him, his back to the window.

She made no move toward him, instead remained in place like a statue aflame. A pressure began to build in his mind, he knew it was her but didn't know what she was trying to do. There was no pain, just pressure. He shook his head as he clapped the dust off his hands before crossing his arms over his chest.

"So what's your plan?" he asked, with a tone of annoyance. "You got me here, now what?" It occurred to him that he shouldn't provoke her but this was beginning to feel like another game, and he was tired of playing.

She didn't answer him with words, instead responded by stepping away from the metal bed frame. Her fiery appearance dying down to reveal the curves of a feminine form. The char broke away to reveal a face he'd only recently become acquainted with, a version of his former self, Kirana. Different from the face he'd seen in his dreams and visions, it was like looking at a funhouse version of her. Her face twisted into an unsettling smirk and the eyes were wrong, empty, adding a disturbing wildness to her once warm brown eyes. The sight was unnerving, he was now very aware of her position in the room; it felt like staring down a wild animal, she felt too close.

Arel did his best to push his discomfort aside. "Presenting me with a version of myself? If you're trying to psych me out, you'll have to do better than that."

Something akin to deja vú came over him, not a memory or vision replaying. It was the tired weight of the repetitive knowledge that they'd done this before. In a different time, a different choice of words but unmistakably the same. He felt it now, the chain that held them together was heavy and the lifetimes past added to its burden. Looking at the evil version of his former self reminded him of the fight between Kirana and the avatar of his sister.

He smirked and shook his head, "I get it," he thought aloud. The annoyance and impatience when Kirana grew tired of dancing around the boy and wanted to end it, he felt that now. He wanted to finish this, he didn't care how he just didn't want this to come around again. The imposter's face shifted into an angry confusion, her smile dropped to a hard line.

Arel was laughing, there was nothing particularly amusing, it was the combination of overstimulation and exhaustion that hit him and he was so close to a release he could feel it, he just had to get through her. He sighed and uncoiled his arms, holding them out at his sides, an open gesture.

"Well?"

Her smile returned.

Just Beneath The Surface

"How long has he been over there now?" Eugene asked, facing Nalini mainly, only signing half his question in anxiety and haste.

"About four hours," Evaine answered.

"And Rú? Where is he?"

Leona pointed to the clouds above the island at the same time a massive shadow swooped down beneath them, silhouetted by the light of the moon.

Eugene nodded silently, before stepping forward and holding his hand out to Leona, "I'm Eugene."

Nalini stepped to the side as he reached his hand out to give him more room. Positioning herself just outside the group, closer to the edge of the dock.

"Dylan!" he called over Eugene's shoulder introducing himself to the new addition to the group, holding his hand up in identification. All heads turned to face him.

It was quick and wouldn't have been noticed if it weren't for the splash. Nalini was gone.

She could feel the pressure of something flat against her back as she sank deeper into the water and looked down to see that she was fighting against the iron grip of two large arms. Nalini kicked and tried to wiggle enough to loosen its hold, just enough to land a hit to the ribs. The more she moved the tighter the arms squeezed, making it harder to hold her breath. She stopped fighting and focused on holding her breath. One of them had to see her pulled off the dock, she hoped at least. Panic began to build in her chest and pressure built between her eyes. She had to do something. The thought of the wine they all drank came to mind, it was supposed to protect all of them, not only Rel, right? She couldn't remember, it was getting more difficult to hold on to a single thought and she lost track of how long she'd been underwater. The pain in her head built to be unbearable and she opened her eyes just in time to see a hand shoot past her face and grab the collar of her jacket. As she felt herself being pulled to the surface the specter released its grip around her.

Leona pulled Nalini up and pushed her so she'd reach the surface ahead of her. It took a minute for Nalini to catch her breath and get her bearings.

The moment Leona broke the surface, she grabbed onto Nalini and began paddling toward the hazy dock, keeping her head on a swivel to keep an eye out for anything that might appear on the surface. Leona let go of Nalini when she matched her speed and they both began to swim as fast as their muscles would allow. The current had taken them farther than Leo had thought.

Dylan and Eugene were on their knees at the edge of the dock, ready to snatch them from the water once they were in arm's reach. Evaine nervously watched Leona and Nalini fight against the rushing water, keeping an eye on the waves around them in case anything breached the surface. At the same time, vigilant eyes tracked her every move through the spaces between the planks of wood at her feet, eagerly watching just beneath the mirrored surface of the water, waiting.

Chapter Twenty-Seven

THE SACRIFICE

"WELL?" Arel repeated aggressively.

A monstrous flicker of delight flashed in the eyes of Kirana's imposter and she held up her palm toward his face. Arel blinked and couldn't see anything, he thought she blinded him until he realized it wasn't complete darkness, his vision began to clear enough to witness a constricted figure floating in the greenish haze.

"Underwater," he mumbled. "What is this?" confusion and anger colored his demand for answers.

He wasn't sure if he was getting closer to the figure or if it was drifting toward him but soon his sight cleared and he was able to make out a face. His heart dropped, it was Nalini. Her eyes were shut and her mouth set in a thin line, the only thing in motion were the strands of hair that moved gracefully over her stone face. He pulled his vision from her face to see what held her motionless, a pair of ghostly white arms. He felt sick, a pain building in his mind and chest.

"This is a trick," he growled through his teeth.

"No," the Djinn finally spoke, he could tell she was smiling. "No, tricks," she hissed.

Arel's confidence was gone, his mind raced with panic, dancing on the edge of despair. He'd never be able to forgive himself if he walked away from this and Nalini didn't.

That was it.

He remembered the conversation in his vision at the shack, he was told he'd need to make a sacrifice. He also remembered being told Djinn are suckers for a deal.

"ENOUGH!" He was surprised by the control he had over his voice. His vision changed at the same time, warm tears fell over his lashes and down his cheeks but he wasn't back in that hospital room. He was standing behind his friends on the dock. Evaine was looking out into the water standing over a kneeling Dylan and Eugene to his left at the edge of the dock. The relief of seeing Eugene was short-lived as he watched the ghouls emerge from the water and begin to climb the poles of the dock.

"Watch out!" he screamed, "Turn around!"

The Djinn let out a low satisfied laugh, that brought his attention back to the reality he was standing in.

"STOP THIS," he pleaded. "TAKE ME! FUCK, I'M RIGHT HERE!"

"Son of Lilith, I don't just want you..." she crooned, sounding almost consoling. "I want to break you."

He felt like all the air was being vacuumed from his lungs and he didn't have the capacity to inhale. He had played into everything she wanted, the hopelessness was numbing. He failed to protect the ones he loved the most.

His last chance was to get her to possess him. When the air returned to his lungs he didn't think, he rushed her, slamming her hard against the brick wall. He put all his weight behind his forearm now against her throat, she remained unfazed. She smiled and slid her hands up his chest and his neck to rest gently on his cheek.

"You will watch them die," she cooed sweetly. "By your own hands, your parents will perish and I will bask in your dying light."

The excitement in her voice churned his stomach but he focused on keeping his mind clear as the hand she held to his cheek began to heat to an unbearable temperature. She wrapped her other arm around his waist and pulled him closer so there was no longer space between them. His first instinct was to push her away but he resisted the urge to fight her. This is what he wanted, he closed his eyes as he allowed her in limb by limb. It was like having currents of electricity running through him, the voltage increasing by every second. Unfortunately, after the initial shock, there was no release, paralysis, or unconsciousness, she wanted him to feel it all. The pain and the heat of fire as it worked through his skin and his bones. She wanted his anguish to be slow, to hear his symphony of screams as her flame devoured him but to her dismay, his eyes remained shut tight and his screams were stifled by a clenched jaw.

She decided she could wait...she wanted to see the hopelessness in his eyes before settling in behind them. She watched with glee as he finally opened them and saw tired sorrow and something else that wasn't quite sadness, it was acceptance. She beamed with satisfaction as she put her lips to his, suffocating him and breathing fire down his throat.

Arel wasn't sure how long this went on, it felt like he'd been on fire for hours. His only focus was surviving the pain and praying for it to subside. Uncertain if it was his prayers, but soon after the pain settled into a steady manageable current he began to feel her in his mind. His entire body was experiencing the painful sting of static, like trying to walk on sleeping limbs. He tried to move but it was as if he couldn't reach the thoughts to command his body. He was trapped in a fog cut off from the rest of his mind. Like a projection in front of him, he was looking at the scene across the river again. He saw Leona and Nalini on the surface of the water swimming to the dock. The sight of his sister alive and well enough to swim lifted the sting of panic he felt before. The hope he needed to focus his thoughts.

'This is my body, my mind,' he thought and was brought back to the conversation he had with The Being. Nothing could overpower *his* will, she wouldn't be able to take what was rightfully his. She was exactly where he needed her to be. This was his chance, she was preoccupied with the success of her plan and making him watch as she hurt his friends.

He focused all his thoughts on the iron flowing through his veins and envisioned his blood as liquid bars. The thought of being made by remnants of a dying star, a part of a celestial body, made him feel strong enough to clear the fog she encased him in. As the fog lifted it was like standing in the middle of a crowded room. He was moving through all the souls she enslaved, frozen still like statues, lying in wait to be called upon, to be used in whatever twisted way she chose. It wasn't long before she came to him, again in the form of Kirana.

"I expected keeping you locked away would be a challenge but I admit I didn't think you'd slip through so soon," she said, unaware and unphased by his plan.

Seeing a manifestation of her made it easier for him to visualize her in a cage, he smiled and the surrounding statues began to fade away one by one.

"What is this?" she hissed, her eyes wide and wild as she turned in place watching her captives escape her grasp before her eyes. "This isn't possible, YOU DON'T HAVE THE POWER."

"You gave me the power when you made my body the arena," Arel said calmly, his tone aired on patronizing. She made a move to rush him and found herself bound by invisible shackles. She looked up at him in astonishment, anger, and, could it be, fear?

"Not as comfortable a prison as a lamp, I imagine, nothing in there that can snuff you out," he said, walking around her slowly.

"Your soul won't survive long enough to be a threat to me, I WILL BURN YOU FROM THE INSIDE OUT!" she roared.

"Well, we'll find out I guess," he said with a shrug. "But here's the difference between you and me, I'm not alone. You won't do to me what you did to Mal, I know what flows through my veins. I am part of a greater whole and have access to all its strength and power, made even stronger by the connections I have with the ones I love." Arel stopped walking and stepped forward to face her, so confident as to lean in and whisper into her ear. "There is nothing and no one that will come to your aid, you are alone." He didn't know what the state of her reaction would be when he pulled back to see her face. Her brows were drawn together and he could tell her mind was busy working on her problem. He stepped back as a calm came over her features again.

"You have me bound," she conceded. "Well done. Cutting the ties I had over those paltry souls under my command must have taken a lot of concentration."

He grimaced hearing the way she spoke about the souls she enslaved to do her bidding.

"You have tremendous focus..." she went on, "Cutting my ties to the islands, you've got almost everything under control..." She smiled as she watched Arel's face contort in confusion. "But you've neglected some things."

In a blink, she had him by the shoulders, "Motor skills."

And suddenly he was awake and falling, she had leaped from the window before releasing her hold on his body. He knew he had been close to the window before she possessed him but she had successfully moved his body toward the window while his focus was away from his physical body. He couldn't be her prison if he fell to his death. Time seemed to slow down as he felt himself falling through the air. He regained his sight as he saw the hopeful silhouette of giant wings sailing toward him, just before hitting the ground.

Where Are You?

Nalini was pulled first from the water, Eugene lifting her with enough strength to send her flying through the air as Dylan merely assisted Leona out of the water and onto the dock. Evaine kept her eyes on the water waiting with Dylan's bat in hand, sure of an assault on the way. Instead, the fog around the dock began to clear and the sound of the water grew quieter. Eugene sprinted back to the SUV to grab the first aid kit that he kept tucked away and grabbed the emergency blankets for Nalini and Leona.

Evaine was the first to see wings flying through the fog over the water.

"Rú's coming back!" excitement coloring her voice. She rushed to Leona to help her to her feet as Dylan helped Nalini up and out of the way so Rú would have enough room to land. He changed his form mid-air and floated down to the dock, landing gingerly with Arel draped over his arms. Nalini ran to her brother and cradled his head as Rú set him down gently. She released a shuddered breath, relieved to see he was breathing.

'What happened?' she thought, knowing full well Rú would understand her and not wanting to lift her hands away from her brother to ask.

"He..." Rú began aloud so they could all hear what happened. "He fell from a third-story window, I couldn't reach him in time," he finished, his voice laden with guilt.

"But he's breathing, we need to get him to a hospital," Leona said, looking Arel over and checking his pulse.

"There's nothing physically wrong with him, I'm taking him to Leila," he decided, kneeling to pick him up again.

"REL!" Eugene cried, now close enough to see what they were huddled around. He hadn't noticed Rú as he was blocked by Dylan.

He moved aside as Eugene approached the group, dropping the blankets before kneeling next to Arel and taking hold of his forearm.

"He's burning up, what's happening to him?" he asked, looking at Rú.

"Oh my God," Evaine gasped, thinking back to the condition they found Mal in. "Did she?"

"We have to get Rel to Leila now. It won't happen to him," Rú affirmed, first to Evaine then Nalini, "I promise."

Nalini looked up at him with guarded eyes before nodding once. She kissed her brother's forehead and allowed Rú to take him from her arms. It seemed as if he were just sleeping, he looked so young to her, the little brother from her memories. The fire in the back of her throat raged as she fought to hold in her tears as she watched Rú change mid-jump and shoot into the sky and the others took off to the SUV.

Eugene wrapped a warm arm around her shoulders allowing her a moment to find her feet before catching up with the others. Rú going ahead without them meant leaving the rest to deal with the hair-pulling frustration of New York City traffic. No one could blame him, the faster he could get Arel to Leila the faster they could figure out what was happening to him.

✶✶✶✶

There weren't a lot of people on the roads and it was the time of morning when the shadows off the buildings were particularly dark. Giving the illusion of nothing beyond the light from the street lamps, a definitive line where light ended and darkness began. Rú wasn't worried about being seen but the setting helped. He landed in the alley around the side of the building, glad to see no one had made it their home for the evening, and hurried to the front doors. They were open.

He breathed a sigh of relief and rushed through the storefront and down the stairs. Nothing was out of place as he made his way through the storefront to the back and only noticed something was missing as he made his way down the stairs.

There was no trace of Leila anywhere, he couldn't feel her the way he could before. Panic rose in his chest as he quickened his pace down the stairs and set Arel down gently on the couch where they laid Eugene before. The door to Leila's herb room was ajar.

"Leila! Leila, Arel needs help!" Rú called out before pushing the door open the rest of the way. The endless room was bare, nothing left but empty shelves.

"FUCK!" he roared, pushing over a row of shelves before walking out and slamming the door behind him with enough force to shake the walls.

He walked back over to where Arel lay to check his pulse and read his energy. He could still feel him but just a portion, like the soul's default settings holding space like an anchor. Where the rest of him was he couldn't tell. He sat down on the floor and leaned back against the couch taking comfort in the sound of Arel's rhythmic breaths and he waited for the others to arrive.

"Where are you, Rel?"

Alternative Scene

Rumble at Riverside: Just Beneath The Surface

Nalini and Leona remained seated as they caught their breath as Eugene and Dylan ran back to the Jeep to grab a blanket or anything else that was warm and dry to wrap them in. Evaine kept an eye on the water in case anything breached the glassy surface, relying on the magic of the protection bag in her pocket.

Nalini waited for Leona to meet her eyes and mouthed the words 'Thank you', Leona nodded. Nalini held out her hand to her, Leona eyed it for a moment before taking it, a silent agreement to let go of the resentment she held for what happened to Mal. When she released Nalini's hand she let herself fall back on the dock, allowing her heart rate to return to normal, comforted by the sound of Dylan and Eugene's footsteps as they made their way back down to them. She watched the dark clouds drift through the night sky as vigilant eyes tracked her every move through the spaces between the planks, countless eyes watching just beneath the mirrored surface of the water, waiting.

Notes

Notes

Notes